Destroyed

Lost in Oblivion

Book 3

RR
RAINBOW
rage
PUBLISHING

Copyright

© 2015 by Taryn Elliott & Cari Quinn

Book Cover Design: Late Nite Designs

Publisher: Rainbow Rage Publishing

ISBN: 978-1-940346-28-1

For Mom, who kept giving me signs that everything was going to be all right. I miss you. Happy Birthday.

For Cari Quinn who is, and always will be, a ninja.

Chapter 1

Ahh, fuck.

Simon Kagan swung his foot out and tried to slap it on the floor. His goddamn foot didn't reach. The track lighting above him spun like the lights on the Pacific Park Ferris wheel.

He shut his eyes against the nauseating view and forced himself to sit up. He scrubbed his hands over his face and found at least two days' worth of beard.

He'd shaved for the promo show in Manlol
hattan. He hated to be a slave to his electric razor, but he couldn't pull off the scruffy look as easily as the rest of the guys in the band. It took at least a week to grow a respectable level of scruff. And by then he was itching to get it off his face anyway.

He lifted the sheet.

Buck naked.

Huh.

That wasn't exactly a surprise. He rarely slept in clothes, but the problem was…he didn't remember getting that way.

The cotton in his mouth wasn't from vodka. He glanced around the room to find a half dozen bottles of champagne.

Nothing ended well for him when wine was involved. Including the head-clanging addition of bubbly.

That was why he stuck to vodka. He knew exactly how much to drink to keep a steady buzz and only tip over into drunk when it was safe.

At least his ass was on superior sheets. He spread his fingers over the suede-soft comforter and crisp high thread count sheets. A far cry from the ones on his bed at the house they rented in the Hollywood Hills.

The pillow on the other side of the bed was dented.

He brought it up to his face and smelled smoke and the powdery scent of something cloyingly sweet.

Simon wrinkled his nose and tossed the pillow down. He stood on wobbly legs and leaned on the paneled room divider. The wood crumpled into an accordion style window shield and his gut rolled again.

New York City opened up in front of him. He flattened his palm against the cool glass and evened out. Lights and the effervescent bounce of pedestrians scurrying across the streets made this city just a bit different from Los Angeles. Not that he'd give up L.A. to save his life—fuck no—but this city pulled at him.

Filled with people and yet the sense of isolation resonated.

He understood that.

Lived it every single day.

And the roller coaster of a tour would be starting in five short weeks.

Part of him itched for it. He was restless and boredom had settled inside his brain midway through the last album. Not during studio time, but the endless drag in between.

Hurry up and wait.

Sit.

Sit.

Sit.

Sing, monkey, sing.

He pushed overlong bangs out of his face and stepped away from the cacophony of street noise that bled through the window.

Were the windows tinted?

He frowned and pulled the dark wood panel across the huge window. Even more effective than blackout curtains.

He'd have to remember that.

The room went silent again. He padded to the mini bar and found the distinctive bottle of his favorite vodka—Crystal Head. Two other unopened boxes sat side by side on the shelf.

Nice.

He splashed the clear perfection into a tumbler and swished his mouth with it. The burn around his gums and down his throat was comfortingly familiar.

The slap of water in the shower finally penetrated his subconscious. He wasn't alone—again, not a surprise with the scent on the sheets. Plush carpeting turned to marble floors the closer he got to the bathroom.

The clear glass stall of the shower gave him an unencumbered view of his guest. Long legs led up to an ass that was definitely a regular visitor to the gym. Bitable to be sure. Dark hair full of suds snaked down her back.

He frowned as she turned to dunk her head.

No.

God, no.

He wouldn't.

He didn't.

A long neck flowed into an elegant collarbone, but he started breathing again when his gaze drifted down to her breasts.

Not hers.

He'd never forget the surprising fullness of her breasts or the peach tips matched her lips—both on her mouth and the exquisite cleft between her thighs.

It wasn't her.

Wasn't Margo.

But Christ, she could have been.

He dragged his palm against his jawline and down his neck. "Fuck me sideways," he muttered when his dick lengthened.

It was always this way.

The second Margo Reece had come back into his sphere he'd been messed up about her. One goddamn night should not crawl under his skin. Women before and way too many women after her—but he'd never been so stupid as to go for anyone that looked like her.

Like Violin Girl.

And now she was on the album. He simply couldn't get away from her. From the sad tones of her strings layered into "Finally", to the surprisingly shred-worthy addition to "Torn To Pieces", she'd burrowed into his head again. They lived in his chest and his head like any of the Oblivion songs. They all crawled in and settled. Some deeper than others.

Hers settled in with hooks. The more he pulled on them, the more they shredded muscle and scraped bone.

He'd gone out of his way to avoid her in the studio and he'd managed it until they'd called her in for another pass at "Finally" and he'd been in the box.

The sucker punch of seeing her.

Like nothing had changed.

Like he'd been back in that fucking vocal closet at Trident's studio. The smell of her in the chair, on his lips, in the goddamn walls. That honeysuckle scent with her musky essence burning on his tongue.

Time bled away as if it had never been.

For fuck's sake, she'd even worn one of her high-collared blouses and black skirts.

He'd gotten drunk for a week straight.

But at least he'd been smart enough to fuck blonds or redheads. Nothing and no one that could remind him of her. Of the way she clasped him to perfection and tasted like a dream wrapped in a nightmare.

He'd drank her out of his system.

Until he'd been told about the release party.

And now he had a very pretty girl in his shower that didn't deserve to be on the opposite end of his psychosis.

Part of him wanted to follow the hard-on swiftly growing. Step into the stall and pour himself into her willing body.

Snatches of their two nights of sex and champagne reminded him that she was very willing. Even if he couldn't remember her name.

She slicked back her hair and smiled.

A perfectly nice smile.

Just not *hers*.

Not Margo's.

Being with second best when he was sober would never happen. He wasn't that masochistic. No matter how hard his dick was.

Before he could open his mouth, his phone bleated out a rooster's cry. He winced. That would be Lila.

She was usually his killjoy.

He returned to the bedroom and swiped his phone alive. Instead of a call, her beautiful face and huge light eyes filled his screen.

"Do you or do you not know how to use a telephone?"

Simon sighed. "Yes, Lila. I do."

"Then tell me why it took you two days to answer?"

He frowned and toggled out of FaceTime to the main screen of his phone. His eyebrows shot up. It really had been.

Fuck.

He switched back and slid his sheepish smile on. "Whoops."

"Don't 'whoops' me, Kagan. We've been searching all over the city for you. The only reason I know where you are is that your credit card company contacted your account manager—namely me—to double check overactive spending."

It was a pretty swanky hotel. In New York City, in the middle of midtown if his view had anything to say about it.

"Had to celebrate."

"Well, celebrate your way back to our hotel this morning. You have two radio shows to do this afternoon and the release party is tonight."

Simon's gut twisted.

She would be there.

He glanced over his shoulder. At least this was one way to move the girl in the shower along.

"Simon?"

He nodded to Lila. "Got it, boss. I'll be back soon."

"Now."

"Would you like me to pan down with the camera? I need to get ready."

"Nothing I haven't seen before, Kagan. Not like you're discerning where you show it off."

He smirked. "It's show-off worthy."

"So you say."

He snorted. "All right, I'll check out and make my way over there."

"Do you remember where we are?"

He frowned. "Now that you mention it..."

She rolled her eyes. "I'll text the address." And then she was gone.

"Simon?"

The voice was higher than he was expecting. Almost child-like. He winced and turned around. No, nothing child-like about her.

He loved women, loved their scents and sounds. But man, he hated a baby doll voice. "Hey, babe."

She sauntered in, an exaggerated swing in her hips. She wore the smallest towel possible, flashing half of her perfectly curved hip and a hint of breast.

All enticing.

Except one thing.

Out of the shower, it was even more apparent.

She had Margo's look, minus the air of sophistication Violin Girl had. For fuck's sake, she even had her bangs.

She walked in front of him, her bold fingers sliding around his half hard cock. "I was hoping you'd wake up and come in the shower with me. We had fun in there last night."

He winced and couldn't hold out against a groan as she stroked him masterfully. "Ah, babe. I wish I could." He stepped back.

It would be way too easy to boost her up and toss her on the bed with a laugh. Nothing different than any other night. A good time for her, one for him.

Everyone went their separate ways with a few orgasms under their belts and a goodbye kiss at the door.

Hopeful dark eyes went wary. "Oh, why?"

"Work calls. That was just my manager on the phone. Time for me to turn into a pumpkin."

She giggled. "Midnight was a long time ago." She dropped her towel and took advantage of his suddenly cemented feet. With far too much practiced ease, she twisted around the head of his cock playfully. He had a feeling that he'd lost most of the last two days with this beautiful woman.

He was such a shit.

But he didn't want her to feel bad about what had probably been a fun Wednesday into Thursday combo. The first stirrings of memory hit him when she grinned at him with her crooked eye tooth. It was adorable. He always liked the inconsistencies of a beautiful woman. Why one woman could lure and another could repel.

They'd met at a bar.

The bar across from the iHeart Radio interview with the band. Where Lila had informed him that Margo was invited to the exclusive party they'd been planning and would be playing with them on the little stage.

He'd been pissed and excited, but mostly pissed. Every time that woman got around him, he got twisted up. And it was the thought of Margo that got him all the way hard and why he pulled back.

Fuck.

He was a head case, but even he couldn't use a woman like that.

"I gotta go, babe."

"Just ten more minutes," she said and rubbed her breasts against his chest. "I like you all clear-eyed. So you know it's me."

Shame slicked up his spine and left a bad taste in his mouth.

"We had a little too much fun the last few days. Now I have to go pay for it."

She sighed. "I guess spending two days with a rockstar is more than most get." She took a step back, grabbed a stretchy black dress off the chair, and slid it over her head. Not a damn stitch under it and she was mouthwateringly tight in all the right spots.

Fuck, Kagan. You are an idiot.

He should be on that like syrup on pancakes—instead he felt a little ill. The dress hugged her from shoulder to knee. She clipped her hair up and turned to him and the kick was so hard, he actually staggered back a step.

She could be Margo's twin.

Fucked. He was so goddamn fucked.

"Are you all right?"

"Fine." He went to the bar and splashed another three inches of vodka into a tumbler before tossing back the liquid fire. "I just need a little hangover cure."

She came up behind him and stroked him from shoulder to ass. "I'd play hooky more often if this is what happened. How long are you in New York for?"

"Just tonight. Then back to L.A."

"Too bad. I have to work tonight." She tugged on his earlobe with her teeth. "I could call in again."

"No. I'm sorry, sweetheart. Tonight is going to be insane."

She pressed a surprisingly chaste kiss against his cheek. "Going back to her?"

He turned his head. "What?"

"Violin Girl."

He dropped his chin to his chest, his fingers digging into the bar.

"It's okay. I didn't mind being your violin girl for a few nights. She's a lucky woman."

"She's no one."

"If you say so." She trailed her fingers over his shoulders and stepped to the side. She gathered her things and left quietly.

Simon swiped his arm across the bar. The shattering glass echoing after her.

Margo Reece slipped into her seat. She tucked her violin case under her feet and crossed her legs at the ankle. The familiar press of the case along her foot should have calmed her.

The flying didn't bother her.

Even going on a job didn't bother her. She'd been jetting from studio to studio for the last six weeks. Any studio work that came into her email or her agent called her about—she went to. She couldn't afford to turn anything down right now.

She smoothed the fabric of her skirt down and laced her fingers.

No, she definitely didn't have the luxury of turning down work.

A woman with a diaper bag, purse, and toddler in tow dropped into the seat beside her. She invaded more than half Margo's space. The little girl on her shoulder wrapped her chubby little fists around Margo's braid. "No, Patsy. Sorry."

Margo tugged her hair out of the child's hand with a wince and tucked herself back against the window. "It's fine."

"She's just discovered hair. It's why I chopped mine off." The harried mother sighed and transferred the child to her other side, but little Patsy had other ideas. Squealing at top volume until her mother set her back on her right shoulder, for instance.

Margo pressed her lips together when a man that had to be pushing three hundred pounds paused at their row. Really? Because sharing the space with a baby wasn't bad enough? Now the baby would practically be in her lap regardless.

She reached into her pocket and took out her phone and Bluetooth headphones. Noise-canceling headphones to be more precise. She tucked the foamy plastic molds into her ears and flicked through her album list to the one she wanted. *Wanted* perhaps wasn't the correct word. The album that controlled her lately. In her car, headphones, even the through the tinny speakers of her phone—it was always on.

In the middle of the night, she curled into her pillow and held herself in a tight ball and forced herself to endure silence just to give herself a break. Only to stumble around in the dark like an addict to find a fix.

Simon Kagan's voice was her auditory affliction.

Music had always been her savior. As a small child, Bach and Mozart had inspired her. The Reece house was cultured. Cartoons and children's songs weren't tolerated. Rachmaninoff had transitioned into Paganini and Vivaldi as the violin had become her life.

There was passion in those composers. She knew this, and they'd ruled her life for so long. She was happy with them — or had been.

Until him.

One song had started her down this path.

How many soundtrack songs had she played on? Too many to count.

Being second chair — *previously* being second chair — in the Boston Philharmonic had afforded her a measure of status, but not exactly a monetary one. She supplemented with studio work. From movie scores to the occasional contemporary song, she'd sold her talent to fatten her bank account.

Working with Oblivion shouldn't have mattered.

It was just another job.

She'd told herself that when she'd taken the job for another album. To prove to herself that they were just another job.

Now it was so much worse. Untried and filled with testosterone more than talent, "The Becoming" had been an anomaly. That first song had been child's play. The rest of the songs on that album were good — more than good. She'd listened to "Burn" on a number of occasions.

Watched live performances that had instantly constricted her lungs like a corset that was laced too tight. Nothing had prepared her this time.

Nothing.

Their album *Rise* had ruined her.

Their music shouldn't be a guilty secret that had bloomed into a far reaching sickness. It had awakened something inside her that she didn't understand or want to face.

But she had little choice now. She'd tried to hold onto her life with her fingernails and no amount of rosin could smooth out the frayed ends of her career.

A hiatus could be explained. Losing her chair...

No.

She wasn't thinking about that now.

The plane began to taxi and the woman beside her tried to calm her shrieking child. Margo concentrated on the sandpaper over silk voice of the man who'd ruined her with a song. She pulled her sweater tighter around her.

It didn't matter where she was, didn't matter how inconvenient it was, her body flushed at the first chord. The lyrics to "Monster" wound around her senses, pushing her nipples against her bra and making her clit pound with the bassline. The feedback echo of Simon's voice under each chorus was like a caress as her spine pressed back into the seat and the plane lifted.

Another time, another chair back...

She curled her fingers around the arms of her seat.

He'd looked up at her with those unearthly silvery blue eyes as he held her against the velvet chair. He didn't know it, but his hand across her belly hadn't been necessary. The first lash of his busy tongue had chained her to that chair. No matter how much she'd railed against it, she'd been lost to him.

She'd never even liked oral sex before that night in the booth. Before he'd shown her what sex was. What pleasure could be.

The same way he showed so many others.

She yanked her headphones out and opened her eyes. She stared into the headrest in front of her, stared until the nubby texture of the material came in clear and she breathed through the memory.

"Hate flying, too?"

"Yes," she said quietly. She hated the flying that she did in her dreams, and when she got caught up in the music. That was accurate enough.

This was going to be the longest short flight in the history of life.

She tucked her phone away into her pocket and pulled out the magazine she'd purchased at the airport. Celebrity gossip and the inane antics of the faux celebrities that social media created had always been fascinating to her. It was so far removed from her life in the orchestra—what *had* been her life in the orchestra.

No.

She wouldn't—couldn't think about that right now.

Guilt clawed at her neck and base of her skull, letting loose enough poison to make her second-guess every decision for the last year. But she wouldn't let it taint this week.

She would feed the swirling obsession that flowed through her blood like adrenaline and be done with Simon Kagan and Oblivion.

Lila Shawcross had invited her to the party and to play on the small stage with them. To rehearse this afternoon and help make the release party a social media explosion.

She'd get her name out then she'd move on to the next phase of her life. This, she could control. And she would. There was no other option.

She pulled her phone out again and launched her thunderstorm and rain app before tucking her headphones in again.

Sleep.

Just an hour.

Resolution made, she forced her mind to quiet.

And because she was a master at catnaps, she did. By the time the attendant made the announcement that they were landing, she'd managed to find a quiet corner of her mind.

When they came to a stop on the runway, she reached for her violin case. The little girl was tucked onto her mother's shoulder, her thumb in her mouth. Both child and mother were beyond exhausted.

Margo couldn't help herself. Quiet and sweet, the child lured her closer. She stroked her finger down her arm to her hand. The child curled her pinkie around Margo's finger, took her thumb out of her mouth and spewed.

"Oh, my God." The woman grabbed the diaper bag and pulled out three baby wipes in a blink. "I'm so sorry."

Margo held up her hand. "Just hand me the wipes." This is why she didn't interact with kids. It never ended well.

She tried to blot out the worst of the mess, but gave up and stripped off her sweater. She handed it to the mother. "If you can get the stain out, you're welcome to it."

"Cashmere?" The woman was dumbfounded.

Margo shrugged. It was all she wore. "Yes."

"I couldn't. I—"

"It's fine. You deserve it as combat pay, ma'am."

The woman laughed. She slumped back into her seat and laughed in a way that made Margo cringe. Taking care of another person was a level of responsibility she'd never had.

Independence, yes. That she understood. It had been instilled in her from the moment they'd laid a rosined bow into her hands. Being someone's everything?

That was too much.

The mother turned her face to Margo's. "Tell me at least one of us will have a good time tonight?"

"I'm going to try."

"Do me a favor?"

Hesitant, Margo nodded.

"Kiss a hot guy tonight and remind yourself that you are an unencumbered woman in New York City. I had that once upon a time."

Instantly, Simon's face registered as clear as if he was standing in front of her.

"That guy—whoever gave you that look."

Margo veiled her eyes with lashes and her bangs. She didn't have a *look*.

"You're young and beautiful. And cripes, I wish I had your body."

She fussed with the thin strap of her camisole. She wasn't used to showing so much skin. The orchestra had a uniform. Her whole life had been a uniform. She hid her curves under skirts and sweaters. She always felt too lush compared to the slim and perfect women in the string section. They were dainty and elegant.

She had to consciously work to keep up the same appearances. All too often her parents had pushed her into diets and monochrome colors to make her belong.

"I hope your little girl will feel better."

The man that kept them squashed in like sardines stood and the line started moving.

"Thanks," the mother said and stood, gathering her things. She tucked the sweater into the bag and slipped out into the aisle.

Margo sat there for a moment longer. A man moved down the aisle. He was attractive, in the suited-up businessman-like way that she usually was interested in.

His eyes widened and he stopped. "Can I help you with a bag or anything?"

"I'm fine, thank you."

His gaze skittered down her neck and shoulders, stalling at her breasts before bouncing back to her face. "Are you sure?"

She suddenly missed her sweater very much. "Positive."

He moved on, with a backward glance then a shake of his head.

She slung her purse over her shoulder and hefted her case. With her head held high, she walked down the aisle and into the terminal. Instead of going right for JFK's departure gate, she ducked into the shopping area.

This was not in her budget but she couldn't walk around the huge airport like this. No matter how much bravado she thought she had.

She drifted toward the classic styles of a designer store. Cashmere twin sets were her stock in trade. Maybe she'd get a color—that was different. Not the grays and blacks she was used to. Maybe a navy?

"That's not you."

"I beg your pardon?" Margo turned to the voice. What was it today? Everyone knew what she should be doing except her.

The tall, well-dressed man came over with a short cranberry jacket. "This."

She shook her head. "Too small."

He held it up in front of her. "Indulge me."

With one eyebrow raised, she stared him down.

"That's impressive, doll. Save it for a man that it would work on. I'm not hitting on you. I just want to dress you."

"Oh."

"Well, not that I wouldn't hit on you. You're as hot as a Maxim shoot in August, but my wife would have my nuts in a vise. And while that's fun on occasion, I'm not in the mood today."

Margo blinked. Not at all sure what to say to that, she turned around and let him slip the jacket over her arms and drape it over her shoulders.

He spun her around. "See?"

She went still as she caught a glimpse of herself in the mirror. Surely that wasn't her. The black pencil skirt and camisole hugged her and gave her an hourglass shape. The short jacket hit her right at the midriff. Instead of making her look boxy as she'd expected, it accentuated her curves and took off five years from her face.

She jumped when he held up a pair of four-inch raspberry-colored ankle breakers. She only paused for a moment before kicking off her sensible pumps.

"That a girl."

Her arches screamed and her calves tightened, but it was exactly what she needed. She didn't recognize this woman in the mirror. She matched the Margo she wanted to be.

A little bolder.

A little surer.

She pulled out her credit card and held it up. "Don't even tell me what it costs. I don't want to change my mind."

"I knew it."

"Hope you work on commission."

"I do."

At least he got compensated for his genius. He came back with the slip and she signed it. He clipped off the tags and dropped them into a bag.

"Kick it in the ass."

She turned to him. "How do you know I need to kick anything in the... ass?" The curse word felt alien on her tongue, but she kind of liked it.

"You're all lit up. Something is up tonight."

She inclined her head. She nodded toward the case on the chair outside the dressing room. "Yes."

"Then it definitely applies."

Her phone buzzed in her purse. She pulled it out and found a text from Lila with the address of the club and time for rehearsal. "I have to get going."

"The skirt is amazing, but if you have a pair of leggings, it would work for this outfit as well."

She shook her head. "I don't really wear anything that tight out of my house."

"You should." He folded his arms over his chest. "Own those curves. I know far too many women that pay for them."

"Don't they usually pay to have them sucked out?"

He grinned. "Heroin chic is going out of style."

She was pretty sure skinny would never go out of style, but she smiled anyway. "Thank you..." She glanced at his discreet tag. "Thomas."

"You're welcome." He held up her case. "What do you play?"

"Violin." She slid her fingers over the handle. The grooves fitted into her palm as perfectly as the fret of her Starfish.

"Your hot factor just jumped about fifteen percent."

"Dare I ask where that put me?"

"Triple digits for sure, Ms. Reece."

"Margo."

He smiled. "Elegant and sexy."

Someday she might get away with just the sexy.

Maybe.

She walked out of the store with an extra sway in her hips. She didn't even have to try to put it there, the heels did it.

Maybe she would fit in tonight with the band.

She reached the baggage claim for her flight and claimed her herringbone pink suitcase before making her way out to the line waiting for cabs.

New York City was dirty and noisy, but there was a level of excitement that Boston didn't have. As if the air was infused with something that wouldn't allow sleep.

By the time she'd made it up the line to a cab, she was almost adept at walking in heels again. It had been a while. She stepped inside and gave the driver the address. She tucked her case on one side and her suitcase on the other. The city was a logjam of cars and pedestrians. The closer they got to Broadway, the slower the approach.

Finally, old world elegance edged the hyper-neon that peeked from down the street. A doorman opened the cab and helped her out.

"Welcome to the WestHouse, Ms. Reece. We've been expecting you."

"Oh." She blinked. Lila sure knew how to pull out the stops. "Thank you."

He took her suitcase and walked her to the gilded door. "Your guest has already arrived and Frank is waiting just inside to take your things." He popped her telescope handle and Margo slid her specially made case along the length.

"Would you like me to bring this to your room?"

"No, that's fine. Thank you." She didn't let her violin out of her sight—ever. *Her guest?* Was Lila waiting for her? "Thank you."

"My pleasure."

Did people really smile like that? Did his face hurt by the end of the night? She knew hers did when she was playing and was supposed to smile at the end of each song.

The lobby was amazing. Crystal, hardwood, and silk everywhere. The dark elegance was touched with cool white marble and a touch of Art Deco design in the front of the check-in desk.

A charming antique key system was still used there and they were displayed behind the desk in lit boxes. A tall man with an austere face and perfectly cut suit came out from a small room behind the desk display.

The moment he caught sight of her, he smiled and his face completely changed. So much so that Margo found herself smiling back.

"Ms. Reece, so glad to see you made your flight in."

"Thank you." How did they know her name?

The tall man slid a slim envelope across the marble counter. "Ms. Shawcross has left your itinerary. When you're ready, please call down to the desk. She's made a car available to bring you to the venue tonight."

Lila thought of everything. She was one of the most professional managers that Margo had ever worked with. It was as refreshing as it was odd. Lila should be running a company, not herding twenty-something rockstars.

"I will, thank you."

"You're in Room 604 with a terrace view." He set a key on the envelope. "The rest of the guests have made their way to the venue."

She spared a glance at her watch. She had an hour before she needed to be there, but traffic was murderous in the city. "If you could have the car ready in thirty minutes, that would be satisfactory."

"Excellent." He inclined his head. "Welcome to the WestHouse, Ms. Reece. I'm Frank. If you need anything, please let me know. We hope you enjoy your stay. "

She nodded with a smile. "Thank you, Frank."

He held his arm out. "Lewis will help you with your bags."

"That's fine. I only have the two."

"Very well, then."

Margo had been in plenty of beautiful hotels before. Being the child of a lawyer and doctor afforded her a world of culture beyond the symphony. She tapped the ornate button to the elevator. The bronze doors, designed in the typical lines and curves of the Art Deco movement, slid open silently and more silk-tufted walls came into view.

For such an old building, everything was remarkably quiet. The ride was smooth and when she arrived on her floor, the silence was pervasive.

She slid her itinerary out of the envelope. In a world where emails and copy paper were the norm, the elegant silvery gray stationery with Donovan Lewis's corporate seal along the top was an anomaly—much like the entire situation. Discreetly-spaced letters underneath the raised seal were the only clue to the fact that it was for a record company.

A company that was very hands-on with their clients.

She didn't quite know what to make of the company or Lila Shawcross and Donovan Lewis. Margo was a classically trained violinist and twice now she'd been invited to work with a band that was as rough around the edges as a garage band.

And yet her strings blended seamlessly with them.

It didn't make sense.

Like that night with Simon made sense? Like your obsession with this garage band made sense?

Her grip tightened on the paper and she had to drag in a breath and force her fingers to relax. No, she wasn't going to think about that. Instead, she focused on the letter.

The entire floor was reserved for the band and Ripper Records, which explained the quiet. Everyone was already at the venue for the festivities. She had to go to rehearsal then was expected to sit for a few interviews with the band.

Music Life was going to film the entire release party and there would be a special airing that Saturday with footage from the New York City and Los Angeles parties.

Why did they want to involve her? She wasn't specifically mentioned in anything on the itinerary.

She slipped the sheet back into the envelope and into her purse. She leaned her suitcase against the wall but before she could open the door, it swung open.

Framed in the doorway stood a five-foot-four burr up her butt. A lovable one—usually—but thorny just the same.

"Hiya, sis."

Margo searched for her voice. "What the hell are you doing here?"

Chapter 2

Simon fit the key into the door. Who the fuck still used keys? The door didn't even bang effectively against the wall. He'd been nursing the mad since he'd checked out of the hotel on Park Avenue.

He was never going to hear the end of it from that little bout of excess. He'd used the sacred corporate card that was only supposed to be used sparingly.

The fact that he'd actually winced at the hotel bill he'd found by the door was saying something. What the hell had he been thinking?

Oh, right.

Blackout drunks didn't think.

Fuck.

As usual, the ever efficient Lila had his suitcase in the corner and his schedule on the bar with a bottle of his vodka of choice. If only it was because she didn't mind him drinking.

She'd learned long ago to put anything she wanted him to see within range of alcohol or food. He hated that she knew him so well, even if it did make him smile.

He opened the bottle and splashed an inch into the crystal glass and read his orders. Interviews by the dozen, about three seconds to warm up, and then rehearsal.

At the bottom in her elegant script was a personal note.

If you show up drunk, I will put itching powder in all of your favorite leather pants.

Simon's lips tipped up into a grin.

He had to give her points for style. He knocked back the glass and pulled off his shirt. A shower was desperately needed. He hadn't quite been able to think after that woman had spilled the words *Violin Girl.*

His shoulders were still itchy.

Enjoying himself with a random woman was one thing—replacing another was a whole level of crap he couldn't look at too closely.

Ever since he'd worked with her in the studio, he'd been losing time. For fuck's sake, he didn't even have to actually *work* with her in the studio.

But he sure as shit hadn't been able to walk away once he'd seen her in that cozy little booth. The memories from the huge studio from the first album juxtaposed over the more eclectic studio that Ripper Records owned.

Both times she'd been the proper little miss with her shoulders and back tightly squared off. Her entire posture screamed repressed, but then she lifted that bow and tucked her violin under her chin and it didn't matter that she could make a coal into a diamond with how tight she was clenched.

Magic flowed out of her fingers. She'd closed her dark eyes, then she was lost in the song. The strings were her conduit.

And he'd been so goddamn hard he'd had to walk it off.

Connection to music was something he identified with. It was the only thing that had kept him together in that shitty apartment with his father. It had been his ticket out of Carson and into Los Angeles, and now it was the only thing he had to focus on.

He didn't want to see that same desperate longing in her face. It reminded him of that night with her and "The Becoming" crashing all around them. Of losing himself in her sweet, clasping body. It reminded him that sex wasn't just scratching an itch, and no matter how many different people he'd bedded over the years, she'd been the only one to make him crave more.

Not just an orgasm.

Not just anonymous arms that would slip away once the sweat cooled.

She'd actually quieted the voices that usually only faded with alcohol or a song. Then she'd walked away without a backward glance.

And seeing her again had dredged all that shit up.

Why they'd added her to the album, he just didn't know. It wasn't like she was going to be on tour with them. It was a layer that Gray and Nick had to try and recreate on stage.

It sounded amazing on the studio track—and they were getting known for that little bit of extra. If that pulled them away from the herd of other artists out there, he'd take it.

He just wished he'd missed her visit.

He'd been doing just fine. He's put her out of his mind. And now he'd have to work to do it again.

With the water set on scalding, he stepped under the spray and let it beat along his neck.

When he was pink as a baby and squeaky clean, he hung a towel at his hips and checked his phone. A list of messages he didn't have the energy to read scrolled by. Then came the texts from Lila and Nick. Just as he was about to click off, Jazz filled his screen.

He sighed and answered the FaceTime request. "Purple Penis Eater, I'm naked. Did you want an extra show?"

A pair of long, purple lashes and wide violet eyes filed the screen. "Ugh. You know my pregnancy stomach isn't up for that kind of thing."

"Because the thought of my manhood would negate Gray's baby mojo, of course."

"You are delusional, my friend."

He pursed his lips and brought the camera closer. "I only speak fact."

She rolled her eyes. "You're late. Lila is going to have your balls for a dinner mint."

"Whoa, whoa. Let's not insult the boys here."

Her raspberry lips curved into a broad smile. "Then get your ass here, Super Slut."

Because the words were hitting a little too close to home right now, he forced his lips up into the smirk she'd been expecting. "I must beautify. Some of us can't add some glitter and be perfect."

"This is true." Jazz's laugh tinkled over the line and he didn't have to pretend when he smiled back that time.

She really was the only one in the band who made life bearable when the road got too endless.

"I'll be there in a few. Charm that Kim chick until I get there."

Jazz rubbed her hands together. "I'll tell her that story about when your pants ripped open in Colorado Springs."

Simon poured another two inches of vodka in his glass to stave off the wine hangover and grabbed his pants off the bed.

"You mean when I got the standing ovation?" He winked and ended the call.

"Is that any way to talk to your favorite little sister?"

Margo's jaw clenched. Wherever Juliet Reece was, chaos followed. "How did you even find me?" She pushed inside and stopped in the middle of the room.

Not because of the pure elegance and beauty of the space. No, she'd have to enjoy that later. But because her room currently had about fifteen different outfits strewn across every surface.

She curled her fingers tighter around her handle. "How long have you been here?"

"About an hour."

Margo shut her eyes. "Again, how did you find out where I'd be?"

Juliet curled into a high-backed chair that was tucked next to a large desk. "Hacked your email."

"You what?"

"You really have to pick harder passwords."

The thought of redoing her makeup was the only thing that kept her from rubbing her eyes in frustration. After a mental bookmark to redo all her passwords, she turned around to face her little sister.

"I thought you were in Paris with Tomas."

"Boring."

Only her sister would call Paris boring. And only her sister could go through men as quickly as she changed her shoes. Juliet crossed her long legs, bouncing her foot to her inner beat—the one that was never still for long.

"Of course I did get a little tidbit of information while I was with Tomas."

"Oh?" Margo set her violin on the desk and gathered up Juliet's strewn clothing to drape it over a chair.

"Naughty sister dear. As if it wouldn't get out that you weren't really on hiatus from the Philharmonic."

Margo froze. The conductor was supposed to give her a few weeks before he'd let that information out. So much for that promise.

All she needed was a little bit of time to line something else up before her parents found out she wasn't good enough. Before her name was struck from the programs and her photo banished to the bottom of the former artists section.

Louis Renard, the conductor of the Boston Philharmonic Orchestra, had never been a saint, but at least he understood lies of omission. At least she'd thought so. It wasn't public knowledge yet, but the string section was particularly gossipy. Especially Tomas, the little snake.

All her years of work gone in a half measure. Now there would be the sly, smug smiles behind her back. The half dozen other people that would be fighting for her place smelled the blood in the water. But all of that should have been a few weeks away.

"Because it's none of your business."

"I'm here for moral support. Nothing more, nothing less."

"You're here for the release party. Let's not get all sibling support system here."

"You wound me." Juliet rose from her chair, making her way slowly and methodically to the pile of clothing Margo had made. She picked up a slinky silver top. In a blink, she pulled off the siren red shirt she'd been wearing and wiggled into the silver. "I'm here to make sure you take advantage of this time. I don't know how you landed the gig with Oblivion, but you'll waste it on actually performing."

"That's what I'm here for."

"Ever the straight arrow." Juliet sighed. "You have a Manhattan A-list club at your fingertips and you're going to simply go there and do your job."

Margo's spine snapped straight.

"See. I can see it in your body language. And that hideous pair of stove-pipe pants. So last year." Juliet hauled Margo's suitcase onto the bench at the end of the bed and popped it open. "Black pants, black skirt that goes to your freaking calves, black pants, more black pants. God, do you even have a clue about shopping?" She looked up and skimmed her gaze over the jacket.

"What?"

"Color. It's a good thing. Makes you look not so stuck up."

"I'm not stuck up."

Juliet's eyebrow rose and a slim copper hoop danced from the arch.

"Please. Your picture is on the wiki page." She yanked out a pair of tights and short wraparound skirt Margo only used as a cover up for when she used the pool. "Aha! This will do."

The fact that it was exactly what the man from the store had advised her to wear only made her seethe — internally, of course. Letting Juliet see that she was getting to her was a surefire way for more abuse.

"I wear those for comfort, not for going out."

"Look, I know you're a bit thick in the leg, but it works for your whole hourglass thing."

"Wow."

Juliet rolled her eyes and tossed the tights at her. "You know you are. You just didn't get the perfect metabolism. Only one sister gets that per family."

She snatched the pants out of the air and kicked off her heels before locking herself into the bathroom. Even that had Juliet's stamp. Cosmetics were strewn across the beautiful marble counter and powders from eyeshadow, bronzer, and something full of sparkles stained the sink.

Margo had left home to get away from this chaos and now it was following her to New York? She'd wanted this one thing to boost her visibility and now her sister would probably screw that up, too.

She gripped the edge of the counter and looked up. The deep pink of the jacket pushed her back a step. She'd seen herself in the mirror at the boutique, but it was still jarring. The black and white uniform had been her life for so long that any other color felt foreign.

Even off the stage, it was easier to use the monochrome palette to blend in. To stay unnoticed and safe.

There was nothing safe about a color like this. She shrugged off the jacket and drew in a deep breath. This was no better. She'd learned to hide her curves under the right clothes. Not to show them off.

The tailored slacks didn't accentuate her hips, they were bought specifically to hide them. Sure, it made her look a size larger, but her mother had showed her how to dress for her problem areas.

And she always did what was best for her family.

Except when you lost your chair because you couldn't concentrate.

Because she hated it.

She stood straighter, and threw back her shoulders until her breasts lifted. The camisole didn't allow for the minimizers she usually wore to downplay her cup size. Before she could talk herself out of it, she unbuttoned the slacks and let them puddle at her feet.

Lush hips and a slim waist filled the mirror. No matter how many medicine ball exercises she did to strengthen her core, or resistance exercises she did to firm up her arms, or miles she ran on the treadmill, or the carefully honed diet she kept to—nothing would ever reduce her hips or the curve of her ass.

Your unfortunate shape can be concealed, Margo.

She shut her eyes against her mother's voice in her head. Her perfect size two mother that had the elegant chill of England in her skin and her blood.

Margo got the bloom of pink under cream skin and the heart-shape face and rear end to match. One glass of wine and she was flushed. She couldn't be more opposite from her mother if she tried. Juliet got all that tall, slim perfection.

If only she'd gotten the skill with the violin, *she* could have been the one aimed toward the stage. But no, Juliet had no love of the classical music that ruled their house. She had all the aptitude with instruments and dance, but she would rather die than let their mother know there was any true love for it in her heart.

Her sister was stronger than her in that regard. Juliet didn't care what anyone thought. Margo cared too much.

What a pair they'd made in that mausoleum of a house.

Juliet pounded on the door. "It doesn't take that long to change. Get out here, I have places to go."

Oh, thank God. Did that mean she wasn't going to push her way into an invite to the party?

Maybe she'd be able to enjoy herself with the anonymity of a crowd and the music she'd been dying to hear again. The studio album kept her demons at bay, but the live music sated the prickly feeling that was only growing with each successive night.

She lifted her sister's bronzer brush and highlighted her cheeks, then darkened her eyes. She slicked a pale nude color over her lips to play up her eyes.

Juliet usually went for glamour eyes and lips with a dark stain, but it was too much for Margo's face. Her bee-stung lips were too much for the look she wanted. If any night was one that she could finally be a different person, it was tonight.

Margo stepped into the silky tights and draped the barely there skirt over her hips. She kept her eyes averted from the mirror and resisted the urge to pull down the skirt.

She felt naked.

So very naked and exposed.

Just before she opened the door, she caught a flash of gold in Juliet's bag. She tugged out the wad of bangles in gold and jet black and pulled it over her right hand to stack up her wrist.

Juliet opened the door. "Would you—Wow." Her dark eyes bulged as she dragged Margo out of the bathroom. "Where have you been hiding all that?"

The urge to say how improper the outfit was screamed in her head, but she simply lifted her chin. "This isn't exactly orchestra wear."

"Not something you have to worry about anymore, big sis."

Margo resisted the urge to smack the smug smile off of Juliet's face. "I do have to go on stage with rock stars. I guess this is appropriate."

"Appropriate? Mar, you look like a pinup and it's glorious."

Margo winced. Exactly what she was afraid of. Too lush, too sexual. She turned to go back into the bathroom and Juliet grabbed her arm.

"Oh, no. We are not wasting this." Juliet snapped Margo's black bra strap. "Do you have anything with color?" Juliet waved her finger in front of Margo's face. "No flaring your nostrils at me. Do you or not?"

Margo stalked over to her bag and opened the hidden zippered area.

"Oh, my God. You have a problem. A very expensive and very fabulous problem with high-end lingerie." Juliet reached around her and dragged the bag down the bed. "This one."

"No."

"Yes." Juliet held up the corset-style shaper.

Margo only wore that when she had to be at the front of the stage during one show a year. It sucked everything in and then she didn't have to listen to her mother rip into her about a diet. But she didn't have the minimizer bra to go under it.

There was no way she could wear it. Everything was so...fluffed.

"This." Juliet spun Margo around and undid the bra she was wearing. "Hey!"

"No arguments. I need to cinch this baby on because you'll go too safe."

"I will not."

"You will, too." Juliet pushed down the stretchy camisole she was wearing and whipped the corset around her naked breasts. Margo jumped when her sister shimmied her breasts into the cups without even touching her. "Relax, I'm not copping a feel."

Margo sucked in a breath as Juliet definitely went to the second set of hooks up the back. "I need to breathe, you know."

"Overrated. This top has maximum boob potential. And the fact that it matches those kickass shoes is a bonus."

"I am not wearing only a corset to this party."

"No, you're not ready for that. But you will have it peek out of this little cami."

With each hook and eye that her sister clasped, Margo straightened. She didn't really have a choice. The thing was made for the posture-challenged so it only exacerbated her own penchant for standing straight.

Because she didn't have the shaper on under it, there was nowhere for her breasts to go. Oh, God no.

Juliet turned her around. "Dang, girl. That is some cleavage you hide under those twin sets and cashmere."

"Shut up."

Her sister's eyes twinkled. "And you even dug into my makeup. I approve. We'll get you the new Naked shadows since we're right near Times Square."

Since she did not have anything like it in her own makeup stash, Margo said nothing.

When Juliet tried to pull up Margo's camisole, Margo batted her hands away. "I can dress myself, thank you."

"Well, at least that part."

Margo turned to the mirror in the room and took a step back. No way could she go out looking like that.

Juliet appeared behind her with her new heels. She dropped them beside her. "Put those on."

Margo sighed and tucked her feet into the four inch stilettos.

"Man, you are going to kill tonight. Are you actually playing on stage with them?"

"Yes." Nerves took flight in her belly. She'd been on stage most of her life, but the thought of standing beside any of them with her violin made her palms sweat.

What if she had to go to the front with Simon?

No. Don't think about it.

Juliet tugged Margo's cami down so that the hot pink peeked from the lace. God, it felt like her breasts were actually going to spill out of the top.

Margo tried to hike it up and Juliet pulled it down in the back. "No. It has to sit right above your hips to accentuate the curve."

"It's too tight."

"It's supposed to be. Lifts and separates baby." She pulled the clip out of Margo's hair. "Now, you're good. And I'm off to meet with my friends. We'll see you at the party."

Margo turned. "I can't get all your friends in."

"Well, how handy that I'm the one who got an invite from them. My friend Lucia works for Ripper Records. She has four invites for the festivities tonight."

"Oh."

"Don't wait up. I might not be back until morning."

Margo sighed as her sister sailed out the door, leaving her chaos in the room without a backward glance.

Perfect.

Chapter 3

Simon slicked back his hair from the shower and slipped on the black button-down shirt that wouldn't make it to show time. But with the five interviews he had to do before they got on stage, he had to have some clothes on.

He jammed his feet in his shitkickers and left the buckles open because he was too lazy to actually fasten them. Taking one last shot of Crystal Skull, he grabbed the key and his phone—though he was more than willing to leave it behind if Lila wouldn't skin him alive for it.

The hallway was silent save for the jangle of his buckles and silver chains at his wrist. He locked his door and the solid clunk of a door opening and closing drew his attention. A woman at the far end of the hall was also locking up.

A curtain of dark chocolate hair fell across her shoulders and back. His eyebrow went up as the woman made a quarter turn. The most spectacular pair of breasts were doing their damnedest to stay inside the corset that peeked over a simple black tank.

His cock twitched in his pants. Pissed because it was another brunette that was making Simon senior take notice, he brought his eyes up and stalled at the fragile chain at her throat.

No.

His tongue burned at the memory of the sandy pearl against his teeth and rolling along the tip of his tongue before her honeysuckle scent had taken over. He looked away.

No.

The key dug into his fingers. He was seeing things.

But dammit, he hadn't had enough vodka to make that mistake again.

He looked again and his cock surged. That familiar hip roll was exaggerated thanks to the mile-high heels she wore and skintight opaque black stockings that hugged every goddamn curve.

The curves that he still could taste. Those curves that could wake him from a dead sleep when he least expected it. A little sash at her hip swung with each step and she jangled like a goddamn gypsy.

The familiar case that was never far from her side bounced against her thigh.

Violin Girl.

Margo.

Only this wasn't exactly the woman he remembered. This woman owned her sexuality and walked like she was going to end up in a locked bedroom for days.

She paused in the middle of the hall and in that moment, he saw the woman from the studio. Uncertain and curious. Her chin tipping up as she walked toward him. The roll in her gait had been tempered, but the rest — oh fucking hell, the rest — was there and lured like a siren on the rocks and he was a willing victim.

No.

Not her victim again.

Hell no.

He tucked his key into his pocket, then made sure to adjust himself for her before crossing his arms. "Well, if it isn't Violin Girl."

"Mr. Kagan." Her chest shuddered for the briefest moment before she squared her shoulders.

"And just what are you doing at my hotel?"

She glanced down at her outfit. "Getting ready for tonight."

His eyes skimmed over her again. "So Lila is giving you the VIP treatment."

She tilted her head. "Looks like it."

The skin between his shoulder blades was on fire. "You sure you can handle our party, Violin Girl. It's for grownups and those that don't wear their chastity belts like an accessory."

"Do you see a chastity belt on me?"

No, what he did see was a tool that would cock-block him then strangle him. Even worse, he saw the writing on the wall. Margo Reece was exactly the kind of publicity stunt that Lila would pull. Margo wasn't coming out on stage to play one or two songs.

"I don't remember seeing your name added to the band roster, Violin Girl."

"Maybe you should pay more attention to the call sheet."

Simon stepped closer and tipped his head. "Is that how this is going to go? Back to our petty little insults." He lowered his gaze to her very full, very lush lips. Just a hint underplayed. So much like the woman he remembered.

Hiding.

Always hiding.

Except tonight, she was just a little bit wild. Unbound hair and a hint of mischief in her smoky eyes. He lifted a lock of her hair that had fallen into her cleavage and wound it around his finger.

The silky straight hair didn't bend. It slipped away to fall back in with the rest around her shoulders. "We didn't necessarily need words, if I remember right."

She sucked in a corner of her lip, which plumped up the rest. The wash of blood under her skin made his cock hammer against his leathers. Instead of taking a step back, she tilted her head the other way and let her lower lip go.

"Do you honestly remember? I seem to recall the burn of vodka on your tongue."

"And I recall the salted honey of your pussy."

Her eyes flashed wide and she did step back this time.

He let his trademark smirk slide across his face and lifted a brow. "Oh, I remember everything about that night, Violin Girl."

"Margo," she corrected.

He swept her hair back over her shoulder and was rewarded with a slight tremble. He remembered that reaction before he ripped her pantyhose open and tasted her for the first time. Remembered that she'd corrected him that night too.

Remembered that she'd walked away.

He stepped aside and bowed, his arm out. "Looks like we're going to the same place." He looked up at her from the shag of his bangs and choppy hair. "Care to join me?"

She lifted her chin and walked ahead of him. "A car is waiting for me."

"I can guarantee mine's better."

"Because you expect it?"

"No, because the fans expect it and Lila doesn't like to disappoint the fans."

Her step faltered a little before she continued toward the elevator, but she shook her hair back and he got a good look at all the curves she hid under shapeless clothes and high collars.

Fuck, he needed a drink.

He unhooked his sunglasses from the inside pocket of his jacket and beat her to the elevator. He leaned against the gold wall with the brass fixture. "We can break in the backseat on the ride over."

"In your dreams."

"Well, I've done it a few times, so maybe a memory?" The minute he'd said it, he wished he hadn't.

She stepped into the elevator and turned to face him. The chilly Violin Girl retreated back under her armor and her almost smile was replaced with serene grace.

He hated that face. It always was followed by a retreating back.

Margo curled her fingers under the bar behind her back. She wasn't ready to see him. She'd been prepared to see him at rehearsal—even at a few of the interviews, but not *there*.

Not at the hotel. Not smelling of that leather and cinnamon combination that lived in her head. Now it was sitting in her damn sinuses because he'd walked right into her space. As if he had the right or the privilege. He hadn't even given her the chance to put him in his place about it. He'd just been there. Too close. The heat and scent of him enveloping her like fingers of fog. Pervasive and overwhelming.

And she'd just stood there like an idiot.

Thank all the sinners that she'd had the heavy boning of the corset to hold in all the proof of her body's traitorous reactions. Her breasts ached and her tights felt constricting. His coarse words and those stunning eyes had bored into her until she'd been all but defenseless.

No, she'd definitely not shored up her brick-and-mortar foundation against the instant softening that happened when he was in her vicinity. But she'd have to do it now. Or she'd do something insane like take him up on the idea of Lincoln Town Car sex.

How many of those restrictive cars had she traveled in over the years?

Between her parents and the few times a year that she worked in the city, she'd ridden in many of them. How many of the cars had kneeprints in them?

She looked down at the floor.

Why did she want to have her own imprint on the floor? This one, maybe, or the car's. Perhaps both.

The elevator door opened and Simon slapped his hand over the sensor. He gave her that head tilt that saw far too much and waited patiently for her to exit. She sailed out of the elevator and Frank came around the desk.

"Your car is here, Ms. Reece and Mr. Kagan. I assumed one car would be fine?"

Margo's fingers itched to curl around the concierge's perfect neck, but manners had been instilled in her long before she'd taken up her bow. "Thank you, Frank."

Simon came up behind her. Too close.

God, way too close.

"Thanks, Frankie. I do love to travel in style."

"Yes, sir." Frank led the way across the marble tile and through the ornate doors.

Simon's hand settled on her lower back. It shouldn't have felt proprietary, but it did. Probably because his lack of distance made it seem all the more intimate.

She didn't want intimate.

It was bad enough that she had to be in the same car. She really didn't need his cinnamon and leather scent to be all over her. Nor the memory of his touch to be so intrusive.

So long ago and yet it felt like no time had passed at all. The memory strong and true as the blinding orgasm she'd experienced—one that had never been duplicated. She'd never been a sexual creature. It didn't fit with her lifestyle. She'd had one purpose—to practice and move up the chain at the philharmonic.

But now there was new purpose and being around this man only made her realize what she'd been missing. She didn't like it. Didn't like how out of control he always made her feel. No matter if it was one day or one hour, or a year, Simon Kagan burrowed under her skin. She couldn't handle him touching her.

Not now.

Not when everything already felt too unbalanced. With her costume, with her lies, and a nebulous goal she was trying to create.

She picked up her step so he didn't touch her, but his long legs ate up just as much marble and sidewalk as hers. And the more he knew she was affected by him, the more he'd try to take.

That part she remembered all too clearly as well.

He beat the driver to the door and held it open for her, but instead of standing back like a gentleman, he framed the door with his body. She looked up at him — those few inches that separated them all that leather and heat.

Don't let him know it matters.

Don't let him see.

His eyebrow speared up as he waited to see what she'd do.

That smug smile full of power and sex. She knew it was the charisma he carried around like a pheromone, and she knew many women fell for it right before their panties hit the floor.

Hers had. As galling as it was, she couldn't deny it.

She kept her face blank as she turned and slid her bottom across the front of his thighs and stepped into the car. The urge to cross one foot behind her ankle in the prim pose that suited her former life was ingrained. Legs together, back straight. She heard her mother's voice in her ear as clearly now as she had from toddlerhood.

Today, she crossed her legs and tucked her knees down against the luxury leather so her calves and heels were on display. The silky drape of her skirt rose high on her thigh, and she tucked her case behind her knees.

She caught one look before Simon shielded his eyes with his shades and sprawled in the seat, his arm across the back. The aviators hid everything and his sardonic smirk was in place, but he tightened one hand on his thigh and his first finger tapped restlessly.

"So tell me, when did Lila invite you to the festivities?"

"A few weeks ago."

"I see." Simon's tapping grew in speed.

She'd said no at first. The season was over at the Boston Philharmonic Opera. Even before she'd lost her spot, she'd have been able to do the guest spot. But playing in the studio was far different from the stage. She was a puzzle piece from a Monet, locking in with a cityscape from Los

Angeles. They weren't even the same genre, let alone time period.

She didn't belong.

But her obsession with the music had to be handled. This seemed like the perfect way. Two days and she could kill the curiosity and burn the remains.

She could get back to auditions and the life she'd been born for.

This fairytale could end.

"I only said yes a week ago. Lila sent me another request." More like a command via a FaceTime call. A sleepless night and a weak moment were all someone like Lila needed to get her way.

And here she was, in New York City to play with a rock band.

"She gets what she wants." He turned to her, the fingertips of his stretched out hand brushed against her hair. He dragged a lock away from her shoulder, the calloused tip flicking across her skin before he gently rubbed the stick-straight strands between his thumb and first two fingers. "It usually works out in my favor."

She cupped her hand around her neck and tugged her hair out of his reach to let it fall down her opposite shoulder and the front of her corset. "We can use this time to decide on a cover song for the set. You can use me."

He tipped his shades down. "Oh, Violin Girl, I'd love to use you."

A flash of memory choked her. Her fingers wrapped around the back of that wide-backed velvet chair as he took her from behind. She crossed her arms under her corset—she didn't exactly have a choice there—and gave him a bland stare.

He made a little twirling gesture with his finger. "Dirty Violin Girl had a thought. I knew the ice princess thing hid a freak."

The way he said *freak*—emphasizing the *k* until it was its own word, its own exclamation—made her bury any reaction. The wild dreams and ache she fought against every night was too close to the surface.

"I'm here to work. My job is to enhance the sound you have and give it another layer. To make tonight and tomorrow night special. No more, no less." She drew her phone out of the small pouch she had near the handle of her case. "There's your songs, of course, but Lila thought I could add to a fun cover song—the strings in 'Kashmir'."

"Yes. Yes, that needs to happen. Nick and Gray would kill that and Pixie wouldn't mind a break on the drums. All preggo and such. But it has a big build — long song, though. We've played it a million times when fucking around. You know, Zep and all."

"Won't take much rehearsal then. It's a good one to fire up the crowd. Open with it."

"Not sure the crowd we play to will be as appreciative of the glory that is Led Zeppelin."

"Yes, but your..." She bit her lower lip. How did you tell a man like Simon that his sex appeal on stage was another instrument? Especially without stroking his ego until he puffed up like a peacock. She was fairly sure he knew that it was his instrument. He'd let go of the guitar and embraced that aspect of himself.

"But my..." He scraped his fingers through his messy head of inky hair. "Spit it out."

She sighed. "You have the sexual nature to pull off the song."

"The *sexual nature*?" He crossed his arms, tucking his hands into his jacket. "Are you trying to tell me I'm sexy? I like it."

"You are well aware of your strengths, Mr. Kagan. I don't need to tell you about them, nor to stroke your healthy ego."

"Not the only healthy thing on me. But then again, you know that."

Her spine stiffened and she glanced up at the driver. As with all drivers, he didn't blink, didn't even have a facial expression beyond bored. But he heard Simon. She knew that for sure.

"What happens between two consenting adults is not what we're talking about here."

"Consenting adults? That's what you call it? 'The Becoming' lured you into the singing booth and what we did couldn't be labeled with something as mundane as *consenting adults*. We fucked and you liked it."

They pulled up to the club. The neon and box light marquise looked garish in the waning sunshine. This was a place for the slick dark of New York under the cover of night. A lot like them.

That studio had been a moment in the dark and with day came realizations. Namely that they didn't fit outside of music.

"It was pleasant, yes."

"I remember you screaming." He turned to her, his fingers digging into her hair to grip her scalp. "I remember that you couldn't get enough."

Her nipples tightened and the ache that curled into her belly awakened like a cherry blossom in April. Achingly beautiful and awe-inspiring, but ultimately, only lasting a short time. That's what they were.

And she needed to remember that.

She curled her fingers around his wrist. The tension there was like her violin when she tightened the strings too much. They'd break and the sound resonated on a sour note.

She needed to loosen that strain. "And then it was done."

The tension receded and she almost smiled in relief. There, that wasn't so bad. Until she saw his face. The almost snarl was gone. In its wake was nothing.

No smug smile, no flirtatious liquid movements.

He drew away and stepped out of the car when the driver came around. He didn't stay, didn't help her from the car. Didn't crowd her at all.

He simply detached.

And her ache came back triple time.

Chapter 4

Simon passed the small group of people at the door. They yelled his name, some even screeched out that they were Sirens. He had a part to play and he was fucking good at it, but he just couldn't. Not now.

Not with that vanilla ice cream-cool voice in his head. *And then it was over.*

He'd do well to remember that. That it was well and truly over. No part of them had been more than a memory. A hazy bit of lust.

How many times had he had just the same moment with other women? Fleeting lust and once he'd gotten to the naked and sweaty stage, there was no other allure. Shitty but true. The semi-pretend moment between two bodies that fed off pleasure and the rush of endorphins.

Then it was over.

She'd been just like he was with so many other women. The taste of it was as bitter as the dregs of a cheap bottle of whiskey.

One of a thousand reasons why he was a vodka drinker.

Clarity to the bottom of the bottle.

It was never anything more than it looked. Just like him.

He was a face.

A body.

A voice.

Most of the time that was enough. He had his friends and he had fame that had snowballed with every passing month. The scent of honeysuckle made him a little stupid, that was all.

So he'd fill his head with something else. Something that he did understand. He turned back to the doorway and saw her there. Filtered sunlight backlighting her until she was just a mouthwateringly curvy shadow.

A shadowy memory—as she should be.

He stalked toward her. The surprise on her face almost made him change direction. Her fingers curled tighter on her case. He didn't stop, didn't even look at her as he breezed by her and out the door.

He planted his smile on his lips and studied the twenty women and one bouncer through amber lenses. "I'm sorry, Sirens. I had to go check in with the boss lady. We have a big party planned tonight." He rubbed his hands together. "Who wants a special pass?"

The small crowd bleated out a chorus of "me"s and he opened his arms. "Phones. I need to see 'em!" Smart phones were whipped out and he tipped his shades down. "Think you can take a video?"

A blond at the front of the pack squealed. "I'd make any video with you."

"Now that is an offer I cannot refuse." He took her hand and lifted the ropes. The crowd surged forward. "Uh-uh. Wait your turn. Each of you can get a two minute video with me. Post it to our page and the five of you with the most comments will be my guest tonight."

He could feel the gaze on the back of his neck. It burned like hellfire. "Hello, boss."

"Simon, we have a schedule to keep," Lila said.

He hugged the pretty blond fan into his side. "I think we'll be doing a few videos and then I will do everything on your To Do list. Let the guys know we'll be doing 'Kashmir' as the cover tonight."

The crowd behind him whooped and hollered. The bouncer crossed his arms and nodded.

Simon grinned at the crowd then down to the fan currently squeezing his ribcage. "Think I can channel a little Robert Plant tonight, sweetheart?"

"Who?"

"Oh, darlin'. We need to educate you on the finer songs of the past that have created the future." He looked over his shoulder. "Someone find that shit on YouTube."

The bouncer took out his cell. "I have it on my phone."

Simon smiled, his lead singer veneer slipping. "That is why you are a cool cat. Turn it up."

The epic song played in the background as he hauled girl after girl into his side and took the time to listen, to smile, to give them a moment. He remembered what it was like to love a band enough to stand out and wait for a show.

He'd even charmed his way inside on more than one penniless occasion. This was why he loved the fans. The skin-to-skin contact, the moments.

The crazy.

He glanced at the door and Lila was still there, but her face was thoughtful now and her iPad was out. Boss lady was on the job. She would play up the spin.

When everyone had their videos and Lila had collected names and usernames and numbers, they both walked back into the dark room.

"By all rights, I should skin you for being over an hour late at this point, but your sales of the album just surged with that little stunt. 'Sugar Kiss' just went from number four to number one on iTunes. Congrats, Kagan, you won't be flayed today."

"Ah, c'mon, Lila. I love when you roast me over the coals. It gets my nipples all tingly."

"Keep you and your nipples to yourself. You have four interviews lined up and thanks to that rather delicious bit of social media prowess, we are very behind. And if you tell anyone I called it delicious, I'll kneecap you."

"Geez, kneecap me, put itching powder all over my manly bits...so evil, Dragon Lady." He covered his lips. "I mean, Lila."

"I know you morons call me Dragon Lady. Daenerys always got what she wanted. I'm okay with the moniker."

"You were watching *Games of Thrones* with us in the studio."

"I couldn't help it. You played it at top volume."

Simon bumped her arm. "You love it. Power, sex, kingdoms, and decapitations. It's all bloody good fun. You'd rock the queen status."

"Damn right." She tapped on her tablet.

He grinned. Lila Shawcross liked to pretend she was a badass, but the band had grown on her. Mostly like a fungus he was sure, but they'd grown on her nonetheless.

He looped his arm around her hip. "So, how many interviewers do I need to slay?"

She unhooked his arm and he heard the whoosh of an email being sent from her tablet. "I just sent you an updated list of people. Now bring your A-game to the party, Simon. You have work to do."

"I'm always playing the game, darlin'."

"That's the truth," she said under her breath. She pointed to a leather booth on the far side of the room under cherry lights. "First up is *Music Life*. Kim and her crew will be filming all night so I figured a bookend of interviews would be best. The rest of the band has already done their work."

"Save the best for last, baby."

She merely gave him a side eye. "Then rehearsal and more interviews."

"Good thing I warmed up in the shower."

She hugged her ever present iPad to her chest. "Oh, and thanks for being sober. I didn't want to have to kill you. There are far too many interviews to reschedule."

Her deadpan deliveries always tickled him. Enough that he'd made it his mission in life to break her. "I had to protect my junk, right?"

Lila just shook her head and headed over to the stage. Simon waved to Deacon and a very pregnant Harper on the stage. He was doting on her as usual. She was sitting on one of the trunks with a bottle of water in her hand as her husband checked over the equipment.

No matter how many minions and roadies they had these days, Deacon still needed to approve the layout. And in a club setting Simon appreciated Deacon's Boy Scout nature. No matter how swanky—and this place was swanky—there was always quirks to a venue. This place was more suited to a DJ, so he imagined the acoustics were going to be a bit of a challenge.

He dragged his fingers over the leather covered frames of the wide U-shaped booths. The perky and delicious Kim Forrester was sitting in the far booth with her camera crew scattered around her. A roving cameraman was following Jazz as she waddled around the bar and took over the space. Probably making a virgin version of some drink from the mixing book that she'd stolen from Harper's stash of recipe books.

Jazz was forever making juice concoctions and putting umbrellas in them. Their Pink Princess had never been a big drinker to begin with, but since she'd grown more pregnant, she was obsessed with frilly drinks.

Simon waved to Kim, the interviewer, and stopped off at the bar. He slapped the counter. "Bartender, I need a drink."

Jazz slid over to him. "Finally decided to join us?"

Simon waggled his eyebrows. "Miss me?"

"Like a rash."

"Aww." He crossed his hands over his chest. "You wound me, Pix."

She rubbed the side of her belly. "What can the kiddo and I make you, Lush?"

"Make me two pretty drinks with vodka."

"Of course."

"Of course," he said with a sly grin. "I have to go entertain Miss Forrester."

"Well then." She pulled out two martini glasses. A worker bee at the end of the bar started to come their way, but Simon held up a hand.

The guy balled his fingers into a fist and stayed still. Jazz Edwards knew her way around a bar. All of them had spent so much time in bars that bartending was second nature—and often a second job—for most of them.

Simon preferred drinking to building a drink, but he'd done a few stints as busboy over the years. He usually ended up in the backroom with a patron, but he started off the night working well enough.

Jazz poured cranberry juice and vodka into a shaker over ice and did a little shimmy. Her wild violet and green sparkly dress moved over her bursting curves.

"Pregnant or not, Pix, you are a picture." He leaned on the bar. "A damn sexy one."

"Put it back in your pants, buddy."

He looked down at his leathers. For the first time that day, all was well and under control. "Look at that, everyone's behaving today."

Jazz rolled her eyes but her lips were twitching. She poured the bright raspberry drink into the glasses and splashed lime into each before tucking little curls of lime rind along the lip. She found two umbrellas under the counter and speared one in each. "There."

He leaned across the counter and made to kiss Jazz but she lifted the vodka bottle in front of him first. He laughed and kissed the bottle for the camera and sauntered off with a glass in each hand.

"Mz. Kimberly Forrester. It's been awhile, sweetheart. I brought you libations."

"Oh, Simon. You are not getting me drunk again."

He slid into the booth and set hers down in front of her. "Are the cameras on?"

"Always."

"I'll behave then." Simon grinned and lifted the glass to her. "A little."

She clinked hers against it. "Congrats on the new album. I've heard the numbers are awesome."

"Gotta love iTunes. We did that preorder party last week and had a bunch of fun."

Kim turned her game face on. "Yes, you did. In fact, the whole album streamed and actually leaked out into the world. Did that kill sales?"

Simon relaxed back against the cool leather. "You know how it goes. People like to find stuff online and listen. I was a poor kid too, so I know how it goes. That's why we kept the album cheap. Our label understands that getting it out there is more important."

Kim being Kim, latched onto the *poor kid* sound bite. He knew these questions by rote. He gave charming stories about his childhood. Lies. Lies were so much easier to believe.

They didn't want to know that his father beat him black and blue most nights. They wanted the Disney version. That he scraped and saved and got out. That music saved him.

At least that part was true.

Music had saved him. Nick and Snake had saved him. The scarred and broken cement parking lots on the fringes of Los Angeles that they'd escaped to with their skateboards and bottles of stolen beer.

And eventually the winding, graffiti-strewn benches of Ventura Boulevard and the beach saturated with people that loved street musicians had saved him. Playing until he was too drunk to care about going home saved him.

Singing saved him.

But she didn't care about that.

No one cared about that but him. So he smiled and told colorful stories about the Blue Rhino and all the dive clubs they'd begged to play in. And when their twenty minutes was up, he had finished another drink—a purple one this time.

Warm with the alcohol and Kim's easy flirting, he went still as Margo's sad violin soared into the huge room. All eyes trained on the stage as Nick and Gray played on either side of her. The familiar strings of the opening from "Kashmir" surged the warmth into an epic heat.

His cock stirred immediately and he downed the last drops of the drink. "Looks like that's my cue. Time to rehearse."

"Thanks for sitting with us, Simon. It's always a pleasure to talk to you." She brushed a kiss against his cheek. The sensory memory kicked in. Her classy flowers-and-spice scent had followed them into a small closet at their Los Angeles apartment during the celebration of their first EP.

Funny how scent always struck the chords of memory that were so often softened with booze. But he remembered that night. And how Kim had wanted a hookup without sex.

She'd gotten off on the party and being seen. They both had. The beginning of his career. The first wrong turn that could have been the end of friendships he cherished more than he would ever say.

A little mutual groping that night. Hell, he hadn't even let her touch him. She'd been too high on the night. He'd fed on that high and had fun with a pretty woman in the closet.

That had been more than enough after Margo had hulled him out and left him to crash and burn. That's exactly what he needed to do tonight.

Have fun.

"I'll see you after the rehearsals for the band interview."

"Looking forward to it." Her bluebell eyes sparkled.

Simon hauled himself out of the booth and crossed the room. Margo pulled her searingly purple violin away from her chin, her gaze warily following him as he climbed the stairs. "Violin Girl had a good idea with Zep, huh?"

Nick stuck his pick onto the sticky strip along his microphone stand. "Always like to get my Jimmy Page on."

Gray grinned. "I know everyone and their mother knows this song, but damn, it's good to play it on stage."

"Yeah, you'd be surprised." Simon rolled up his shirtsleeve to his elbow and shook out his bracelets. "This hot twenty-year-old outside had no idea who I was talking about."

"Yeah, I heard you were stealing my video thunder out there, Super Slut," Jazz yelled from behind her kit.

"What can I say? They all wanted a piece of me." He moved to his mic stand. He always had two on the stage. One back by Jazz's drums with a regular mic on it and his retro box microphone from their club days. When he was on stage, he needed it cupped in his hand. The age of it added a little distortion to his voice that was part of his sound at this point.

He'd had the damn thing rewired three times since the last tour. Hank, his tech guy, was pretty much the only one who could fix it. And it was pure perfection right now.

He cupped his hands around the cool metal. "Start from the top."

Margo lifted her violin and the notes soared. He closed his eyes and let the song take him. The lyrics filled his head and spilled out effortlessly. He usually downplayed his voice during rehearsal—saving the real deal for the crowds.

But they were doing an abbreviated set so he didn't have to worry about it. The idle chitchat and scrape of dishes and glasses faded to the background as the song rolled him under.

He paced the stage and unearthed slinky Robert Plant memories. Margo's violin elevated the song. Gray and Nick played back-to-back and Deacon was doing his metronome sway.

Jazz twirled glowing green sticks as she kept the beat, watching Deacon for clues for the pace of the song. Everything was as it should be.

Save for Margo.

She matched him in all black except for the bright pink that drew the eye to her spectacular breasts. So much her and yet not. A new breed of prim musician just waiting to bust out of her mold.

And because the song seemed to cry out for it, he stalked her around the stage. They held eye contact as the song built and his voice got raspier with each chorus. He swayed forward and she arched back until they were one unit in the song.

Like the ebb and flow of thrusting inside of her. They matched up so effortlessly. By the time the song ended, the room was silent and the cord of the mic was wound so tightly around his wrist his blood throbbed with the restriction.

Much like his fucking pants.

The wolf whistle and claps brought him back and he shut down that heady connection with her. Those dark eyes slayed him and moved him. He turned with her at his side and they both bowed.

He itched to curl around her so he crossed the stage to Nick instead. They rolled through the new songs and then one more cover. He coughed through the middle of "Closer to the Edge" from Thirty Seconds to Mars so he pulled back to keep it fresh for the show.

It was a crowd pleaser and a sing-a-long song. They wrapped up rehearsal with "Nailed" and "Sugar Kiss" from the new album.

"Don't you want to do 'The Becoming'?" Jazz asked. "Margo hasn't done it live yet."

"That's fine. I know it by heart," Margo answered before he could.

"It's different live," Nick chimed in.

Simon pushed up his sleeves. "Let's wing it. See if the magic happens. If not, we'll practice double time for tomorrow night."

Margo nodded and uncapped a bottle of water and took a long drink.

He had to turn away from her long, graceful neck beaded with sweat. Even with the lights at a minimum, it was hot on stage. He'd be swapping out the dress shirt for a tank for the show that night.

But for now, he took the front stairs to the floor. "I have to do a few more interviews."

Anything to get away from the stage. He turned up the wattage on his smile as a redhead crossed to him.

"Amazing rehearsal. Tonight will be epic."

"I hope so, darlin'."

"I'm Bobbi Matthews with Z100."

"Oh, right. We did an acoustic set on your show two weeks ago."

"Yes. It was such a hit that we wanted to come down and cover your release party."

"Happy to have you."

"I have a few questions, if that's okay."

He looked over his shoulder at Margo still on the stage talking quietly to Lila. She was blotting her neck with a towel. He turned back to Bobbi. "Absolutely."

Anything to get his mind off that stage.

Margo's chest was still tight and her heart was in her throat. This stage made the philharmonic feel small and boring. The mishmash of instruments and the way Gray and Nick swapped out guitars like there was an endless supply in their trunks fascinated her.

She had a half dozen violins herself, but she'd only thought to bring her Starfish. If she'd had the wherewithal, she would have brought her classical as well.

"Kashmir" lent itself to the classic style she used on the Boston stage—*had* used on the Boston stage.

No more.

This was her only stage for the foreseeable future.

And already she didn't want to let it go. The adrenaline and endorphins were still bubbling under her skin. She'd never felt more alive or free.

"Amazing stuff, Margo."

She turned to Lila. "Thanks. I didn't know this would work. I had my doubts."

"Just wait 'til you feed off the crowd. You and Simon already have magic."

"No. It's just the music."

"Music is sex and sexual power. And you both exude it all over the stage. I can't wait to see it tonight."

No pressure. Margo tucked her violin in its case. "Let's hope the crowd doesn't think it's too weird."

"I was surprised you didn't do 'The Becoming'. It's their biggest hit. Though 'Sugar Kiss' is definitely gaining strength there."

Margo concentrated on the snaps to her case so she wouldn't have to look her in the eye. "The Becoming" was too much. After the Zeppelin song, her body couldn't handle that along with the memories.

Once tonight would be enough.

"I think Simon wanted to go for an organic groove there. Not to rush it."

Lila made a noncommittal noise.

She had a feeling that this woman's bullshit meter was about as astute as her mother's. Her mother was going for a gold medal and Lila was definitely in her league.

"It feels good." She hadn't meant to own up to it. In fact, she didn't really want to even think it. But Lila had amazing contacts and if she was going to make a life as a studio musician, she wanted one of the most influential women in the music scene to be in her corner.

Ripper Records might be small, but Donovan Lewis was a force in the business world. What he was involved in was noticed, whether it was music or brokering a deal. She'd do well to remember that and getting on Lila's good side was a necessary evil.

No matter how much her belly jittered with it.

"I had a feeling." Lila hugged her iPad to her chest. "Your magic in the studio was translatable to the stage with just a nudge."

"I'm not sure about that." Margo's gaze followed Jazz and Gray as they came together like polarized magnets. As a unit, they moved to Nick and Deacon. The four of them were so easy with each other. Like the instruments were just a conduit for them to have a reason to be in the same space.

Add in the fire of Simon's voice and nothing could stop them as a group. Simon was the front man that all bands wanted. He owned the stage and could interact with each and every member of the band individually without breaking stride.

But it was how he connected to the crowd that was awe-inspiring. Even here when it was the jaded industry people with tech people crawling around doing their job.

She'd watched them stop and turn to the stage. His magnetic personality and innate sexuality drew the eye whether you were male or female.

And when he'd faced her and turned that power on her, she'd had no choice but to come out of her shell. Her music reached for him just as she had. That night in the studio had been similar.

The bass that exuded sex and the giving power of two bodies over-rode any protective instinct she'd had. "Kashmir" had done the same. The symphonic composition had been created for strings — both classical and electric.

But his voice was the truth that the song required.

Led Zeppelin's truth had always been in the music. Regardless of egos and drugs, there had been a core talent. And Oblivion had that with each successive album. Each one was more special than the last, but the truth was the stage.

She'd sneaked into more than one show since she'd contributed to "The Becoming". Never letting on that she was there, never intruding on that dynamic.

But now that she'd tasted it, she wanted it.

On a level that she'd never known with the symphony. Shame should have followed that thought, but it just couldn't.

Music was music, whether it included a conductor or a lead singer that owned the crowd. There was no sense of camaraderie in her old world. Only who was better, who would be remembered, who would bump another from the top spot.

This was a relationship. If Gray took the lead, Nick would follow it up with a duel. Not to only one up each other—though she had a feeling there was a little rivalry there—but because he wanted in on the action. Wanted that song to sink into him, too.

That was what she'd missed in all her years with the Philharmonic. And she'd soak it in tonight and tomorrow and hope it was enough.

To have just a small moment of that magic in her life was worth it.

Chapter 5

Simon gargled with salt water—heavy on the salt—with a vodka chaser waiting for him. He'd talked himself blue with the last of the interviews. He'd tried to take a backseat in the band interview, but the shenanigans had been too heightened with excitement as the club filled.

Lila kept interjecting numbers and the overhead screen was a live feed from the iHeart Radio's release party coverage from the club. All of it was feeding the frenzy.

Nothing like their last album.

This was much more fluid and fun. And the stark difference between Ripper Records and Trident was even more obvious. Lila and her staff had created the perfect venue for them. The lights and the murmur of people was the buzz he lived for. As much as he loved the bigger stages they'd been playing as of late, the clubs would always speak to him on a visceral level.

He braced his hands on the side of the sink as the door opened behind him. "Oh. I'm sorry."

Margo's huge dark eyes met his in the mirror. Her hair had been smoothed down around her shoulders again and her ample cleavage trapped the shorter strands that fell forward.

Hair that he wanted to wrap around his hand and use to drag her mouth to his.

The fact that he wanted it so badly had caused him to knock back his drink and snap the glass down on the porcelain a little too forcefully. "Ready for the stage, Violin Girl? Think you can keep up with the adults?"

"If there was an adult in the room, I could answer that question."

He turned and untucked his tank from his back pocket. Her eyes skimmed down his chest once before arrowing back up to his face. "Like what you see?" His buckle was open for him to tuck the shirt in. Well, for as long as it lasted on his body. He hated when shirts bunched up. Hated wearing clothes on stage, period. They were too tight and restrictive when he wanted to prowl around.

But it was much more effective to take them off for the crowd and to play to the screams. He knew how to play the game. Hell, he lived for the game. The other twenty hours in the day were merely killing time so he could get on the stage.

He needed to tour again.

Needed to feed that addiction.

They'd been off the road for too long now.

But the way he felt around Margo could mirror that. And he hated her for it. Those moments in her arms had been as thrilling as the stage. Enough that he'd offered himself to a woman for more than a night and she'd run as far and fast as possible in the opposite direction.

He hated her even more now that he'd seen how affected she really was. Here she couldn't hide it. When they were alone, she couldn't hide behind a cool mask.

He moved closer until her honeysuckle scent teased his nose and tried to draw him closer. Mixed with smoke from the machines and the spice of something else. Cloves.

He leaned into her hair where it clung.

"Why, Violin Girl, did you sneak away for a clove cigarette?"

She flushed. "Of course not."

He walked around her and sifted his fingers through her hair until it fell down her back. "I haven't smelled that scent in too many years to count. I didn't know anyone actually still smoked them."

She tried to move out of his space, but he curled his arm around her waist and spread his hand across her midsection. In the mirror they lined up, her shoulders easily tucked in against his upper chest. So similar in height that his cock brushed against her high, rounded ass.

He kept his grip loose enough that if she really wanted to get away, she could.

But she didn't.

And he knew she wouldn't.

She closed her eyes against the way they looked together in the glass. Because she lied. She knew just how good they were together.

What he wanted to know was why she felt the need to lie.

"You see this, right? Know it's good." He brushed his lips against the shell of her ear. "And yet you walked away without a second look."

"It would have been just another few hours of sex. What would that have accomplished?"

"Why did it have to accomplish anything? Why couldn't it just feel good and right?"

"Is that all that matters to you? What feels good at the time?"

His hand drifted higher to the cup of the corset and the heavy breast he knew filled his hand to perfection. But he didn't go there. There wasn't time, no matter how much he wanted her right then and there.

Hated that he wanted it, but God, he did.

"There's nothing wrong with feeding that side of you, Margo."

Her eyes flashed open. He said her name so rarely. Because it tasted like salted caramel under dark chocolate on his tongue. And now he added the heady scent of cloves to her sensory memories.

"I don't have the luxury of feeding that hedonistic side. I have obligations."

"And those feelings are too messy, aren't they?" He stared at her in the mirror. "Wouldn't want to deal with messy feelings, right?"

"It was sex."

Her posh voice almost had a British edge to it. And the way she spit out the words like she'd never say them unless forced helped to control his runaway dick.

A fundamental difference between them.

He'd do well to remember that.

He slid his hand away and zipped up his leathers. "And sex is bad, right, Violin Girl?"

"No, but it has its place."

"A dirty moment in time that needs to be erased?"

"No."

Her emphatic *no* made him meet her gaze again. "Then what was it?"

"A fantasy."

And that's all he was good for. He pulled the cotton tank over his head and tucked it in before buckling his pants. It was surprising how much he needed to be reminded of that.

"Well, then let's get out there and let me do what I do best."

"Simon, I didn't mean—"

"Oh, but you did." He opened the door and rolled his neck as he headed out. The stage was dark and house lights were beginning to dim.

He put Margo in her place. At the back of his mind where dreams and memories got to rest under the reality of his function in the band. He was the face, the body, and the voice.

He met up with Lila where she stood at the bottom of the stairs. "You're late."

"I had to warm up."

Lila looked over his shoulder as Margo came out of the bathroom. "So I see." Margo walked up. "Have a good show."

Simon hit the stairs at a dead run. Adrenaline replaced the want of a single woman. This mistress he knew and could trust. Some nights were rougher than others, but she was always there for him.

The stage.

The music.

He slapped Nicky on the back as he passed and took a quick look to make sure his friend was set. Stage fright was a reality in Nick's life, but a controlled one for the most part.

The first shows were always the hardest for his best friend. He was a little glassy-eyed, but there wasn't the leading edge of panic. Determination won out tonight.

It would be a good night.

When he passed Gray, the houselights went completely down and the murmuring crowd broke out into applause. Gray and Nick exploded into "Renegade". One of the first songs that they'd all collaborated on. The song was loud, powerful, and unapologetic.

Simon wrapped his hand around the mic and used the stand to dip down as the lyrics curled in his belly and out his mouth. He smiled for the legion of cameras, the faces, the guests both famous and not. Like the A-listers from the Tribeca scene and social media storms with their dead eyes and interest in only what the cameras could provide.

Those were his target tonight.

He always had one.

To win over the jaded and self-involved was his goal. He wanted every arm up and all eyes on him. The low hanging lighting rig was his playground.

When the guitar solo started, he scooted to the back of the small stage and tapped Jazz's cymbals before taking his other mic.

"Simon," she said with that air of warning.

He waggled his eyebrows. "Gotta give them something to remember."

Lila tried to catch his attention from the side stage but he kept his eyes on the prize. He ran to the front of the stage and leaped for the rig.

The crowd gasped and two security guys scrambled from the back. Thankful that he'd started using Deacon's pull-up bar when he was bored, he lifted himself up and monkeyed his way onto the farthest arm of the rig.

It was made to hold thousands of pounds of equipment and he knew it could hold one hundred and seventy pounds more. He was lean and agile as opposed to Deacon's massive size.

He let one arm dangle free with his mic and the crowd surged forward. Drinks forgotten, camera phones up and filming. "We're here to party tonight. You get to hear our new shit and I want you to know the words by the end of the night. Do you hear me?"

The deafening scream was just what he needed. He glanced to the back of the room to the huge screens. The cameras were on him and sending out to the live stream.

As the song wound down and "Monster" started, he tucked his mic into the front of his leathers. The metal slid against his belly and crowded his cock until the leather creaked.

He swung in on the stage and landed in a crouch before he prowled the space, changing out his portable mic for his box. He curled his fingers around it and his lips brushed the familiar metal.

The growl at the chorus came from his gut. When he stood, there was Margo in his path. He crowded her as the lyrics swirled between them and they did a minor dance compared to "Kashmir" from the rehearsal.

Then it all changed when she leaned in and her smoky voice came in at the end of the chorus with the rest of the band.

His eyes widened and he melted back away from her into the shadows of the stage as the lights went down for the show's first cover.

Simon's heart drilled against his sternum as the drums to "Closer to the Edge" came out of the night. He lifted the mic to his lips. The lyrics falling out as they always did. Like they escaped him without his permission.

The song was to pull the rest of the crowd in. He surged to the front of the stage and held the mic up as fists rose to follow his directive.

The lyrics were like gunfire and the piano parts that hadn't been in rehearsal swelled up and layered in.

He spun around. The song was too drum-heavy for Jazz to play the keyboards. Margo stood behind the keys. It was a simple song from that standpoint, and the sound had always been missing from their versions of it.

It was just that much more because of her addition. He stalked the stage and went forehead to forehead with Nicky as he sung the next verse. Both their voices blending into the slight distortion.

He mussed Nick's shaggy hair and bounced away to the front of the stage to drag the crowd in again. With Jazz's powerful drums behind him, the club was completely his. The houselights were bright to the back of the house as they extended the song for another round with a hand gesture from him.

Lights twirled and the crowd screamed for them.

He hopped down into the crowd and let people sing with him from the first row. His cord only went so far. When he felt the tug of the end of his feed, he stopped. The crowd rallied around him, jumping as Gray and Nick dueled out a final battle cry from their axes.

Deacon stood in his spot at the center of the stage with his arms up until the crowd died down then he held a hand out to Simon.

Goddamn Gigantor hauled him back on the stage and they did a quick, fierce hug before he landed in the center of his band.

Of his family.

The lights went down to a moody blue and red that were the signature lights of the club and he fell into "Undertow", their epic "The Becoming" type song on this album and one of Gray and Nick's songs from the cabin. It taxed his pipes with long drawn out notes that he could only do when he was well and truly warmed up.

Flowing into "Echoes" until the midpoint of the set. He stood in the center of the stage and stripped out of his tank and tossed it into the crowd.

His chest bellowed with the need to catch a breath. "How are we doing?"

The blond from outside earlier was up front. She'd won one of the coveted spots from the impromptu video contest. He sat down in front of her. "Hello again."

She pushed back her sweaty hair. A refreshing woman that wasn't afraid to get involved in a show. Most of the pretty girls made the least amount of movements so their makeup and hair survived until the end of the night. So they remained the glossy, too perfect version of a fan. Ones that he never went for at a show these days.

He'd had his fill on the first tour.

Now, he wanted the one who knew the lyrics instead of just wanting a piece of his fame. He didn't mind the fantasy, but he hated being *only* a fantasy.

He wasn't quite sure when that had changed.

"Melissa, right?"

She nodded. "What song do you want to hear, Melissa?"

"'Too Still'. It's my favorite."

His eyebrows shot up. "We rarely play that one."

"I know. That should change."

He grinned and lifted her hand to his mouth. "You got it." He spun on his butt and stood. "Think you can make that happen?" he asked Nick. It was his song.

Nicky grinned and the achingly dark chords flowed out into the darkness. Simon swiped his hand down his dripping chest and caught a towel that came sailing from the side stage. He wiped off his mic and then his chest before dropping it at his feet

The long intro melted into lyrics that were one with the darkness of Carson and their past. He snapped his mic into the stand and fell into the old and felt it juxtapose with the new.

The growth of them as a band instead of loosely connected musicians forced into accepting an amalgam of Nick's vision over theirs. In the early days of Oblivion, Nick had been the principal songwriter and he was damn good.

But it was a sad song of being alone. And none of them were alone anymore.

When he finished the song, he gave Melissa a thumbs up. "That was a nice trip down memory lane. But I think we need to kick it up a notch, yes?"

He lifted his hand up and fingers splayed as their single started. "Sugar Kiss" with the dirty lyrics that had culminated into a hot video he'd never thought they'd do.

But it fit.

The pieces of Gray and Jazz and the band as it was now.

Up against the wall
Or on the floor
I'll take what I need
Anytime at all

He dredged up the sinewy vocals reminiscent of Axl Rose's good years and added the sex dripping honey. He dragged his hand down his chest and to his belt as he ground his hips against the mic stand with a laugh before unhooking his mic and kicking the stand out of the way.

The rest of the set flew by with the last of the new songs from the album until they had to play their biggest hit. The epic flavor of "The Becoming" was something he'd been dreading the entire night.

He'd ignored Margo as long as he could.

She'd played on the outskirts and came into the center stage with Deacon during one of their new songs that she'd been a part of, but this is where it had all begun.

This was where he'd fallen.

Picking up those pieces again required all his concentration. He turned to Margo as Deacon's bass teased out of the smoke and strobing lights.

Her bow sliced out of the night. The silvered edge caught the light and he was lost. He sang to her and only her. They circled each other, the echoing lyrics bleeding into her strings.

Jazz stood in the back as the drums acted as a heartbeat to match Deacon's bass. She sung the verse under his chorus. The new addition to the song that they'd practiced at the end of the last tour.

That had made the song theirs instead of the soundtrack version it had started out as. Her sweet, pure voice soared and his seedy darkness quivered under the bass line.

Then there was Margo.

The final piece.

The bombastic part they hadn't ever had on stage.

Instead of allowing the crowd a break, a breath—even a moment—to recover, the seesawing bow of Margo's instrument slipped into the iconic start of "Kashmir".

The first verse was hers.

She owned it and he had no choice but to give it to her. Until the "Oh"s of the song started. He shut out that intense stare. The too big eyes and their swimming emotion. Emotion which was usually veiled under polite indifference.

This Margo was the one who'd come to him in that booth.

He backed out of the moment, returned to the front of the stage, and rocked out to the song that they killed.

The rehearsal had been magic.

The reality was hedonistic.

When the lights went down and the crowd screamed for more, Simon stumbled back to his band mates for the bows.

Escape.

He needed it.

He jumped into the crowd and led the charge to the bar with a war cry for booze. He needed to be away from her and the voodoo that was them in the middle of a haze of music.

Margo escaped to the backstage area after the show. She just didn't fit in with the band dynamic. Jazz was in the center of them all like a happy puppy.

Simon had escaped like a demon was on his back. The fearless way he jumped into the crowd and onto the lighting rig had stalled her heart a few times. She didn't know if he had absolutely no regard for his safety or he was just that confident in his surroundings.

All she knew was that her corset was pinching every rib and she was so very tired of only taking half a breath.

"Where do you think you're going?"

Margo stopped at the side door. "Backstage to change."

"No, you are going to mingle." Her sister hooked her arm through hers and dragged her down the side stairs to the ground floor.

"I can't breathe in this thing, Juliet." She was tired and exasperated and just uncomfortable enough to snap at her.

Juliet's eyebrows shot up. "Feisty. I like it."

"How did you get that pass?"

"Gave a roadie a blow job."

"Oh my God."

Juliet laughed and dragged her deeper into the crowd. "You're adorable. I just dropped your name and got one."

Horrified, she stopped in the middle of the floor. "You didn't go to Lila."

"Nah. I just told the scrawny dude that follows her around like a puppy."

Margo tried to place the name, but there had been way too many people in Lila's charge today. No way could Margo remember any of them. "Juliet."

"Now don't get that prissy tone with me. Not after you just rocked it out of the park with the band. Seriously. I've never seen anything like it."

Margo flushed. Damn English skin. Why couldn't she have perfect skin like her sister? Margo felt like a melted candle and Juliet looked like she just walked off a photo shoot. "It was pretty amazing."

"Yes. And now you need a drink."

"Now, I need to get this corset off before I faint," she growled.

"Oh." Juliet tipped her head. "You do look a little peaked."

"Great."

Juliet dragged her to the VIP bathrooms and flashed her laminated pass, sailing through the doors to the huge mirrored room with five sinks and four stalls. Three were occupied.

"Take that off."

"I don't have anything to change into."

Juliet whipped off her T-shirt. "Give me your little tank top."

"I can't wear that shirt." Margo looked down at the baby doll-style shirt.

"Sure you can." Juliet turned her around and lifted off the camisole.

"Seriously?" Her wide dark eyes met Juliet's in the mirror. "Anyone could come in or—"

A blond came out of the stall with her perfect waterfall of hair and body-hugging pink dress over a size two body. She went to the sink and washed her hands. "Great corset. Wish I had the boobs to pull one off."

"It pushes up anything you have times two." Horrified, Margo snapped her mouth shut. What had gotten into her tonight?

The blond laughed. "I need a water bra to make anything of my tits. And your girlfriend—"

"Sister," Juliet interjected.

"Huh. You two are totally built differently."

Margo tipped her head back. "To my eternal struggle."

Juliet snorted.

"Your sister is right, that shirt will never fit with her rockin' tits." The blond took the baby doll shirt and opened her purse. She pulled out a tiny makeup case and unearthed a pair of small scissors. She cut a notch out of the shirt and then ripped it open wider. "Now try."

Juliet slipped Margo's camisole on. Her red and black lace bra peeked out, but her sister wasn't exactly flat-chested. Just not quite as endowed as Margo.

Margo quickly pulled on the T-shirt before her sister could unhook the last of her corset.

"Unleash the Kraken," Juliet said with a flourish as she whipped off the corset.

Margo's unencumbered breasts filled out the cotton and stretched it to the limit, but it held.

The blond and Juliet both nodded. "Now you are ready for the dance floor," the woman said.

Juliet laughed. "You so aren't paying for any drinks."

Margo just stared at herself in the mirror. "I can't go out there like that."

"Honey, we only have these tits for so long in our twenties. It's time to take them for a test drive."

The T-shirt was too small. It showed off her midriff and was tight at the shoulder and of course, the chest.

Juliet undid a hair clip from her belt loop and wound Margo's hair into a messy knot. She jammed the clip under it so her usually stick-straight hair was a mass on top of her head, making her neck look even longer and her eyes bigger.

"Okay. Now you're ready to go kick some ass."

Before she could say another word, Juliet was dragging her out of the bathroom. "I can't—"

"If I hear you say 'you can't' anything else tonight, I'm going to scream. You can. You are a sexual woman who has been hiding behind a violin and under an Oxford shirt for far too long. You were on stage with a *rock band* tonight. A band that is just about to hit number one on the charts, I'm pretty sure. The night is yours, Margo. Go out there and take it."

She lifted her chin and let her sister drag her into the throng of people.

They made it to the bar and before she could open her mouth, a martini glass was sitting in front of her.

"From the guy at the end of the bar," the bartender said with a smile.

"What did I tell you?" Juliet punched her arm. She waved back at the guy.

Margo lifted the glass and swore under her breath as the guy came down the bar.

"Now be cool. You just need to flirt a little. If he's a creep, you just blow him off."

Margo's eyes widened. "Is that what you do?"

"All the time."

"And how long is 'all the time'?"

Juliet rolled her eyes. "I've been going to clubs in Boston since I was seventeen."

Margo choked on the strong drink. "How?"

Juliet shrugged. "Mom and Dad were never around much."

"I didn't know."

"How could you? You were always practicing or in class."

Before she could say anything else, the man from the other end of the bar came up to them. "I had no idea a violin could be so incredibly hot."

Juliet leaned on the bar, her back to the guy. She rolled her eyes and turned to him. "Never heard of Lindsey Sterling?"

The guy was attractive enough, but his face was rather orange with self-tanner. He'd paired an off-the-rack suit with a fifty-dollar shirt with French cuffs to make it seem much more than it was.

Margo took a deeper swig of her martini. And he probably had a small dick if the bling on his wrist and pinky finger were anything to go by.

God, what had gotten into her tonight?

She tried to pay attention as he told her he was a PR person from some firm in the city. By the end of the second martini, she'd ascertained that he probably was a junior executive with a corner desk near the bathrooms.

Juliet was having a little too much fun with him. Her sister was obviously baiting him for the drinks he was providing.

The gin was going to Margo's head—especially since she had barely eaten. "I need some air," she said to Juliet.

Her sister flipped off her all access pass. "There's a corridor right through there. They'll let you back in with that."

"Thanks."

The room was a million degrees and there were just too many people milling around. The band was set up on a dais with a long table and tons of food and water, but she hadn't felt right going up there. She was just a visitor.

Margo trailed her fingers over the steel walls and grommets that were part decoration, part construction. Industrial all the way from floor to ceiling. The glowing red and blue lights were making her dizzy as she fuzzed with alcohol and fatigue.

Her only focus was the corridor she was headed toward. It was roped off with a VIP sign over the doorway. She skimmed around people and ducked under the velvet ropes.

She didn't know they actually still had velvet ropes anymore. New York City, ever the glam under the slick. The holes in the steel walls teased her fingertips as she used the support to keep steady.

The noise brought her around first.

The club was so very loud, but here it was almost insulated. She heard the sigh followed by a groan.

"Turn around, Margo." She took a step back when she caught two people wrapped around each other. But her feet wouldn't move.

Long legs ending in heavy, unbuckled motorcycle boots tried to dent her consciousness. Were those familiar?

She couldn't focus. Not when long fingers pulled a woman's knee up on his hip and slid under her denim skirt to cup her bottom.

The man's other hand was in her wild blond hair. The grip was strong and sure as he dragged her head back so he could get at her neck.

The woman moaned and ground herself against his front.

Turn around.

Turn around now.

But she couldn't.

The slash of a nose and furrowed brow with ebony eyebrows locked her feet in place. Wild silver-blue eyes rimmed in smudged kohl zeroed in on her.

He stopped for a moment then dragged his teeth over the woman's chin and to her lips.

Memories flooded her belly and thighs, instantly pulsing between her legs. Simon.

His eyes never strayed from hers as he licked his way into the woman's mouth. She sucked on the tip of his tongue and his attention wavered for a moment. The fingers that were under her skirt tightened and she saw the bunch of knuckle under the material.

Was he touching her? Or just gripping the flesh there?

Why couldn't she look away?

Chapter 6

Simon tasted peppermint schnapps on Melissa's tongue. The exuberant fan had cornered him at the bathrooms and asked for a signature, then asked for a hug and a kiss.

Somehow it had become more than that.

He'd dragged her down this hallway to get the memory and taste of Margo out of his system and he'd almost succeeded.

Until now.

Until she'd appeared at the end of the hallway to the side door. Her bee-stung lips bright red as she scraped her teeth over the lower one, her gaze riveted on him.

On *them*.

The instinct to pull back and away from Melissa was strong. So strong that he forced himself to deepen the kiss.

If Violin Girl wanted to drive him crazy tonight, she was succeeding. On stage when they were so in sync, off stage when she tried to pull the veil of class over her shoulders like a shawl even with a corset and black skirt that barely covered her ass as her costume. And now here, watching him.

The lust lit her dark eyes like a gas lamp.

He hadn't had nearly enough vodka to keep her in that shadowy, fuzzy realm that he liked to keep her.

No, he could see perfectly clearly as the blue and red lights glowed off the too pale skin of Margo's arms and neck. And the shirt that was obviously making a valiant effort at keeping her tits in check.

Too bad the hot pink and black Oblivion shirt was stretched so tight. He might have been able to put an end to the madness until her nipples tightened under the cotton like bullets.

His grip tightened on the Melissa's hair and she groaned in reaction. Completely into this. And he was performing.

Again.

For *her*.

Guilt throbbed under the pulse of blood that filled his cock. The girl in his arms didn't deserve to be a replacement for Margo.

Because she was.

He could see it now. And why could he see it? Because he was too goddamn sober for this shit.

Simon dragged his lips down Melissa's neck again. His teeth sunk into her shoulder as he pushed her bra strap out of the way.

Turn around.

GO.

He urged her in his head even as he dragged his tongue over Melissa's pulse point before latching his mouth around that throbbing vein.

There was something so fragile and consuming about feeling life under his tongue. Probably why he loved the taste of a woman.

Some men hated the thought of getting between a woman's thighs. He loved it. Each one of them tasted different. Some more memorable than others.

Like Margo with her honeyed spice and smoke flavor.

And now he knew the scent of cloves would stick to her skin.

Would it change the taste of her?

Would he ever know the taste of her again?

He lifted his fingers from under Melissa's skirt and brought them to his lips.

Margo's lips went slack and her hand went to her neck. In the process, she rubbed her forearm across her tight nipple. He wanted her to tug on it.

To pull it away from her skin so he could watch it snap back tighter and redder.

He slid his hand down between them and under the girl's skirt. She was wet for him. Hardly a surprise since she'd been grinding against his dick since he'd led her down the hall.

Margo's fingers gripped the long column of her neck and her chest heaved.

Was she wet?

Would he find that silky rich come between her thighs, soaking her panties?

Was it from watching him with this girl? Or was it a memory of that long ago night?

Melissa panted against his neck as she held onto him while his fingers circled the plump lips of her pussy and teased her clit until her cries echoed down the hall.

As one girl fell apart in his arms, the one he'd always wanted finally stumbled back. She disappeared around the corner and he concentrated on getting his partner off.

The ability to lose himself in her scent and touch was gone.

She smelled of hairspray and roses.

Innocent mewling at his ear as she shuddered in his arms.

He slipped his hand from her panties to curl it around her hip and let her sag against him. She kissed down his chest and into his open shirt.

The lower she went, the more his cock stirred.

She wrapped her fingers around him through his leathers. But he caught her chin before she could slide down the line of his belly to his buckle.

He drew her mouth up to his. "Not tonight, baby."

"Are you sure?" Melissa looked up at him with her eager blue eyes.

"I liked making you feel good."

"I've never come with a stranger like that." Her lashes lowered and her smile was hesitant. "I couldn't."

"Obviously you could."

"Only with you."

He heard the worship and eased back. "Ah, no, darlin'. It's just the moment. The stage and the excitement." He brushed a kiss over her forehead. "I got a little carried away."

"You could have whatever you wanted tonight."

Simon shut his eyes against that thought.

No. No, he couldn't have whatever he wanted tonight. Who he really wanted had just walked away.

Again.

This time, he'd chased her away.

How many nights had he lost himself inside an eager woman? Now more than ever, he should take Melissa up on the offer.

But he couldn't. Not with that look on her face.

This wasn't a woman who knew the score. She was a girl with stars in her eyes.

"I have to get back to the band. Do my thing for the cameras."

"Oh." She nodded. "I understand." She curled her fingers into his hair and reached up on her toes for his mouth.

Because he didn't want to crush her, he kissed her. But he didn't allow her to deepen it again. He forced his lips to curve into a smile as he nudged her gently away.

He walked her down the hall and urged her into the crowd with a wave. He could see that she wanted to say more, to keep him engaged, but he needed a minute.

Simon ducked into the bathroom and took care of business then washed his hands, washed her scent and her feel off his fingers. He couldn't have that imbalance clogging up his already fucked-up head.

Margo's heated stare and a strange woman's scent on him at the same time was too fucked up for him just then. He cupped the clean water into his hands and over his face, into his hair and let the droplets slip down his neck and into his shirt.

"What the fuck are you doing?"

Nick stood in the doorway. "Talking to yourself?"

Simon swiped his hand over his neck. "I'm in here hiding."

"Have you been in here the whole time? I've been looking for you."

"Nah. Just washing up a little."

"Some young thing on your cock?"

Simon grinned in spite of himself. "Not quite."

"Losing your touch?"

"Like that could happen."

Nick laughed. "Whiskey dick?"

"Number two reason I usually drink vodka."

"Because you're an uncouth bastard. Only girls drink the clear booze."

"You keep telling yourself that."

"I will, with the eighty-year-old bourbon I have stashed in my bar."

"Now that I could get behind."

"Nope. Not for the likes of you." Nick came over to the sink that Simon stood at and slapped his arm. "I'm here to collect you for a photo op."

"Eh, fuck."

"I had the same sentiment, but Lila beckons and I answer."

"Ain't that the truth," Simon muttered.

"What was that?"

"Nothing."

"Got something to say?" Nick crossed his arms over his chest.

"Nothing worth mentioning," Simon said with a waggle of his brows.

"Then you ready to blow this joint?"

"Picture op then beer pong?" Simon asked hopefully.

"Hell yes."

Helluva better alternative than schmoozing with a room full of people. Once the show was over, he wasn't interested. Either a babe to fall under or over, or his bed as a solo project.

Didn't matter which happened as far as he was concerned.

But tonight he'd go with a belly full of beer and insults. It was a helluva lot easier.

Margo escaped the party with her dignity in tatters and her body on fire. Sleep had been elusive—not shocking—since she was so wound up she couldn't even think, let alone settle.

She sighed as her phone buzzed. With one eye open, she read her sister's text.

> Had a blast.
> Behave in L.A., but don't behave too well.

Margo rolled onto her back and dropped her phone to her chest. The fact that her sister had texted Margo an hour before her alarm was supposed to go off meant Juliet had far more fun than she had last night.

She stared at the ceiling of her room, counting the bands of shadow from the balcony that she hadn't had time to look at, let alone stand out on.

And because that was much more appealing than brooding in her very big, very empty luxury bed, she slipped out and across the room to the sliding door. Lemon-tinged skies peeked from the crowding spears of steel and glass that made up Times Square.

She opened the door and let the cool morning air in. The rattan couch on the small patio was inviting. She swiped the throw blanket off the bottom of the bed and wrapped it around her shoulders. The sights and sounds of the city had never really stopped, but this was a different version of New York City.

This was the business of the city. Commuters coming in to work the shops and the corporate buildings that constantly crept into the tourist areas because they were all running out of space.

Everyone wanted a piece of New York.

Except her.

She'd been happy in Boston. She'd made sojourns into the city for her career—working in the studios, both small and large, that littered the boroughs—but she'd never wanted to stay. Never felt part of it.

She liked the history and winding streets of Boston. Liked being in the know about the small eateries, hidden diners, and the off-color shops that wound around the tourist traps. She knew New York City had the same places, but she'd never been tempted to find them.

But she did like to listen to the city sounds. That was one thing she always looked forward to. She curled onto the couch and tugged the pillow under her cheek. She'd just enjoy that anonymity for a little while before she was herded onto Donovan Lewis's private plane.

She almost wished she hadn't been invited into the inner circle. Even coach was preferable to spending hours on a plane with Simon. The early hour meant that maybe he'd spend the entire ride in a vodka-induced sleep.

It was easier than facing him.

Not after what she'd seen. What she'd watched with fascination and longing. The sounds lived inside her head and had followed her into the restless night.

Abandon.

Lust.

Pleasure.

God, so much pleasure.

She could have gotten past that. Could have turned away and given them their privacy.

Are you sure?

She squeezed her eyes tighter against the vivid memory behind her eyelids.

Maybe.

Maybe she'd have been able to turn away.

But not after he'd met her gaze. Not when he'd made sure she could see exactly what he was doing and where his hands had been.

Not when he'd given that young woman a thigh-shuddering orgasm while his eyes were on Margo.

She tucked her knees up against her middle until she was a ball. Then she could ignore the way her body flared to life again. As if he was standing in front of her and not a memory.

God, she didn't need that back in her head.

As if it had left.

She covered her face with her hands and was about to roll off the couch and return to her room when she heard the giggle.

"I swear this kid is going to be a pro soccer player."

"Did you get any sleep last night?"

"Kinda hard when you were snoring to beat the band."

"I was not."

"God, right there. I gotta tell you, big guy, if you didn't have those magic hands, I'd have killed you in your sleep."

Margo heard the deep chuckle. "You love my big hands for more than lower back massages."

"Those hands are why I'm the size of the state of Texas."

"Nah, you're beautiful. I always liked basketball. Now my wife is carrying around one."

"Try beach ball."

"Perfect beach ball. My beach ball."

Margo gripped her small pillow. She didn't want to stand up and interrupt Deacon and Harper's sweet dialogue, but it was hard to hear it. She'd never had that.

The baby thing she'd pass on—no aliens coming out of her body, thank you—but the rest...

Margo couldn't even imagine a man talking to her like that. Simple adoration lingering in his tone, indulgent pacification of a pregnant wife's distress, and most of all, closeness.

Relationships were hard when she was in practice mode all the time. The Boston Philharmonic didn't have a huge season so she was constantly on call for studio work. She could have taught, but she didn't have the temperament for it.

So instead of looking for someone to spend her life with, she was usually trying to beat out the other violinists in the orchestra, as well as the ones in her field.

The orchestra was often used for scores, but they didn't need all the chairs filled like they did for a concert. It was specific to what the movie music director needed or what the producers and studio needed for album work.

None of it was guaranteed, and the entire business was contingent on a résumé that was constantly out of date. And her own reticence to put herself out there.

These were the only moments where she wished for something more, when she heard the soft murmurings of a male voice and the answering flirty byplay of a woman.

She didn't even know how to flirt back with a man like that. For God's sake, Juliet had gotten all the flirty genes and doubled down with them at some cosmic blackjack table.

The only men Margo had been involved with had been hand-picked by her mother and father for social functions. She'd had the rare hookup in college, but music had been her focus for as long as she could remember.

And where had that gotten her?

Replaced in the one job she'd been tailor-made for.

She pressed her fingertips against her eyes. *No.* Now wasn't the time to think about that. It was time to go in and get ready to go.

To forget about how unsettled her future was. She had some time to figure out what she was supposed to do. Her parents were in Europe for their annual trip and weren't focused on her career.

She peeked over the half wall to the next balcony and caught Deacon drawing Harper back into their room. The way he drew her close even with her rather large belly in the way made Margo look away.

That was a man that wanted to put his hands on his wife no matter what.

She'd never really wanted that before. Saying goodbye was a fact of her life. Small projects didn't allow her to stay in one spot, until the season started. Then it was too much togetherness, too much competition.

Too much hate.

Some of her contemporaries flitted in and out of beds, but she hadn't wanted a part of that. When the undercutting was as prevalent as the talent, it took the desire away as far as she was concerned.

But seeing these people who honestly loved each other under the snark and the music was different. She wasn't sure she liked how it made her feel.

Jazz and Gray, Harper and Deacon—both of them married and pregnant. It seemed incongruous to the lifestyle, but they made it work.

Everything about them as a band shouldn't work.

Maybe that was why she got sucked in every single time she lifted her bow to play with them. Some magic fairy dust that only existed when she was in their sphere.

And now she was being fanciful. So not like her.

Maybe the fairy dust was more like PCP, she mused she rushed through a shower and plaited her hair in a travel braid. She glanced around the room and made sure the last of her sister's left-behinds were packed as well.

A knock on her door had her snapping out her bag and sliding her violin case down the double barrel handle.

"Shuttle for the trip to the airport in five!"

The voice was familiar, but it wasn't one of the band or Lila. Maybe one of her assistants.

She opened the door to find Gray and Jazz racing down the hall, her sparkly purple hard-sided case to Gray's jet black with red racing stripe.

"Hey! Preggo handicap."

"You only want a handicap when it suits you," Gray answered and double backed to take her case and steal a kiss. "Hold the elevator," he called down the hall.

Nick slapped a hand over the sensor. "C'mon, my favorite duck."

Jazz stopped in the middle of the hall. "Carry me."

Simon came out his door and stopped in front of her. "Piggy back for Miss Piggy."

"I should smack you for that, but I want the ride."

Gray stood at the elevator. "That's truly pathetic, Mrs. Duffy."

"It's a long corridor," Jazz said and draped her arms over Simon's shoulders.

"Must be desperate times if you're willing to ride on Simon," Gray said and crossed his arms.

"Well, my husband doesn't love me enough to carry me," Jazz said with a pout.

Margo tried not to smile at their antics, but they were like a bunch of puppies tumbling around and on each other.

Lila opened her door and sagged against the jamb. She had on a large pair of amber sunglasses. "It's too early for them to be so loud."

Margo walked with her down the hallway. "I assumed they would all be dragging their way to the airport."

"Jazz and Harper catnap like no one's business. They'll be out before we get off the runway. Simon probably hasn't gone to bed yet and Gray and Nick will end up at the back of the plane with guitars and headphones or playing a video game."

"And Deacon?"

"Deacon will herd them in and herd them out, watching over them the whole time."

"So, you liken Deacon to a border collie?"

Lila gave a tight smile. "If the hair fits."

Margo nodded. "Interesting group."

"They grow on you. Mostly against your will, but they grow on you nonetheless."

"Well, thanks for letting me on the plane with you guys. It's better than flying coach."

"I'll remind you of that when Nick and Gray are arguing over lyrics and Jazz is tapping on every surface because she can't sit still unless she's unconscious."

"Or making a baby," Margo said under her breath.

Lila laughed. "Or making a baby. They are bunnies, but thankfully our social media queen is usually too busy with interviews and research or reading baby books to bounce off the walls quite as much as she once did."

"How are you guys going to work the tour?"

Lila waved to them at the end in the elevator to go ahead. The car was full.

Simon stood in the middle of the car, his fingers wrapped around his suitcase handle in front of his crotch. His eyebrow winged up as the doors closed.

Margo swallowed down nerves and the irrational need to drag him out of the elevator and toss him off the building. He knew what he did to any woman. That cocksure attitude was as attractive as it was annoying.

"We're splitting the tour into two legs as we usually do. The first will be abbreviated, of course. Their timing could be better—the ticket sales are amazing and the record is getting way more downloads than we thought it would. Hell, *Rise* got four stars from *Rolling Stone*."

She rarely agreed with *Rolling Stone* magazine's critics, but Margo had to concede this one. Considering the album was in her ears every time she stuck headphones in, it was a fair assessment.

"And you couldn't get someone to fill in?"

Lila stopped and turned to her. "Have you met these people? If I dared to give them that as an option, I might get stoned."

"Business is business."

Lila slid her shades down her nose. "It's nice to hear that from another person in this crazy group, but it just shows that you're on the outside like me. No one could replace Jazz. Not even if Stuart Copeland said he'd sit in."

"I suppose that's true." Margo reached for the elevator button set into the Art Deco plate. "That would be a sight, though."

"That it would."

They waited in companionable silence as the elevator made its way back up to them.

"I got the idea you were enjoying yourself on stage last night."

Margo curled her fingers around her handle. "I did, yes."

"A much different dynamic than the philharmonic."

"It is." Margo resisted the urge to fidget.

"You're off for the summer?"

"The season is over," Margo answered vaguely.

The doors opened. "So it is." Lila walked into the elevator and didn't say another word on the ride down.

Margo recognized the tactic. It was one that her mother used often. Dangle the carrot and get her to ask or offer up her services for whatever they were looking for.

She was tired of reaching for carrots.

If Lila wanted to ask her something, she could damn well ask her.

Margo strode off the elevator and across the lobby to where the band was gathering for the shuttle. Deacon and Harper were already down in the lobby and a carton of orange juice in Harper's hand told her they'd actually gone down for breakfast.

She wished for coffee but followed everyone onto the huge white shuttle van that the hotel provided. There were two bucket seats at the front and three benches. Gray and Jazz took up one bench, Harper and Deacon the other.

Lila dropped into one of the bucket seats in the front, speaking to the driver about which part of the private airport they were leaving from.

Before Margo could get into the other chair, Nick took it.

Fabulous.

Simon was sprawled along the last bench seat with his arm along the top. So similar to their Town Car ride and yet so much different now.

Before they could forget that there had been skin and moans between them, now they were far too fresh.

Even if she wasn't the one that had her flesh licked and sucked at. She lifted her chin and sat down on the far end of the bench.

"You like to be close and yet not too close, don't you, Violin Girl?"

She stared straight ahead. She would not let him bait her. No way, no how.

He flicked the end of her braid. "Aw c'mon, Violin Girl, I'm just playing."

"Leave her alone, Singer Boy," Jazz said on a yawn.

Simon's eyebrow lifted.

"See, how's it feel to be called your instrument?"

"Terms of endearment, Pink Penis Eater."

"Can you punch him, G? Just once. I promise I won't ask again." Jazz waited a beat. "Today."

Gray sighed. "Don't make me bruise my knuckles so early in the day, Simon."

"Man, it's gang up on Simon day."

"Deserve it," Jazz said with a hand flourish over her head.

Twenty minutes into the drive, Margo started to relax. Simon looked out the window but didn't interrupt or engage with the rest of the band while they halfheartedly teased one another.

It was early even by Margo's standards. By the time they pulled onto one of the exchanges toward the airport, the van was quiet. They all shuffled off, grabbing their suitcases from the side storage.

A young guy not much older than Jazz was loading the undercarriage of the plane with their gear and everyone left their suitcases to him.

Just before the cargo person took her suitcase, she rescued her violin case.

"Not good enough to go in with our gear?" Simon tucked the tips of his fingers into the tight black jeans he was wearing.

"It doesn't leave my side." Margo knew she was being a little territorial, but her instrument was an extension of her. She never let anyone handle her Starfish.

Ever.

She climbed the stairs after Gray helped Jazz inside. Definitely not a prop jet. This was plush and worth a few million in her estimation. Gray and burgundy leather stretched across couches and captain chairs. The back of the plane was transformed into a bar with a large television, with game consoles discreetly tucked under the speakers.

Everything a man could want. And incongruous to what she thought Donovan Lewis would be about. The television, yes — he probably watched the stock market like crazy.

But the games?

Was that just for the boys? Because the men of Oblivion were definitely more boys than men. In some ways they were hardened with life, but in others they were still very much guys in their twenties.

Nick and Simon made a beeline for the back of the plane and had the television on before their onboard bags were stowed. They just dumped them into what had probably become their space after a few flights.

Simon on the couch, Nick in the captain's chair.

That was interesting in itself. Nick seemed to need a space all of his own. She'd noticed it on a few different instances now. He very much liked to be a part of the group and in the center of it.

"You watch them like a science experiment."

Margo jumped. "I..."

"It's okay. It's how I was when I first started managing them."

"How did that happen, anyway? Don't you work for Donovan Lewis? Not the band."

"We like to cultivate our clients. These guys need a little more hands-on than Donovan was comfortable with."

Margo tipped her head. "You went to bat for them."

Lila's face smoothed into an expression that didn't give one iota away.

"I did what the company needed."

Hmm.

Margo wasn't entirely convinced. And part of her liked Lila all the more for it. It wasn't often that she met a woman that she could identify with.

Before Lila could back up, Margo touched her arm. "It's good they have you to look out for them."

Lila looked away and lifted her chin. "Ready to go?"

The band had gotten themselves situated. The pregnant women were set up in reclining chairs with blankets over them. Harper was already half asleep. Deacon was reading on his tablet and Gray was fussing over Jazz.

The pilot advised them that they would be leaving in ten minutes. Tired didn't seem to be a strong enough word for how Margo was feeling, but she was too wound up to settle.

Again, this was completely the opposite of how she normally was. Travel and killing time was a large part of her life. She was good at traveling.

Determined to settle down, she tucked herself into the corner of one of the couches. With the ledge behind her, she tucked her case into the small space and took out her phone and headphones. It seemed wrong to listen to her music of choice when they were right across from her.

But part of her problem was that she hadn't indulged in her rituals. She rolled her sweater into a ball under her head, put her headphones in, and started the album from the beginning.

Chapter 7

Simon rolled to his feet. Three hours of zombies was enough. He'd gotten most of his aggressions out on the murder and mayhem that video games provided.

Gray and Nick were in it for the long haul. He guzzled one of the half dozen bottles of water that Lila had stashed on the plane for them. Hydrating was a new thing. He was used to either hungover or drunk, with not much in between.

This album was much more taxing on his vocals so he had to actually remember to take care of himself. The last song of the night last night reminded him of that.

"Kashmir" was tough for anyone, even Plant, to sing. He'd felt the crack during the last verse and had pulled his mic away before it had gone out to the speakers and to the people.

He'd rather look like he forgot the lyric than his voice couldn't hack the song.

He finished the one bottle and immediately opened another. Which of course made him realize he'd been sitting too long. He made his way to the front of the plane for the bathrooms.

He'd all but forgotten that she was on the plane.

Right, like you could forget.

Simon curled his fingers on the bottle until the plastic, and the water dribbling down his fingers, let him know to dial it back. She was curled into a ball on one of the couches.

His couch to sleep on, usually.

With her sweater under her cheek and her phone clutched against her chest, she looked like a little girl. Until he got a better look at that lush mouth.

Nothing about that made him think of a girl. No, that mouth was all woman and incited far too many thoughts about his cock. He walked past her and closeted himself into the bathroom.

Get a hold of yourself, man.

After the first pressing concern was taken care of, he washed his hands and cupped water over his face. Even unconscious, she coated his skin like a sunburn. Hot, sensitive to the touch, and goddamn annoying.

Getting his hands on another woman should have cleared those cobwebs, but he'd let Melissa go without taking what she was so eager to give him.

Because of this woman.

One more day.

Then he could put her back into her place. A memory. A memory far too entrenched into a song he had to sing every goddamn day, but still a memory.

A soft knock at the door pulled him out of his funk. "Just a sec."

"Sorry."

Fuck.

He knew that voice.

He opened the door and because she was inhabiting his brain and his sleep, he figured it was quid pro quo to make her just as uncomfortable.

Margo with her back up kept him focused and put her in her place in his head.

He lifted his hands to the top of the doorway and leaned out. "Couldn't wait your turn, Violin Girl?"

Her huge dark eyes were heavy-lidded with sleep. Her defenses were down and he immediately wanted to pull back. This Margo was one he'd never seen before. Curious Margo, impassioned Margo, music Margo—all of those lived in his brain. But all of those facets of her were enhanced with emotion.

This was a woman who hadn't put on her layers and shields yet.

Her gaze drifted to his neck and his mouth then to his eyes before she curled her lower lip behind her teeth. Then she seemed to realize what she'd done and she retreated against the wall of the small cubby that made up the bathroom area.

He stepped out and rested his hand on the wall beside her head. "Nervous?"

"Why would you get nervous from me being half awake?"

"Not me. I meant you." He chuckled. "Why else would you back up a step?"

"To let you pass." Her chin lifted. "You know that archaic thing called manners."

"Yeah, we don't know much about those now do we, Violin Girl?" He lowered his head until his cheek brushed hers. "Uncouth rockstars and all."

She shivered and he wanted so much to bury his face in her neck. The honeysuckle scent of her urged him closer, clogging his brain and dissolving any better judgement.

His knee slid between her thighs. When she laid her hand on his belly, he stilled. Instead of pushing him away, her thumb slipped under his shirt and through the arrow of hair above his zipper.

"Playing with fire," he said into her ear.

She turned her face so her lips brushed his ear. "Which of us is the flame?"

He drew back and looked down at her. She didn't try to look away, didn't veil her eyes, and didn't even try to hide behind her many cool masks.

No.

There was naked need there.

The kind that he remembered from that day and even more damning... the kind that echoed inside of him. As if there was no other option, they moved closer. There were only a few inches difference between them. She was tall and stacked in ways that made him itch to possess.

He drew her minted breath in and their lips hovered between touch and tease. Part of him didn't want to connect. The almost kiss was strung so tight between them.

He flicked his tongue along the divot of her upper lip and the shaky breath could have been hers or his own. When her fingertips curled into the top of his jeans, the light scrape of her nail along his lower belly made him groan.

"Christ, get a room."

Nick's disgusted voice had her ducking under his arm and flying into the bathroom.

"Well, shit," Nick muttered. "I needed to go in there."

Simon thunked his forehead against the wall. "Jesus."

"You think it's smart to go there again, man?"

No. Nothing about what he'd just done was smart. His iron-hard cock had other thoughts, but the head on his shoulders was trying desperately to drag his thoughts away from anything that included Margo and a kiss.

Because they never stopped at a kiss.

Hell, they rarely kissed. The one time they'd gotten together they'd been too aggressive to actually kiss much.

But fuck, he'd wanted to taste her.

He brushed by Nick and dropped onto the couch. Her phone lay on top of her sweater, the headphones trailing over the seat. His fingers itched to lift one of the earphones.

Was she listening to some classical masterpiece, hip hop, or rock? Enya?

"Fuck it." He lifted one of the earphones to his ear and jammed his thumb into the bottom button of her iPhone and pressed *play* on the screen that lit up. Even in a locked position, music would play.

"The Becoming" filled his head. He flicked out the earbud and stood.

Why the hell was she listening to that? The new stuff he could understand. She needed to learn it for tonight. They were adding more violin to the pieces that hadn't required it from the studio sessions.

This song, they knew.

Had she been drowning in memories, too?

He moved back to the big screen where Jazz was playing Mario Kart with Harper. Both women maneuvering their controllers with a belly in the way.

As far removed from his yo-yoing feelings about Margo as possible.

"I play winner."

"You're going down, Super Slut." Jazz's eyes were wide and had a maniacal gleam in them as she passed the finish line with her bonus points stacking up.

Harper tossed her controller at Simon and he caught it right before plastic met his inconveniently hard dick. He sat down and pulled his shirt out to pool in his lap.

"You're going down, Pix." Harper gave him a small frown but he just grinned up at her. "I'm going to smoke your rather pathetic score."

Harper's face smoothed. "Rematch."

"You got it."

Margo dug through her bag at the hotel in Los Angeles. It had been a long ride into the city from the airport and again they'd taken over a floor of a swanky hotel.

This one was glass and steel without the old world flair of New York. Much more slick and glossy like she was used to in Los Angeles.

Ripper Records had spared no expense on the hotel. It was luxury at its best with sheets that boasted high thread counts and down feather pillows and comforters.

White over gray with a pinstripe wall in the darker gray. Leather and chrome, marble over glass in the bathrooms.

Beautiful.

Cold.

It seemed even more jarring because she'd been on a slow burn for hours now. She could still feel the silky hair of his belly, the warmth of his skin, his cinnamon breath filling her mouth.

No defenses could have withstood that kind of attack.

She'd continued telling herself that after she'd returned to the belly of the plane. She avoided the couch and sat with Lila. Both of them quietly reviewing things on their phone.

She'd seemed to know that Margo needed the quiet and no questions.

Margo had read a book for the rest of the flight. What book, she had no flipping idea. The words had kept her mind busy but she hadn't retained a damn thing.

She'd ridden with Lila to the hotel and left the band to travel together. Simon's gaze had trailed her from stairs to concrete, to blacktop to leather interior.

His eyes had burned through the silk of her blouse, the summer wool of her pants. There'd been no escape after that move in the small hallway.

She hadn't been able to hide the want. And she was so good at hiding it. She curled her fingers over the high-necked camisole that she usually wore under a suit jacket.

It left far too much of her shoulders and back visible to wear it alone.

Except tonight.

She'd own tonight. There really wasn't anything else she could do. If she didn't burn off some of this, she was fairly certain she was going to lose her mind.

She showered and wound her hair up into an intricate twist. She added a gold ear cuff that she wore on special occasions. Playing the violin meant she couldn't wear a lot of earrings, but she did like the effect.

It climbed her right ear with a flourish of diamonds and aged gold leaves. She played up her eyes with liquid liner and a pale shimmer over the arch of her brow. She stained her lips a deep wine red and covered the matte finish with a mirror shine gloss.

Her sister's bangles were still tucked into her travel case so she stacked them along her arm to jangle and flash against the jet black silk she wore. Two condoms also had gotten into her bag and she was damn sure she hadn't put them there.

"Juliet."

She shook her head, but tucked one into the pocket of her skirt. She was feeling too dangerous tonight. If she was going to do something stupid, at least she would do it with a level of intelligent preparation.

Her arches still hadn't forgiven her for the last evening of heels, but she stepped into her suede heeled boots anyway. One more night of torture.

A column of black over the English rose of her skin.

She'd match Simon tonight and whatever happened after that would be that. She was tired of staying inside the lines.

Chapter 8

"If one more cell phone is stuck in my face, I'm going to break it."

"Quit your bitching, Nicky. This is the first of many weeks of interviews." Simon tipped a bottle of water to his lips, drained it, and uncapped another one. His damn throat was like sandpaper from the interviews.

"Don't remind me."

Interviews and press were a necessary evil and for the most part Simon didn't mind them. The release of *Rise* was definitely a lot more intense than anything they'd done yet. He didn't want to own up to how many times he'd checked their rankings on iTunes.

And now they had another mini-concert to showcase the new songs. No matter how many times they practiced the new songs, they still felt fresh to him. Like they were finally finding who and what they were supposed to be as a band.

Lila came up behind them and crouched between him and Nick. Jazz was holding court at the end of the buffet tables they'd brought out for them to sign posters and albums—actual vinyl records—for the fan giveaways.

Simon knew his own signature was little more than an S and K with scribbles at this point. He'd done at least a hundred of them between interviews.

She set a new package of metallic Sharpies on the desk. "I thought you might want to know, that little clause in your contract?"

Nick's face grew wary. "Yeah."

"Now, Crandall, stop looking at me like I'm about to take away your new toy. This is the good clause."

Nick sighed. "I'll be the judge of that."

Simon tucked his hands under his arms. "Whadya got, beautiful?"

"See. This one knows how to butter a woman up."

"By all means enjoy his buttering," Nick muttered, his eyes going cool.

She rolled her eyes. "Your clause was a bonus if you hit gold status and *Rise* has officially hit platinum twice."

"Holy shit," Simon said and leaned forward. "That has to be a better one, right?"

"It means each of you gets a two hundred and fifty thousand dollar bonus."

Nick sat back, his face completely blank.

Simon punched him. "Holy fuck!"

Nick's eyebrows drew forward and he stood and excused himself.

"I thought this was good news," Lila said.

Simon swiped a hand down Lila's back and watched his best friend head for the side door. "It is. I do believe Nicky boy is going outside to barf."

"What?" Lila spun on her ever present four-inch heels. "Why?"

Simon cupped Lila's face and laid two huge kisses on either chick. "Because we aren't used to getting good news. And *that* is epically good news."

Lila batted his hands away. "And that equates to tossing his cookies?"

"He's an odd dude." Simon pressed a hand to his own jumping belly. "Can I tell everyone else?"

"Yes."

Simon stood and helped her up. "We couldn't have done it without you, Dragon Lady."

"I doubt that, but I'm very glad I helped."

He looked over her blond head to find Margo coming down the side stairs. She was all in black again, but this time it was a mix of vamp and innocence. Both of the traits that seemed to pour out of Margo when she let the musical side of herself free.

She turned to the side and the slinky silk she wore hugged her curves. She lifted her arm to point to the stage and a hint of purple teased from the side of her blouse.

So much skin and yet so very covered.

She turned and went back up the stairs. As the little pleat at the back of her skirt kicked up, he glimpsed the stretchy band of lace at the top of her inky thigh-highs.

Jesus fuck.

He turned away and pushed that thought of his mind. That wasn't going to help anything. It was bad enough that he had to do a ninety minute set with her knowing she was wearing garters.

He was a dead man.

When he could breathe again, he turned his attention to Jazz. "Pix, where'd Gray get to?"

"He went to get me a juice. I'm feeling a little spin-ish."

Simon cupped her elbow and dragged her around the table. "Sit down."

"I said *ish*, not actually spinning. I'm fine." She laughed and cupped her hands over her baby bump. "I'm fine, Simon."

He looked over her shoulder and saw Gray walking quickly across the club from the bar.

"Oh good, you got her to sit." Gray came around the table and crouched beside her. "Orange pineapple."

"Two of my guys waiting on me. Look at that." Jazz took the bottle of juice and uncapped it before taking long drink. "My sugar just got a little low, don't wig out you two. I burn more calories with small fry than I do alone. And you know how much I eat alone."

Simon shrugged. "She can out eat me on a good day."

"Exactly."

"Well, how about some good news."

Jazz shifted on her chair to sit up straighter. "I like that kind of news."

"We just hit double platinum."

"No way!" Jazz jumped from her chair and tackle-hugged Gray. "That's like two million downloads or buys or whatever, right?"

Gray lost his balance and the two of them landed on the floor, Gray taking all of her weight.

"Oh, shit." Jazz was laughing so hard she was squealing.

"Better news—remember that clause in our contract?"

Jazz curled herself into Gray's lap. "There were a lot of clauses."

"This is the bonus clause."

Jazz spun in Gray's arms and wound her arms around his neck. "Oh, holy shit. That's awesome."

Simon lowered his voice. "Two hundred and fifty large—each."

Jazz burst into tears.

"Whoops." Simon patted her shoulder awkwardly.

"What did you do to Pix?"

Simon looked up at Deacon. "Gave her some good news."

"It doesn't look like good news."

"Happy tears." Jazz sniffled and reached for Deacon's hand. He pulled both Gray and Jazz off the floor.

Jazz threw herself into Deacon's arms. "We got this amazing bonus for our record sales."

Deacon stroked a gentle hand down her flashing braids. "Is that so?"

"Two hundred and fifty thousand dollars, dude!"

Deacon's hand stilled. "Each?"

"Yes." Jazz bounced back. "I can't even. We can get our house." She turned and threw herself into Gray's arms. "Babe, we can buy our house." And then the tears started again.

Simon jammed his hands in his pockets. He knew they were supposed to be good tears, but man, there were a lot of them. Then Harper walked over and the lot of them were squealing about houses and babies and he decided it was a good time for a break.

He wandered out to the main part of the club. New York had been slick blues and red and this was industrial rust. Copper and dark browns with moody lights.

He liked it better. It was gritty and honest. The building had been through a few different incarnations and you could see it in the layers of the place. The ghosts of the past that were looking for something.

Like him.

Rough, rusty spots that had a bit of a spit-shine, hoping for better. A catwalk that hung above the bar and looked down on everything. Helluva vantage point for the show.

That's where he'd go.

His arms ached to climb up there and get a look at the surroundings. But that would have to wait. Lila was incoming with her ridiculous heels and suits that shouldn't belong at a rock show and yet...she did.

She'd quickly become important to all of them, even if he wanted her schedules to burn in the fiery pits of hell. She was miles better than their old manager. At least Lila played to their strengths instead of trying to force the band into the mainstream version of a typical release party.

They weren't there to schmooze. There was some of that required, of course, but for the most part she wanted them playing up to the camera and building the buzz. She didn't trot them out in front of a row of reporters and hope for the best.

She hand-selected bloggers, YouTube sensations, and even some of the smaller fry people that had supported them in the beginning. She was damn savvy and the fact that she was a brain trust on top of it all seemed incredibly unfair to all the other people in the music business.

They had to work hard to keep up.

"Mr. Kagan, you are late for an interview."

"Sorry, was dealing with the Kleenex commercial that is our pregnant drummer."

"Oh." Lila flicked a glance over at the still sobbing Jazz. "Do I need to go over there?"

The fact that every part of her expression clearly wanted him to say *no* urged him to tell her *yes*. But he couldn't do that to her. Lila didn't deal well with tears either. It just caused her to bark orders.

"Nah, she's good. They're all excited about the house money you and Ripper Records just added to their nest egg."

"Oh. Well, that's great." Her brow furrowed.

"Yeah, I can tell by the look on your face."

Instantly, her forehead smoothed. "I aim to increase their wedded bliss."

He barked out a laugh. "No you don't. You see the white picket fence and three more babies."

"Plenty of women have had babies and careers, Simon."

"And Pix will be one of them. Don't worry, she doesn't know how to be away from her drum kit for long."

"You seem very sure of yourself."

"And you should stop drinking Nicky's hater-aid."

Lila hugged her iPad to her chest. "Excuse me if I worry about your careers. You are just exploding onto the scene now and you guys are going to disappear in a few months. Are you sure I can't convince you to find an interim drummer?" Her face was earnest and serious all at the same time. "It would solve a lot of problems."

"The band doesn't work without Jazz and you know that."

Lila sighed and looked at her peep-toe shoes. "We could try it."

"We could try it, but it wouldn't work." He laced his hands behind his head. "Then where would you be if we had to back out?"

"Backing out isn't a good idea." Lila's gaze turned determined. "Not a good idea at all. The insurance is a nightmare and every contract we sign with a venue could come back and bite us in the ass due to the revenue they'll lose if we miss a show."

Simon's hands fell to his sides. "What if someone was sick?"

"Let's just keep everyone healthy, shall we?" She tried to walk by and Simon caught her elbow.

"What if something happened?"

"Let's put it this way. The tour is your major moneymaker. Missing just one show could set you back half a million."

"Half a..." Simon swallowed. "That much?"

"Between what you get to play from the venue, the merchandising, and what they have to go through to return tickets…yeah, it's not good."

Simon frowned. The business side of music was a fucking buzzkill.

One of the dozens of minions that were crawling all over the space walked by with a bucketful of iced water bottles. Simon snaked one out of the huge red bin with a quick smile at Lila. "I'll just hydrate now."

"Good thinking."

Simon squashed the minor tickle that had been following him around since rehearsals. The half-dozen interviews hadn't helped calm it down either. When the club got near capacity, he escaped to the VIP bathroom section and turned all the hot taps on.

Twenty minutes before curtain meant he really needed to warm up. The problem with being the lead singer was that most people wanted to talk to him more than the rest of the band. Which meant he taxed his voice.

When they were doing regular shows, he was able to do the morning radio calls and then rest for the remainder of the day. This week had been nothing but talking.

He needed to kill it tonight. This was his home turf and people were watching, but not just because Oblivion was from the Los Angeles area. An equal number of people were waiting for them to fail.

And failure wasn't an option. Not now. Not when they were *this close* to making something of themselves. If they rocked out enough, they could write their own ticket.

They didn't have to worry about venue insurance. And a quarter of a million bonus would look like chump change if they continued on the path they were on.

Pushing it all out of his mind, he went through a few of the scales that worked for him and kept an eye on the clock.

Deacon opened the door and slipped in. "Hey, Pretty Boy. How's the warm-up? Sounds good from outside."

Simon turned off the taps as he made his way down to the last sink. "Between the cover song we're doing and the one from the Twitter contest, I need all the help I can get."

Deacon took care of the purpose for his visit and met him at the sinks to wash. "You can sing 'Jet City Woman' in your sleep."

"Lyrics are easy. Hitting Geoff Tate's lower registers then quick highs... yeah. I'll have some of Harper's famous tea on stage tonight, that's for sure."

Deacon slapped him on the back. "I'll take care of it."

Simon turned off his tap. "Ready to do this shit?"

"Hell yes."

He followed Deacon out and they circumvented the crush of people to find the stairs to the backstage area. Deacon swapped out his dress shirt for a Doors T-shirt.

"Hey, there you are."

Simon turned to Jazz's voice. "Hey Pinky." He flicked the peek-a-boo locks of hair she'd deftly arranged in her dark hair. Since she'd gotten pregnant, she'd been having a little too much fun with the fake hair since she couldn't dye her own.

"I got a present from a fan for you."

"Oh yeah? Is it sexy?"

She rolled her eyes. "Is that all you care about?"

He chewed on his bottom lip and paused. And because she got even more exasperated, he nodded. "Mostly."

"Normally it just goes in the crazy box, but man, this was way too cool. Especially with the song we picked for the cover." She snapped out a ripped out T-shirt. The fan had even torn out the sides like he preferred.

"Jesus. You'd think she...*she*?"

Jazz nodded. "Yeah, it was a woman."

Simon wiggled out of his shirt and tossed it on a guitar trunk.

"Geeze, Simon."

He took the shirt from her and arched one eyebrow then the other until they danced. "Nothing you haven't seen before, Pix."

"I see your chest almost as much as my husband's."

"Clothing is restrictive," he said with a shrug.

He tossed the shirt over his head. "This, however, is not. Awesome." He looked up and Margo stood in the sidelines, her dark eyes heavy-lidded as they skimmed down his body.

Jesus fuck.

Thankful that the shirt was a little long in the front, he tugged it over his buckle to hide his instant reaction to Margo. "Like the show, Violin Girl?"

Instead of the embarrassment he was going for, he saw only interest in her eyes. "Creative use of Michael Hutchence's face," she said.

He grinned and turned around. "Even better from the back."

Jazz ticked her nails down the sliced back. "I need to do that to some of my shirts. It's hot under these lights and the tadpole definitely kicks up my temperature gauge."

"Not sure you can call it a tadpole when you're carrying around the equivalent of a soccer ball."

Jazz socked him in the arm. "Rude."

Simon reached over and patted her little Buddha belly. "Adorable."

She slapped his hand.

He laughed. A much better state of affairs than the mood he'd been in during his warm-up.

"On in five."

Simon ushered Jazz into the backstage area and let Margo go ahead of him as well.

"Last minute change to the setlist."

Simon groaned. "If I have to try and remember lyrics again, I'm gonna kill ya, Nicky."

"Nah, just rearranging."

"Thank fuck."

Simon scanned the page. "Starting with 'Sugar Kiss'. That's different. Why?"

"Kim got us on iHeart Radio's live broadcast."

Simon's eyebrows shot up.

Nick blew out a nervous breath. "Yeah. My sentiments exactly."

"That's a little more than the live feed we were doing from our website."

"Yeah. We're moving up 'Jet City Woman' too since it was the Twitter winner. Blast the social media shit out of the sky tonight."

"Buzz, buzz, buzz."

"You got it." Nick shook out his hands. "I'm gonna go throw up. I'll be back in a minute."

Simon shook his head. Nicky was not kidding. He probably was going to go heave out whatever they'd had for lunch.

He scooted backstage to the dressing area and grabbed the Crystal Skull bottle on the dressing room table and a small stack of Dixie cups.

When he got back out there, he snagged a bottle of pineapple juice from the stash Lila had waiting for them between songs.

"Okay everyone, band huddle."

"One minute, Simon. You don't have time for speeches," Lila said.

Simon set out seven cups on Deacon's bass trunk.

"If you splash booze on my bass, I'm going to kick your ass."

"Chill out, Demon." Simon splashed a little more than a shot in six of the cups then pineapple juice in the seventh.

"What if I wanted pineapple juice?" Deacon asked.

"Too bad."

Deacon sighed and picked up his cup.

Simon nodded to the last cup. "You too, Violin Girl."

"I'm not part of the band."

"You are tonight."

She set her bow down on the trunk and picked up her cup.

"Everyone in. You too, Lila." Simon lifted his cup and they all tapped paper together. "To the next phase."

"The next phase," everyone repeated.

Lila tossed her shot back without a hiss or a wince. Her sac was a helluva lot more impressive than Gray and Deacon, who both made faces.

"Cups." Lila held hers up and everyone tucked theirs into hers and grabbed their instruments.

He poured another for himself and grinned when Margo held her cup up for another. "Need a little liquid courage tonight?"

"I like vodka."

"Ever a surprise, Violin Girl." He splashed two fingers in her cup and they both tossed it back.

"Give me that." Lila took the skull-shaped bottle from him. "Go. Get on stage."

"Ready for one more night with us crazies?"

Margo nodded. "More than."

"Then let's do this."

Margo drew her bow across her strings as Simon curled his entire body around the microphone and his stand.

The man never stayed still. He slithered against the chrome like it was a lover. She remembered how those hips had moved, the innate fluidity of his inner rhythm. And she wished for a little more of the vodka.

Maybe that would take the edge off.

Because watching Simon all damn day had left her skin too tight for her body. The heavy air under the lights seemed oppressive. Screams rending the air seemed shrill and over the top.

Or maybe it was just her.

As "The Becoming" hit its peak, she came out to the spotlight with Simon as she'd done the night before. The first time she'd been in a trance. Simply existing in his sphere and following his cues.

Tonight she played up the push and pull game they'd played the first time. This time she slid behind him until they were shoulder-to-shoulder, her hips following his as the song got darker and sexier.

Deacon's bass was her central line into the song. He was the constant, Simon was the wild card. The song ramped up, Nick's guitars came to the forefront and then Gray's blew them both out of the water.

She tried to melt back into the darkness. This song was going out into the internet ether with their rabid fans soaking up each chord. But Simon didn't allow that.

He dragged her in front of him, and his hips never stopped the slow seduction against her. His arm banded across her midriff and they moved as one. The crowd below lost their collective minds.

Maybe she had as well.

She had no choice but to stay in the moment. Was entirely sure she couldn't do anything else anyway. She felt the stiff length of him bumping against her and tried to resist his voice in her ear.

They created a darkly sensual dance between them, and her violin answered his words as if the conversation was on a different plane.

He swung her out as the song ended and then dragged her in tight until she had no choice but to let her violin dangle against her thigh.

As if in a distant time and place, the crowd screamed in reaction.

He palmed the back of her neck and dipped her. His nose and the barest hint of lips trailed up her neck before he put her back to rights and the heavy bass of "Jet City Woman" filled the room.

She escaped his touch, the madness that had bespelled them, and managed to play her part in the layers of the epic cover song. Simon prowled the stage and pulled the crowd in like a lover.

As easily as he'd dragged her under, he left women mesmerized in his wake. His old-style microphone became an extension of him. His lips caressed the guard, and his moans translated to screams from the crowd.

And as the song ended, he dropped to his knees and mimicked the pain of the narrator. It was his gift. Their songs were catalogued in a different part of performance for Simon. No less powerful, no less entrancing in their own right, but when he sang someone else's song, he became a chameleon.

When he popped to his feet, the crowd swelled forward and women reached for him and men hollered out their battle cries. Women wanted to fuck him and men wanted to be him.

It was a heady experience to behold.

Simon clipped his microphone into the stand and swiped his hair back. "Good goddamn! This is why we do everything in L.A., man. This crowd. Fuck yeah!"

He put his hand up to his mouth. "Whoops. Sorry, iHeart. I got a little carried away. That six second rule always saves our asses, huh?"

Margo shook her head and tucked her violin under her arm.

"Thanks so much for peeking in on our release party." He held his arm out to his right. "Nicky boy and Grayson, come take a bow."

The two of them stepped into the spotlights and waved.

"Demon, get your Gigantor ass out of the shadows. Give my ridiculously tall friend a hand, huh?"

Deacon draped his arm around Simon's neck.

"Think we should give them one more?" he asked Deacon.

Deacon leaned into the mic. "Not sure they can handle it."

"What do you guys think?" The crowd blasted him with screams and Simon fake stumbled away from Deacon. "Holy shit. Maybe they can." He stood on the drum riser. "Jazzercise, what do you think?"

"I think you should sing 'Monster'."

Simon looked over his shoulder. "Whadya think?"

The crowd screamed and he pointed at Margo. "Violin Girl, start us off."

Startled, Margo lifted her bow and started off the song as they'd rehearsed.

Sometime toward the middle of the song, she noticed that the camera crew had lessened. It didn't seem to matter that the cameras were off Simon. He poured everything into the show just the same.

A heavy sheen of sweat coated her arms by the end of the night. Her back ached from the heels, and her heart still raced in time with the last song.

When the house lights went down, it felt like they'd only just begun even as her body said otherwise.

A single violet-tinged light shot out of the night and the murmuring crowd settled as Simon held his hand up. "Thank you so much for making tonight amazing. We'll be out to schmooze and booze with you momentarily, but we've got one more song tonight." He slid his hand under the shirt that was molded to him with sweat. "This might give you a clue."

Then the light went out and she cradled her violin against her chin for the opening chords of "Never Tear Us Apart".

Simon sang the first verse in the complete dark. His voice morphed into a fair mimic of Michael Hutchence with his own spin.

The lights slowly lifted until they were all awash in a purple glow with a roving disco ball splash as Simon's fluid performance entranced.

Though a jazzy saxophone had been part of the original version, they'd modified her strings to suit the melody. She came forward and her lights went pink with a heartbeat pulse around her.

The slow song built until there was nothing but guitars and drums pounding out around Simon as he got the crowd to sing with him. The iconic INXS song bled into the raunchy, gritty guitars of Guns n' Roses.

Simon stripped off his shirt and raced to the edge of the stage, then dropped to his knees. He rolled onto his back and screamed out the lyrics with a raw edge that made Margo wince.

He wouldn't be able to talk later.

But the crowd lapped it up. They moved as one and sang back at him for every line. Los Angeles anthem that it was, everyone knew the song.

By the time it was over, the party had started.

And same as last night, Simon jumped into the crowd and led the charge to the bar. He slapped the countertop and a line of shot glasses flamed to life.

Gray and Nick played the hell out of the guitar solos, each of them dueling over the riff-heavy song as the crowd went wild.

Simon blew out his shot and tossed back two of them before running back to the stage to finish the song. The fans and radio people, the famous and pseudo-famous all joined in for the last chorus.

Margo got pulled forward with the band as the song closed out. Deacon scooped her up and dropped her next to Simon as they waved and bowed.

Somehow her arm ended up around Simon's back. He was slick with sweat and vibrating with excitement. He looked down at her, but the smile she was expecting was missing.

His eyes burned with a flame similar to the shot glasses making the rounds at the bar. She shivered and pulled away as the band dispersed.

Jazz jumped and hugged everyone, including her. There was nothing but the high of the show, the crowd, and a night of success.

Why did she want to escape?

True, it wasn't her success, but she'd enjoyed the way that the band had allowed her into the inner circle. The interaction of the fans was a high she couldn't deny.

She should allow herself to be pulled in, but she only wanted escape. Her heart rate was hummingbird-fast as she climbed the hidden stairs to the quiet corner she'd found after rehearsal.

The stairs to the catwalk over the bar. Now that the show was over, the lights had been brought down and shadows and strobe lights bounced around the room in a heady pulse that echoed the excitement of the night.

People were talking over one another and Oblivion songs were piped in with a current radio hit in between each song. She curled her fingers around the textured paint that splattered the iron bars and rivets.

No one knew she was up there. She wasn't altogether sure that anyone cared. Her purpose had been fulfilled for this part of their promotional tour.

She wasn't sure how to feel about that.

She'd gotten exactly what she wanted. The exposure had garnered interest and her email was peppered with new offers that her agent was getting for her and studio work. Her untimely dismissal from the Boston Philharmonic might be just what she needed for a different career.

She had Oblivion to thank for that. "The Becoming" had ruined her for the staid and true songs that had molded her childhood, but in the end, that song had given her so much more.

"Hiding?"

Margo shivered at his voice. "Watching."

"Is that what you like to do?"

She closed her eyes against the throb of reaction that flared to life again. Escape had been too much to ask for. Not when Simon was in the picture.

"Sometimes."

He came up behind her, curling his fingers around the bar on either side of her hands. "Is it the people below that you like or the dancers in the cages?" He tucked his chin over her shoulder and steered her gaze to the far side of the room.

Under the throbbing bass of the song, she noticed two women book-ending the second bar with a little extra entertainment. All the lights and the crowd's focus centered on the two dark-haired women with thigh high boots and leather bikinis who gyrated with the songs.

"A little obvious, don't you think?"

"We are in L.A.," he said with a purr.

"The home of excess?"

"That might be Vegas."

"That's greed."

"And the looks on their faces below don't include greed?"

"I'd say the greed would be the executives under Donovan Lewis. Here, the commodity is lust and excess."

Simon laughed. "Is that why you're up here? Too good for those emotions, Violin Girl?"

No.

No, she definitely wasn't.

She'd been living with the lust part for weeks now. It was inconvenient and messy and she hoped to hell that she could leave it behind with the experience, but she was beginning to wonder.

"I saw the need in your eyes tonight." He slid one arm around her and tucked her back against his hips. "Felt it in the way we moved together on the stage."

She let out a shaky breath. "A moment of madness."

"Is that all we'll ever be?"

I don't know.

He moved his hips in time to the syrupy tempo of the song piping out into the crowd. Conversation and milling bodies, laughter and shouts, light and shadow—all of it fed into the insanity that made her move against him.

He hissed out a breath and his arm tightened across her hips until they moved as one. "Is this what you want?" His hand slid lower as he skimmed his fingers along the hem of her skirt.

She let out a shuddering breath.

"Under the cover of shadows, with the crowd right there." He tucked his fingers into the band of her thigh-high and scraped short nails over the skin until he reached the line of her panties. "Are you wet?"

She nodded.

"Are you wet because of me?"

The moan that tripped out of her chest couldn't be hers. It *wasn't* her. It was her when she was with him.

A new kind of Margo.

He nosed his way along the line of her neck, behind her ear. "Tell me you want this." He pushed the front of her panties to the side and sneaked under the elastic. His grumbling voice thickened when he pushed the pads of his fingers under the swollen flesh that hid her clit. "I need to hear it, Margo."

Her knuckles went white with her grip on the iron support bar. "Yes. God, yes."

He flicked his tongue over the lobe of her ear and drew it into his mouth as he sunk two fingers into her. "All those people under us. All they need to do is look up and they'd see me finger-fucking you."

She let out a breath and undulated against his hardness from behind and his invading fingers from the front. "Let them."

His laugh was low and harsh in her ear. "My naughty Violin Girl likes that idea."

"Harder."

He drew his other arm around her and gripped her breast through the silk camisole. He tucked his chin onto her shoulder and tugged at the strapless bra she wore until the tip of her nipple peeked over the top.

"Watch," he said.

"Watch what?"

"The people."

She tried to turn her attention to the people below, but her gaze kept straying to her breast. He plucked at the distended flesh, gently at first then twisted tighter as she fed him with moans and groans in approval.

"Not me, watch the crowd below."

Margo cried out as his other hand opened her lips and strummed a nail over her clit. He didn't quite stroke her as she needed him to.

No, he left that to his never ending tug on her nipple through silk, first one then the other as his breathing increased against her ear. He let out a growl as her flesh dampened even more.

"I'm not even inside you and you're soaking my hand."

"Simon."

"Again." He coasted two fingers around her clit.

She pressed her head against his shoulder. "I need..."

"You *need* to say my name again."

"Simon." She bucked against his hand. "Simon, I need..."

"Need what?"

"Need you." Her blood boiled under the surface and her skin was an electric conduit that jumped with each touch.

"Need me to do what? Give you an orgasm? All it would take was a few more of these." He tugged at her nipples roughly and she blew out a breath. "Or maybe here? Is this what you want?" He dipped his fingers inside of her and caught her clit between them.

The friction made black spots haze over her vision. "Oh, yes."

"Is that what you want?"

"More," she said brokenly. "*You.* You, I need you, not your fingers."

He groaned. "I didn't come prepared for this kind of party."

"My pocket."

"There's a pocket in this tiny thing?"

She ground back against him. "Yes." His fingers slid away from her and she groaned in relief and distress as he dug into her pocket.

"Were you holding this the entire night?"

She nodded.

"You wanted this?"

She always wanted this.

Wanted him.

He speared his fingers into her hair and pushed her head down to look at the floor of people. "Did you come up here for this?"

"No." She'd needed to get away from Simon, but now all she wanted was the feel of him filling her again.

"But you want it now?"

"So much."

He dug into her pocket and the crinkle of plastic then the unnaturally loud echo of his zipper made her sag against the bar.

He kicked out her feet and jerked up her skirt. "Are you sure this is what you want?"

She heard the anger there. She wasn't sure just *why* it was there, but she was too far gone to puzzle it out. She reached between her legs to his fingers, pushing them away from his cock. "Yes."

She lifted onto her toes on her already high heels. He pulled her panties to the side and thrust inside of her.

She bit back a scream and returned her hands to the bar.

"Is this what you need?" His voice was lower, his tone darker.

"Yes."

He snapped his hips forward and lifted her even higher onto her toes. He gripped the bar in front of her, placing both hands between hers for leverage. And fucked her.

There was no other word for it.

This wasn't lovemaking. This wasn't even a hook-up. This was raw and real and dirty. His breath was harsh against her neck, then came the leading edge of pain as he scraped his teeth down her nape to the high collar of her camisole.

He skipped over the material to get to her shoulder as he ground his pelvis against her backside. His length and the broad head of his cock hit all the places she remembered and some that she'd never known could come alive inside of her.

He brought one hand up the front of her from clit to belly then to breast. His touch rough, his calloused fingertips warring with his softer palm until he left behind his own branding.

She pushed back against him. So close. Her body fairly vibrated with the jarring thrusts as the head of his cock kept battering her from the inside out.

He slid his hand higher and his fingers curled around her throat as he held her still, his mouth at her ear. "I know what you need. This, between us, it's always what you've needed."

He dipped his fingers of his other hand under her skirt and found her clit.

The barest hint of a grip on her throat, combined with his busy fingers, and she was lost. She prayed that she didn't scream his name.

Though no one would be able to hear it over the drowning beat of the music, though they were hidden in the rafters of shadow and red light and no one could see, he would know.

If she let that scream of surrender out, Simon would know.

And that terrified her even as she chased it.

Chapter 9

Simon dragged in a breath and tried to hold onto sanity. Suspended over a crowd of people with cameras as he sank inside Margo's fisting pussy was not the way to hold onto sanity, but he'd been lying to himself since he'd climbed up here. What was one more?

He felt her swallow under his fingers, vibrated with her keening moan as her pussy spasmed around his cock. He thrust into her again and again until his thighs burned, until his spine flamed, until his balls drew up tight with the need to come.

He tried to hold out.

Knew that as soon as he came it would be over. She felt too good and he'd wanted her for too damn long. The guttural groan he unleashed as he let go was too honest, too raw.

She sagged against the bars of the catwalk and still he had the unyielding urge to drive into her again. To imprint himself all over her body.

And he hated it.

He wanted to pull back, wanted to keep the pleasure from her. Hated to give her this power when this had been her plan all along.

Maybe not here but tonight she'd been ready for something to happen between them. He couldn't even say why that pissed him off, but it did.

Because he'd seen her itinerary and knew she was on a flight tonight. Knew she was leaving again. And he'd tried not to give her the satisfaction. Tried to walk away before he did something stupid like this.

But she'd been standing there alone and the endorphin rush from the show was still bubbling under his skin.

She'd still been under his skin from the show.

And he'd pushed her buttons. The anger from wanting her as if no time had passed had landed him here. His cock still wet from her. It didn't matter that latex was between them, her silky heat was on his fingers, had transferred onto his leathers, and the scent of them together was back in his head.

He tied off the condom and backed away. Because he couldn't take the thought of her walking away from him again, he stuffed himself into his pants and turned away from her.

He got three steps away.

"Simon."

He stopped. He didn't turn back. Couldn't have any more of her in his head right now.

"I..."

He fisted his hand at his side. When she didn't say anything more, he strode across the catwalk to the stairs. He slid down the railing and pitched the condom in the garbage.

"There you are."

"Not now, Pix."

"We have a photo op."

"Fuck the photo op." His voice broke on the shout and he swallowed the need to cough. His goddamn throat was on fire.

Jazz backed up a step, her hand instantly covering her baby bump.

"Fuck. I'm sorry."

She held up a hand. "It's fine." But the wariness didn't leave her eyes.

"Just give me a minute. I'll be out in a few."

She just nodded.

He turned away. "Jazz, I'm sorry. It's not you. I just...need a minute, all right?"

"Sure, Simon."

He took the stairs at a dead run and crossed the sea of people like a shark in the water. Whomever was in his path seemed to know that he wasn't to be fucked with.

Lila waved him over in his periphery, but he ignored her. Just before he hit the bathrooms, a woman stopped in front of him. Slim and an almost colorless blond, she was the antithesis of Margo. The urge to snarl at her was like a living thing inside him.

Instead he flashed the wicked smile he used in interviews at her. "Do me a favor, get me a vodka tonic, hold the tonic and meet me back here in five minutes."

"Can do."

"Christ, I hope she's old enough to order," he muttered as he slammed the door open. He went right to the sinks and dunked his head under the stream. Icy cold and cleansing was the key to getting his head back in the game.

He cupped handfuls of water and rinsed his mouth. He hadn't even gotten his mouth on hers, but that honeysuckle and mint scent had infiltrated every part of him.

He flipped his hair back and hissed at the cold rivulets of water that soaked his T-shirt. He scrubbed away the remnants of the black liner he wore on stage until his skin was pink and raw.

Awesome for pictures.

He gripped the sides of the sink and stared into the mirror. "It was just sex. Just fucking. Nothing else. Pull it together."

Resisting the impulse to smash his fist into his reflection, he left the bathroom. The blond was waiting for him.

"Well, hello sweetheart."

"Your vodka tonic, no tonic," she said with a giggle.

He took the tall, thin glass from her. "You have my eternal gratitude."

"I'll take a kiss instead."

Simon laughed and leaned down to brush her cheek. The young woman turned her face and he got a very thorough, very tongue-intensive kiss for his trouble.

When he pulled back, he caught a movement in the crowd. Margo's eyes locked on them. This was nothing like the moment in the corridor from New York.

There wasn't a wild, voyeuristic flavor between them tonight.

She backed up and the crowd of dancers and minglers swallowed her before he could take two steps after her.

He wanted to chase her, to explain, and because he wanted to do that so very badly, he stopped in the middle of the crowd.

What would be the point?

She'd still be on a flight in a few hours. She'd still be one more memory he'd have to fight to find sleep.

He drained the vodka on the rocks and pushed the glass into the first outstretched hand he could find and made his way over to the crush of cameras.

That was exactly where he should be. Not chasing a woman who didn't want to be caught.

He smiled for the camera that zeroed in on him and dug his phone out of his pocket to take a picture back. And because his job was to post selfies and stupid pictures, he opened his Instagram program and winged the picture off into the ether with a quippy little comment about photos.

"Where's Margo?" Deacon asked. "We've got to do those pictures."

"She had to run to catch a flight," Lila chimed in.

His smile faltered for a minute before he hung his arm around Nick's neck. "Helluva show tonight, huh?"

Nick allowed the affection for about three seconds, then shrugged Simon off. "C'mon, man."

"Just giving the photographers what they want."

"Why are you hugging up on me? Nobody wants to see that."

"Oh, you'd be surprised," Jazz piped up.

"I do not want to know," Nick said.

"Good, because you don't have time for that." Lila raised her voice. "Everyone line up."

It was time to work.

Margo dropped her keys into the bowl on the table inside her door. It felt like forever since she'd been inside her house. Between the studio gigs and the trips into Los Angeles and New York City, she hadn't seen her own bed in well over two weeks.

She opened to door to her music room and set her violin into its slot between her Stradivarius and her 5-String Realist. Which, in hindsight, she should have brought with the Starfish. She'd honestly thought they would bring her out for the three songs she'd worked on and that was it.

The fact that the band had utilized her as an asset, not just a guest star had been thrilling. Deacon seemed to be their mastermind at putting the songs together cohesively.

To an impressive level. So much so that the little part of her that had been composing in her head got really loud.

Not good.

That wasn't her job. She was an accomplished violinist who was hired on because she was skilled in learning songs in a very short time. Not for her composing skills.

Even if she'd had a lot of input for the three songs she'd done with them. *No.*

She closed the door firmly on her music room and moved to her living room. Her far too quiet living room.

Quiet had never bothered her before. She picked up her phone and sent off a text to her friend Siobhan. Maybe she could go out to lunch with her tomorrow.

Her phone rang in her hand.

"Hey, Siobhan."

"Is everything okay?"

"Of course."

"It's after one in the morning. You never text that late."

Margo closed her eyes. "I'm sorry. You were probably sleeping."

"No, I'm actually out with some people from the orchestra. Do you want to come out and meet us?"

"I...yes."

"You do?"

The fact that her friend sounded so surprised cinched the decision. She was tired of holing up and working more than having fun. "Yes. Yes, I do."

"Great. We're at Callahan's off—"

"I know it."

"Well, we'll see you in a little bit then."

"Thanks for calling to check on me, Siobhan."

"Of course I would. We've been friends for a long time. I worry about how isolated you get."

She swallowed hard. Things like friends and socializing had never been on her radar. At least socializing beyond the kind she did for networking.

Being around Simon and the band had been eye-opening.

Everything about Simon had been eye-opening.

She cleared her throat. "I just got in from Los Angeles. I don't have time to be isolated."

"That's not what I mean and you know it."

"I know. Well, let's make some changes then, huh?"

"Excellent idea."

Margo hung up and went to her closet. She pushed aside the sweater sets and skirts that made up her wardrobe for the symphony.

At the back of her closet, she found the high-waisted pencil skirt that she wore so rarely. She could hear her mother's voice lecturing in her head that it was too revealing, hugged her too-curvy figure, and sexualized her.

It was the skirt she'd been wearing when Simon had taken notice of her over a year ago.

Flashes of the studio and now the catwalk wrapped around each other until her skin flushed. If that's what it felt like to be wanted, then she couldn't find a reason to put that Margo back at the back of the closet.

Dammit, she was tired of hiding who she was under frumpy clothing. Maybe it was time to use a little of her savings to update her wardrobe.

Maybe it was time for a lot of changes.

Chapter 10

Simon spun his glass on the itinerary page. The sweat rings from his ever present bottle of water smudged out the city. Not that it really mattered. They'd been trotted out to every major city for the last few weeks.

But they were finally in week four.

Acoustic gigs, small garage band gigs, hell, they'd even played a converted armory for a late spring festival. Anything to get their name out there and build buzz for the tour.

Tickets were selling out.

For *them*.

On a freaking headline tour.

It was insane.

Just last year they'd been the opening act and this tour they were in talks to be one of the most sought after tickets of the summer. The album had actually hit the top three on Billboard for two weeks in a row, only falling off to the stay in the top ten.

He walked to the window. On the street below there was a crowd of people—mostly women. Every city had the same scene. With increasing numbers, they were getting stalked at every hotel. He was still trying to comprehend it all.

What the hell had changed? Was this album so very different from the last one? It didn't feel like it. And still, this was so incredibly nuts.

Jesus fuck, it was just weird to have a room to himself. He'd been living in Nick and Deacon's pockets for years now. Once the tour started, they'd be back to the buses, of course, but even then it would be a big change. They had the married and babies bus, then the one for himself and Nick.

The budget for the tour was increasing as well. If he got one more update from Lila about what the stage was going to look like, he was going to bust his hand through a wall. All he cared about was his mic and a place to run around.

Okay, so the ramps that they'd had built were kinda cool. He had complete access to the stage from back to front, and around Jazz.

They were going to look at a set-up at the end of the week and then they'd have a week to rehearse and figure out the setlist, what worked, what didn't, lights, and all that happy horse shit.

Singing to an empty amphitheater wasn't his idea of a good time, but he'd do it. The fact that he didn't have much choice was only part of it. With each successive mini-show they did, he was learning that he couldn't just scream out a song and bounce back.

It was fucking annoying.

He glugged down another bottle of water and watched the people wander into the street. The bar across the street was either taking the overflow or creating it, he wasn't quite sure.

He wanted to be out there. They were in freaking Boston, for fuck's sake. The bar capital of the damn world and he was stuck here.

He had an early radio show to rest up for. Between the shows and the interviews, he was constantly talking or singing. He hadn't been able to just chill out and drink a beer.

Or sing a cover song.

He loved singing their stuff, but man…there was something about the way a room lit up with an old tried and true song.

He'd been mostly singing to ugly carpeting and soundproof glass. The inspiration factor had been about minus five hundred. The little shows were good, but they were rushed through five or six songs then pushed on to the next city.

Right there, with those people down on the street is where he wanted to be. He uncapped another bottle of water and tipped his head back.

"Fuck it."

He grabbed his leather duffle that he'd been living out of and dug through to find a shirt. He grinned when he found the burgundy rolled up T-shirt. Not one that he could wear to the radio shows Lila had set up for them.

But damn well fun for a night out. He unrolled the once black pants that had faded to a charcoal gray with a million washings. His favorite non-stage gear. Before he could talk himself out of it, he stripped off the ratty sweatshorts he wore around the hotel and dressed.

He scooped his hair back and grabbed a condom, his wallet, and his phone. Maybe the pussy fairy would like his shirt and get him laid. He paused before he went through the door. Maybe a little bit of a disguise to at least get outside.

Or at least through the lobby.

He snagged the Fedora off the desk, thought better of it and went to grab his suspenders. No one would recognize him.

Maybe.

Fuck it. Who cared if they did? He needed to get out of his room.

He snuck out. On the way down the hall, he heard the low murmurings of Deacon and Harper talking, Nick's music, and Lila on the phone as always.

He just might make it to the elevator without anyone paying attention. The doors opened and he slid inside. Just as they were closing, Nick stuck his head out of his room and gave him a "what the fuck" look.

Simon waved and grinned.

His phone vibrated in his pocket. He pulled it out.

Where the fuck are you going?

Simon grinned and typed back.

Escape. If you don't see me by dawn, send a search party.

Before he could even send back his text, he saw the reply coming through.

And I'm not invited?

Sure you want to incur the wrath of Dragon Lady?

She's not my keeper.

Simon grinned. Nick so wished Lila was his keeper. At least of his dick. The boy had a serious case of blue balls over her.

Not that he was one to talk.

He hadn't been able to seal the deal with a chick since he'd gotten his hands on Margo again. Maybe tonight would finally turn that around.

A bar, too much vodka or beer to be smart, and the streets of Boston might be just what he needed.

I'm headed to the bar across the street. If you dare to wade through the groupies, meet me there.

You couldn't wait?

Right, so both of them could try to hide who they were? Was he high?

Your disguises suck.

And yours don't? The hat doesn't work for anyone, jackass.

Simon grinned and typed back.

Just has to get me out the door, son.

He jammed his phone in his pocket and hurried through the lobby. He stopped at the desk. "Hi. Is there a side door out of here that won't set off the crowd?"

The girl behind the counter's eyes went wide. "Um. Hi, Sim—Mr. Kagan."

"Simon is fine, sweetheart."

She cleared her throat. "Right. Um, sure. If you go down that hallway to where the pool is, there's a side door. You'll have to go around the building, but at least there's no one back there. At least last time we did a walk-through."

He drummed his fingers on the counter and waggled his eyebrows at her. "Awesome." He looked down at her tag. "Thanks, Ashley."

Before she could stammer out a reply, Simon moved down the hallway to the scent of chlorine and the unnatural humidity of the indoor pool area. He might just take a dip on his way back in.

Sure enough, there was a side entrance at the end of the hall. If he was stalking someone famous, he'd go for the side door, but private property practices were probably enforced. And that was where he cashed in.

Ca-ching. Empty of screaming fans.

He skirted the edges of the parking lot and snuck across the street. There was a shit ton of people out. And on this side of the street, it definitely wasn't for Oblivion.

Well, at least not all of it.

He slipped into the crowd and pulled down the brim of his hat, keeping his chin down. He jammed his hands into his pockets to look like a college kid. The closer he got to the bar, the more he realized it was an honest to God pub.

He knew Boston was full of them. Had seen them out the windows on the drive in. And now he could get in there and enjoy a pint or whatever the fuck you did in an Irish pub.

Whatever it was, he was game.

He stopped when a pair of very scuffed, very large black boots came into his line of sight. "Nice Docs."

"Ten bucks, college boy."

And Nicky said his disguises sucked. Simon dug a crumpled bill out of his pants. He wasn't used to carrying cash anymore. Everything was expensed lately.

Bingo. A twenty from his allowance yesterday. Ahem—per diem. As far as he was concerned, it was a goddamn allowance. Not that he'd ever had one as a kid, but he got the reference.

He didn't tip his hat up, just forked over the cash. The dude grunted and gave him two fives back. Simon tried to go around him but the guy clamped a hand around his arm.

"ID," he mumbled.

Ah fuck. Maybe Mr. No Neck wouldn't recognize his name. He fished out his California license and handed it over. The guy's eyebrows rose then looked from him to the license and then back. Instead of saying anything, he just grunted and gave him back the license.

Simon fought his way to the bar, but it was like moving against a tide with six feet swells. The prize was a beer. And it damn well better be a good beer.

Music swelled out of the back of the bar. A deep baritone of a male voice that made the hairs at the back of his neck stand up. That was some Barry White shit right there.

He sung of the hardships of Boston, the life, the streets, and of course, the Irish. Because what would an Irish pub be without the stories of the people? And under it was a sad bit of strings. Guitar and fiddle layered until there was nothing but emotion.

As he was standing to pay, the song moved on into a lively tune. He tapped his foot to the alt-country sound. He liked all sorts of music, even if rock was his purest love.

After taking a healthy sip of his beer, he wandered the room. College kids eight shot glasses deep on what should have been a four maximum night were being a little rambunctious, but not enough to warrant a bounce just yet. Four blonds in a row were dominating the secondary bar at the corner of the room. They were all tanned legs and short shirts or shorts — hell, even by his standards, he hoped a few of them were actual shorts. Have mercy.

But the rest of the room was fixated on the small stage at the far end of the room. A redhead with the most freckles he'd ever seen was belting it out on the mic. That was the Barry White-sounding dude?

Damn, son.

And beside him was a girl in a skintight fawn-colored skirt. She had hips that made a man want to grab on and take a ride for hours and hours. And she moved with the music like it was feeding an inner part of her.

Goddamn, *finally*. He thought his dick had taken a vacation on him.

No one had gotten him revved since Margo.

His gaze traveled up to the sleeveless white bit of lace that hugged her tiny waist and generous breasts and he froze.

Dark hair tumbled forward and covered half her face, but he knew that mouth. Had lusted after that mouth for weeks. For fuck's sake, years.

No, goddammit.

She sawed her bow across her strings so fast that her heavy, usually pin-straight hair was full of loose curls that hid her beautiful face.

What it couldn't hide was the passionate way she lost herself in the song. As if it was going to come out of her damn soul.

Like when she was on stage with him.

He recognized that drugging pull of Margo in the middle of a song where the melody had taken hold. The singer barely kept up with her fiddling. Because no way was that the smooth, sad song of the violin he was used to.

This was hyper and folksy with just a little bit of grace. Fuck, she was amazing.

The song ended and she flipped her hair back, her chest heaving as if she'd run a mile.

Or fucked him blind.

Dammit.

No.

He was not going to picture her naked again. Fuck all, he didn't even have the full naked in his memory, anyway. They were too busy pushing clothes out of the way to get to the pleasure.

Like a drug.

A drug that would have a million dollar street value. Anyone would want that endless loop of lust, fuck, release, and repeat.

He sure as shit did.

No matter how much she messed with his head when it was over, he wanted inside her again right now.

Damn the consequences.

"That was our new friend, Margo. Man, we do love when she comes in to play with us."

The crowd clapped and hooted. And the flush of happiness on Margo's face hit him low. As amazing as she'd been on stage with them, he'd never seen that smile before.

Pure enjoyment.

With him, it was intensity and just like they were having mind-blowing sex in front of thousands of people. Here, it was the simple glow of enjoying her instrument and a crowd.

Why the hell did he want to do just about anything to see that smile on her face?

Such a fool, Kagan.

He finished his beer as they did another song. The band flag behind them touted them as a Flogging Molly cover band. The crowd seemed to love them.

Christ. With all the cities they'd been to, why did he have to find her in the one random bar he'd escaped to?

He hooked his thumbs along the straps of his suspenders and tried to give his cock a pep talk about the virtues of finding another pussy to fill.

That one was trouble.

Too bad his dick wasn't listening.

It wanted that pussy.

That woman.

And the appendage was about as stupid as its owner.

"Holy shit."

Simon stilled with his thumbs at the middle of the straps. Jesus.

The lead singer hopped down into the bar area and weaved his way around tables. "I can't believe it."

Ah, fuck. He hadn't been paying attention to his disguise. He'd just kept moving forward like a freaking lightning rod looking for its next power source.

"It's Simon Kagan from Oblivion."

The room started talking all at once and people got up from their tables. Oh, shit.

Simon waved. The best thing to do was move forward and get to the safety of the stage. He'd never been afraid to jump into a mob of people, but they were usually making room for him, not crowding in.

The crowding thing was new.

He was still undecided if he was a fan of it or not.

He met the singer in front of a table right near the three stairs that separated the dais from the bar floor. "Hey, man."

The ginger dude with a beard that put lumberjacks to shame held his hand out. Simon gripped his hand and the guy slapped his arm. "This is awesome. Would you sing with us?"

"I really shouldn't." He was supposed to be resting his voice tonight. He'd really overdone it that week with the morning gigs.

"C'mon. The crowd would love it."

Simon's gaze found Margo on the stage. He wasn't used to the more classical-looking violin that she was holding. She usually played the purple Starfish one.

This was a small room and she didn't need the amplification of the electric. Her long, graceful fingers were curled around the neck of her violin.

Was that unease he saw in her eyes?

He climbed the stairs and went right to her, crowding her in until his boots bookended her mile-high heels. She was nearly the same height as he was now and she didn't back up.

He lowered his mouth until he was a breath away from her lips before detouring to brush his mouth over her cheek. "Nice to see you again, Violin Girl."

Ginger Beard clapped. "Oh, shit. You know each other?"

Simon stepped back and slid an arm around her back. "Margo has done some studio work for us."

"Wow. This is awesome. Well hell, we all have to play now, right?" The singer of the band turned to the crowd. "Right?"

Beers in hands and loud cheers hit the rafters. Simon leaned into the mic. "Think you have a guitar I can borrow?"

"Yeah, man." The guy turned to a bandmate and an old Gibson acoustic was handed forward. Simon slid his fingers over the fret board with a grateful sigh. This was what he missed.

He loved running around the stage unencumbered, but some nights he missed his acoustic. With an adjustment to the height of the guitar against him, he settled the strap against his neck and across his body.

"I'm sad to say I don't know a Flogging Molly song well enough to play. How about a cover?"

The crowd cheered and started shouting out songs. Simon took the mic stand and slipped the guitar around his back. "All right, how am I supposed to figure out what you're saying?"

Margo stepped up beside him. "I have a request."

His cock went rigid in an instant. He turned his face to hers. Her dark eyes dropped to his mouth before she licked her lips. "Vivaldi?"

"No, smart ass."

His eyebrow winged up. "Did you just swear at me?"

"I did."

"I like it."

"You would."

He nodded. "Pretty much."

She sighed. "Request."

"Listening," he said into the microphone.

"Well, you are in Boston…"

He lowered his hand to the strings and plucked out a few notes. He stared at her as he opened his mouth and the first verse of Boston's "More Than a Feeling" rumbled out of his chest.

She laughed and lifted her violin to her chin. An echoing set of strings matched his guitar note for note.

Ginger Beard picked up the electric guitar part, while Simon focused on the acoustic. He concentrated on his fret board so he could pick out the notes. It had been a damn long time since he'd fallen into a song.

Three long weeks at least.

Since her.

And because that was so close to the truth, he slung the guitar around his back and leaned into the crowd. They screamed back the words and he pulled the mic away from his mouth as he battled back a cough.

Damn that guy from Boston could sing the high notes. He cleared his throat and followed through with the last verse. And by the grace of Callahan's loving crowd, they lifted their voices through the end of the song.

He laughed and clapped against his arm. "That's what I'm talkin' about." He hauled the guitar back up in front of him and strummed the first few notes of a famous singalong song.

He waved to a roving waitress and motioned to the water bottle on the stool. She nodded and rushed to the bar. Way too much singing and talking this week. He lowered his pitch and wiggled his hips to take the focus off how shredded he sounded.

The group of people cheered and three girls stood on their chairs in the back, pumping the air as they sang "Jessie's Girl" back to him.

As if they'd been playing for years, Ginger Beard came up to the front and played the solo. Simon picked up the rhythm section of the song and brushed his lips against the microphone. Not his mic, but it did well enough, especially for a bar. He smiled broadly when Margo leaned in and shouted out the words to the song.

Simon leaned over to Ginger Beard and said the first Journey song that came to mind. The guy threw a startled look his way, but nodded.

He followed suit when the guy went for the long, distressing notes. Simon curled his fingers around the mic and as his voice cracked, he pulled his mouth away and held it out to the crowd. When the waitress came back, he wiggled his fingers at her for the bottle.

Margo gave him a look before she touched his arm.

He shrugged her off and uncapped the bottle as the bar sang the well-known lyrics to "Don't Stop Believing" for him.

He didn't want to look weak or incapable in front of this woman. Pouring every ounce of energy into hamming it up for the crowd, Simon strutted down the stage and then turned to find Margo in his space. Her expressive dark eyes searched his face.

When he crowded her space and curled his arm around her back, worry turned to heat. She lifted her bow again and he turned them in a circle.

Margo's bow bounced and her gaze never left his. The classic rock song was so entrenched in his brain that he didn't even have to think about the lyrics. They just fell out of his mouth.

Their feet moved together as if they'd done this forever. Too intense, too perfect—just another reminder of how good they were and how quickly she ran off.

He dragged his hand across her lower back and cupped her ass before he moved to the other side of the stage. The tickle in the back of his throat was back and he held up his arms for the crowd to sing.

Thank fuck they were right there with him. He clapped against his arm, then fit the mic back into the stand and clapped for real. "You guys are awesome."

They thundered to their feet and cheered, whooped, and hollered.

"I gotta go."

The resounding *no* from the crowd made him smile and stack his hands over his heart. Another song and he'd crack for sure.

He scanned the crowd and spotted Nick at the back. "But I spy with my little eye someone who might like to take over."

Nick's arms fell to his sides. He mouthed, "You fucker," and waved. "Only if I don't have to sing Journey."

Ginger Beard waved him up. "Guys, Nick Crandall from Oblivion is here too."

Nick trudged through the crowd and tried not to shrink away from all the people pawing at him. He had a black ball cap on that covered his blond hair, but he hadn't bothered with that much else disguise-wise.

Simon lifted the guitar off his head and placed it around Nick's neck. "You prick."

Unrepentant, Simon waggled his eyebrows. He downed half the bottle of water before burying his face in his elbow to cough.

"You aren't getting sick, are you?"

Simon shook his head. "Just tried to reach too hard for the Steve Perry notes."

"You and your stadium rock."

Simon slapped his arm. "You love it. They don't make guitar solos like that anymore."

Nick lifted a shoulder. "True." He turned to the mic and tipped his head. "You guys know how to rock?"

They screamed back an affirmative and Simon jumped off the stage.

Nick leaned away from the mic. "Where are you going?"

Simon turned around and mimed that he couldn't hear him. His best friend's eyes blazed fire and he held his arms out in the universal gesture of *what the fuck*.

Simon did a thumbs up with each hand and Nick smiled weakly at the crowd. And because he didn't have time to stress about it, the song took him over and Nick had the first verse of "Back in Black" pouring through the sound system before Simon escaped to the side exit.

Margo tucked her violin into her case and placed it under her chair at the back of the stage. She scanned the crowd, catching Simon heading outside.

The frustration in his eyes tugged at her. She'd only seen him struggle with his voice once, but there was no doubt it was happening again. He'd covered it well enough by making the crowd sing louder and longer, but she knew the signs.

She just wanted to make sure he was all right. Like any good musician would. Like any friend would.

Not that she could exactly call Simon a friend. A few good orgasms didn't exactly put them on a friendly basis. Not when all they did was walk away from each other after said orgasms.

Fool.

She pushed through the door marked *deliveries* and found an alley. No sign of Simon. The door shut behind her before she could catch it. "Dammit."

"Following me, Violin Girl?" The eerie blue of a phone lighting up cut the dark. Simon stood against the brick side of the building, his hawkish features and the shadows from the Fedora accentuated by the low light.

"I wanted to see if you were all right."

"And why would you care?"

The zing of danger in his voice caught her off-guard. Simon was usually sarcastic and playful. He was the definition of the guy who had walked in the bar with his T-shirt slogan, *Pussy, the most expensive meal you'll ever eat*, emblazoned over his chest.

Tongue-in-cheek.

Nick was the guy who was more sardonic. His comments a little more biting.

"Of course I care."

"Funny, I don't ever get that vibe from you. The only thing you care about is my cock. Is that why you came out here? I'm in the same town as you so you want a bounce? Not sure you'd like what you got tonight, Violin Girl."

"That is not why I came out here." Her clit pounded like a heartbeat at the tone in his voice. And that simply wasn't allowed. She'd finally gotten herself back to an even keel since she'd played with Oblivion.

Finally had been able to turn the sound down on her overactive dreams that included a mashup of stage time and Simon's hands on her.

Oh, they still came nightly. And even some nights she found herself with her hand down her panties to ease the ache, but she was dealing with it.

"I'm in a dark mood tonight, Margo."

She closed her eyes at the way he said her name. Not the sly Violin Girl. No, this was his lips and rough voice curling around her given name. He used it so rarely that her system burned in reaction.

"Why?"

His phone light extinguished, leaving them in the dark. "Because I'm pissed that I still get hard when you're within three hundred feet of me. Because I'm tired and miss my cat."

She huffed out a laugh. "Your cat?"

"I miss my bed." She heard the scuff of his feet over the debris of the alley. "I miss my sanity. I miss banging a random woman to ease the tensions of the day."

She frowned. What did that mean? She'd seen YouTube videos of his exploits in the towns he'd visited. A weakness she couldn't seem to get a handle on, but seeing him in a video eased the late night visits in her dreams.

As if her mind's eye could be sated with a taste of him and let her rest. Sometimes.

It didn't always work.

If she touched him again, she knew it wouldn't work for a good long time.

But she'd seen him with women. Seen his hands on them, his mouth—even right after he'd had sex with her, he'd had his mouth on another woman. This wasn't a man that would ever be able to be faithful.

It didn't matter. She'd gotten what she needed from him and they'd both known it wasn't going to be anything more than a few stray minutes on that catwalk.

She'd gone after him because it felt wrong to end it like they had. But seeing him with that woman had sewn up her regrets and second thoughts.

She'd been able to walk away again.

This alley with him and that dangerous voice certainly would set her back for weeks. When Simon touched her, everything inside her came alive. She couldn't deny that she wanted it again.

But she could control herself.

"I do believe that you could walk into that bar and get your wish."

"I can get a woman whenever I want, Violin Girl."

She clenched her jaw. "Then why are you bitching about it?"

"Oh, the ice princess has a little fire in her belly."

"I'm not sure exactly who you think I am."

"I think you're a well-bred, moneyed young woman who has been following a plan since she was in her...what? Early teens?"

Margo took a step back.

He advanced, his eyes glittering in the dim light from the street. "I think fucking a rockstar wasn't in the plan, but you can't help but want to slum it sometimes."

"That's not it."

"Oh no?"

"No," she whispered as he caged her in with an arm over her head and one against the wall at her hip. He didn't touch her—mostly. His worn pants brushed her knees and his belly grazed hers.

"Tell me, Margo. Why would you come after a man like me in a dark alleyway if you didn't want to fuck?"

"I didn't say I didn't want to..." She swallowed. The words felt right and wrong at the same time. She wasn't a prude, but she had been trained since birth to keep crass words out of her vocabulary.

"*Fuck*," he said with a hard K. "If you're going to do that with me here and now, you best be able to say the word. Because there's no gentle touches in me tonight."

Part of her wanted to know why. There was something there that he wasn't saying, but she didn't have any right to peek into that private domain. Not when they were only *this*.

Sex.

Fucking.

Sinful pleasure that she'd never known before and would never know after him.

Simon with his jagged edges and broken past.

Just Simon.

She slid her hand under his T-shirt and up to his chest. She pulled back as her nail skimmed over something metal.

Simon groaned.

Margo pushed his shirt up. Had she missed that before? He was always behind her, always pushing at her until she unraveled.

And she loved it.

It was raw and God, it felt good. But she'd seen him without his shirt many times before, and she would have remembered a piercing.

He hissed as her thumb traced over the ring.

"When did you do this?"

"About a month ago."

She pulled her hand away. "Oh, God. Is it still healing?"

"Yeah." He held her hand over his nipple. "Feels good."

When he hissed again, she stopped. It didn't sound like it felt good.

"A little pain can feel good, Margo."

When his fingers tightened on her hips, she thought he might have something there. "What if I don't want you to be gentle with me?"

"Want to walk on the wild side with the bad boy from Oblivion?"

She wasn't used to his rough voice, or the sharper edge to it. Simon usually had a sleepy, sexy quality to his speech. Like he'd just rolled out of bed. This Simon was almost harsh. "I just want you inside me," she said without preamble. "I want you, Simon."

"Jesus fuck."

His mouth was on hers, his arm around her back, crushing her to him until he'd emptied her lungs and taken all her air. He dragged her skirt up and found her pantyhose. He pushed it up higher until he could get both hands under there. The rending of material echoed to days past.

That night he'd been impatient to get inside her as well.

The cool night air kissed her inner thighs, then it was all Simon. His fingers pushing at her underwear as he cupped her.

"*This*. Is this what you want?"

"God." She clutched at his upper arm.

"Tell me, Margo. You want me to fuck you?"

She whimpered when he slowly slid two fingers inside of her. She lifted her hips to give him better access, but he stopped.

"Tell me, Margo."

"Yes. Yes, I want you to fuck me."

He growled into her neck. "That voice. That upper crust accent. I want you to fuck me, Simon." He swirled his thumb around her clit. "Say it."

"I want you to fuck me, Simon."

He moved quickly. So fast that she didn't have time to ready herself or her back for the brunt of his invasion. The zipper, the crinkle of plastic, then he lifted her knee up on his hip and levered himself inside her.

And no, he wasn't the least bit gentle.

His fingers dug into her hips, his mouth sealed over her neck and the harsh suction of his lips with a bite snapped her closer to the edge. He'd marked her. She knew there would be something there, along with the tattoo of his fingertips on her hips.

There would be reminders this time.

She coasted her nails up his neck and pushed the Fedora off his head to get to his hair. And because she wanted him as insane as she was, she slid under his shirt again and found the piercing.

"Ah, fuck."

Her shoulder burned where the brick abraded her skin, where the elastic of her panties dug into her, and at her neck where he kept scraping his teeth like she was going to give him something. But she was dripping. He took her without care or consequence. As if he was driving a demon out of himself and into her.

Her leg shook and still he came at her.

No flourishes, no laughter, just him battering into her until her skin was too sensitive to take anymore. She gripped his shoulders and cried out, surprised when the orgasm enveloped her like a black hole.

"*Yes.*"

His voice was raw and the friction built until there was nothing but darkness and Simon and an unending orgasm. She wasn't built for this.

Shattered.

Broken open.

Forever changed.

Damn this man. If she hadn't known, if she could have stayed blissfully ignorant, then nothing would have changed.

He pulled out of her and she felt him doing something with the condom, but she was too frayed to care. Her leg dropped to the ground and she slapped her hands on the brick to stop the slide into a quivering mass on the pavement.

She expected him to walk away. This is what she'd wanted, of course. She'd asked for it. But no, he came back and leaned into her, touching her forehead with his.

He said nothing.

Just stood there with her until their breathing evened and the night sounds intruded. Until someone opened the door.

"Oh, man. How long were you out here, guys?" The waiter lit a cigarette and drew in a deep lungful of smoke. He jammed his foot against the door to keep it open. "Aren't you glad I came when I did?"

"Yeah, man. Thanks." Simon bent to pick up his hat.

The crash of piano and horns, the guitars and screams penetrated the moment, reminding her that nothing about this was right time, right place. She let Simon hold open the door for her, and she held her head up high as she sailed down the hallway.

"I need to use the ladies."

Simon nodded. "I have to get back to the hotel."

She nodded. "Of course."

He curled his fingers into a fist. "This is stupid." She flipped her hair over her shoulder and he crowded her. "Margo."

"What?"

He traced his thumb over her shoulder. "Fuck. Did I do that?"

"It's nothing." She pulled her hair forward.

"Dammit, why didn't you tell me?"

"I was a willing participant, Simon. Everything you did to me I wanted."

"You wanted to bleed?" His face was incredulous as he crushed his hat between his hands.

She tipped her head. "I wanted someone to want me like that." To see her as a woman, not just an instrument. Not just a tool. A woman.

"Someone?"

"Do you need to hear that it was you?"

Simon's eyes glittered.

"The millions of adoring fans aren't enough. Do you need to hear that one more woman can't resist you?" Angry at him, at herself, and the fact that she couldn't feel this way with anyone but him, she pushed at him. "*You*. It needed to be you."

He curled his hands around her upper arms and drove her back into the wall.

She winced and he tried to back up. She could see the horror on his face. She gripped his belt loops. "You're right about me. I had a plan. I've always had a schedule, a goal, an endgame. And now I'm starting over.

And I like this feeling." She brushed her thumb over the rigid muscles of his belly and the ultra-soft line of hair above his zipper. "I'm not ashamed to want more of it."

He cupped her face, his fingers twining in her hair. His eyes blazed a silvery blue that haunted her dreams. Seeing them again, the way he looked at her—it would follow her for days. "You make me fucking nuts."

"I like when we're nuts."

He brought his other hand up to frame her face. "Then come back to my hotel."

She twisted her fingers into his suspenders. "I don't think that's a good idea."

"Why? Because that would make it real?"

"Actually, that's pretty much it."

His nostrils flared and his brows snapped down. "I'm good enough to fuck in an alley, but not a bed?"

"I've had guys in a bed. I want this." She knotted her fingers into his shirt. "I'm tired of being traditional."

Simon blew out a breath. "And I'm your ticket to non-traditional, huh?"

"Golden ticket."

"At least there's that." He leaned into her. "Well, if you're not going to use my bed for some exceptional gymnastics, then this is goodbye." He coasted his mouth over her chin and to her neck. He skimmed down to the vee of her shirt and flicked his tongue over her cleavage. "Goodbye perfect boobs."

She pushed him back. "Pig."

He looked down at his chest then stuffed his hat back on his head. "This is obvious."

"The shirt is a bit much."

He shrugged. "I like the expressions on people's faces when they figure it out."

"You would."

The smirk she'd been missing slid across his face as he hooked his thumbs into his suspenders. "Never a dull moment, Violin Girl."

The warmth in his voice when he said that made her tuck a hand behind her back to steady herself. Simon could make anything feel like a sexual innuendo, even playing with a pair of suspenders. "You guys are almost done with the promo stuff?"

He nodded. "A few more days then we're off to someplace in upstate New York to rehearse."

"Where?"

"Gonna come find me?"

She rolled her eyes. "Just wondering."

"Someplace with an S. Horses—lots of horses are there or from there. Something."

Her eyebrows rose. "Saratoga?"

"Yeah." He frowned. "How did you pull that out of your head?"

"Saratoga Racetrack, and it's one of the most famous outdoor venues for the ballet and orchestra."

"Ah. Violin Girl knows her classical."

"That I do."

"Then if you get a wild hair to visit the venue, you know where I'll be."

She snapped his suspender. "You never know."

But she did know. This was one more goodbye, but at least this one was civil. He turned on his heel and headed toward the crowds and the music, to the streets of Boston that wanted him and his band.

Watching him go shouldn't leave her ready to chase after him.

But it did.

Chapter 11

Margo skimmed her email as she sipped from a wide red mug of French roast on her back terrace. Three possible jobs and a message from her mother that she was studiously ignoring were the only things worth reading.

Summers were notoriously busy for her since that was when she made most of her money with the studio work. So she could ignore her mother for a few more days, thank God.

When her phone chimed, she debated ignoring it. For the first time in weeks, she was actually enjoying her solitary cup of coffee. No restless night to recover from, nothing on her schedule. A day to herself.

She didn't want to examine the fact that Simon and last night's impromptu concert had a large part to do with that. She simply wanted to enjoy her afterglow.

When a second message popped up, she sighed and glanced at the phone.

Please don't be Mother.

Lila Shawcross.

What did she want?

She frowned and picked up her phone

Are you home?
Are you alone?

Margo thumbed back a *yes*. Almost immediately there was a reply.

Then open your door.

Surprised, she moved back through her house to the front. She checked the peep hole and swung the door open. "Hi."

Lila was on her stoop but she definitely didn't look like the usual woman who was barking out instructions and reminders. She wore white shorts and a navy and white striped cotton shirt.

Margo glanced down at Lila's feet and was dumbfounded to see Chucks.

"Don't look at me like that. I don't wear a power suit every day." Lila pushed by her and inside.

Margo gripped the door and stared after her. "I don't think I've ever seen you in flats, let alone shorts."

"Yeah well, I'm here in a non-professional manner."

Margo closed the door and followed her into the vestibule. "Okay. I was just having coffee, would you like some?"

"Is it a day ending in Y?"

"Touché. Come in." She led her down to the kitchen. She unhooked a poppy red mug from her company cups and filled it with the last of her French-pressed coffee. "Black, right?"

"Damn right."

Margo set a mug in front of her. "Well if you're not here for business, what can I do for you?"

Lila cupped slim, ringless fingers around the mug and tapped her forefinger on the handle. "Can I be blunt?"

"I'm not sure you have any other mode."

Lila lifted her mug and smiled over the rim. "I like you." She took a sip and her wide blue eyes went heavy-lidded. "And I'll pay you five thousand dollars a week just to make me this coffee every day."

"My one vice." Margo nodded to the back. "Why don't we go out on the patio so I can finish mine?"

"Lead the way."

Margo held the door for her and caught Lila looking around at her house. "It was my grandmother's."

Lila's golden brow rose. "Was I telegraphing?"

"Well, I'm sure you know what a studio musician makes. Add in the Philharmonic, and it still wouldn't cover this place in Boston."

"No. It wouldn't. Especially when you were dismissed from the Boston Philharmonic," Lila said as she sailed through the door.

Margo's fingers tightened on the doorknob. "And here I thought we weren't going to discuss business."

"I didn't say that." Lila sat on the rattan couch and crossed her elegant legs.

Margo perched on the matching chair at the end of the oval table. "Okay. Since you obviously have a plan for this visit, care to share?"

"May I?" She nodded as Lila pulled Margo's laptop toward her. She typed for a moment then spun the screen to face Margo.

Callahan's filled the small video player box. Margo's heart skipped a beat and her lower belly pulsed as the camera focused in on her and Simon making a small circle around each other.

Intense and prowling, they were the center of attention for the videographer. She glanced down at the name of the video — *Since when is a violin player this hot?*

The audio was questionable with the level of background noise and shouts, but the video was certainly the important part.

"Yes, Simon came in and played."

"Did you call him?"

"God, no."

"So this wasn't planned?"

"No." Margo crossed her arms. "What are you angling for, fifteen percent or something?"

Lila put her mug down and gave a delighted laugh. "Oh, that's perfect."

"What's with the interrogation, then?"

"It was a roundabout way of asking you if this was planned or just happened." She picked up her mug again and leaned back on the couch and looked around. "I like this set-up." She wiggled her fingers. "All New England chic."

"I'm glad you like my postage stamp backyard."

"Brrr. It just got chilly." Lila's wide cornflower eyes sparkled with humor. "Look at the other videos."

Margo sighed. "So, a few people took videos. That's what people do when famous people are around."

"Indeed they do. But there are over forty videos from that one show and look at the views. Hell, even the crappy videos have tons of them."

"And that means what, exactly?"

Lila sighed. "It means whatever chemistry you and Simon have on stage translates to salivating fans." She tipped the mug back and frowned when she got to the bottom. "More?"

She started to stand and Lila waved her back.

"I'll get it. You keep looking."

Margo scrolled down and saw the views and the comments. Some were obvious troublemaker types, but on the whole, there were a lot of people excited to see Simon play on stage with her. Some that were shocked that a violin player could be so cool, others that couldn't get enough of Simon dirty dancing with her.

In the comments, there were other links to their release party videos. She leaned forward at the sheer number of posts on the sidebar of the site.

Hundreds.

Thousands of views and shares.

Their rendition of "The Becoming" seemed to be the most watched video. And that was from the second night in Los Angeles. Back to back, they were one with each other on the stage and when he circled her to come at her from behind, her body reacted.

Stiffened nipples and a throb so deep inside that she shut the laptop.

"Pretty amazing, huh?"

Margo lifted her mug and took a healthy swallow, saying nothing.

Lila came down the three stairs and settled on the couch again. She'd changed out the standard red mug for a huge black one from her cupboard. "You can't deny that was awesome stuff."

"I hope it translates to sales for them."

"Oh, it did. We actually rebounded from the top twenty on Billboard to top five again."

Margo swallowed. "That's great. I'm happy for them."

"You know what it also sparked?"

"No, but I have a feeling you're about to tell me."

"Don't look so glum, Margo. This is a good thing. We're releasing the video from the Los Angeles show this week as a fan club marketing tool. I have a feeling it's going to go viral."

"And what does that have to do with me?" She set her mug down carefully.

"Tell me, what exactly do you have planned for this summer?"

"Studio work. I've gotten a lot of great offers because of the work I did with Oblivion."

"You should have. I put your name out there as the one to call for violin work."

Surprised, Margo gripped her knees. "Thank you."

"Don't thank me. I wish I hadn't."

"Why?"

"Because I don't want there to be any reason for you to turn me down."

"I—what?"

"The band is heading to Saratoga, New York to rehearse for their summer tour. I want you to go down and rehearse with them. See if that magic is still in effect."

Margo stood. She tapped her thumb with her middle finger as she paced the little square of shale patio. "Why?"

"Would there be a personal issue as to why you wouldn't want to go?"

Margo stopped and met her gaze. "Why would you ask that?"

"Because you two are damn sexy and that usual translates to naked time."

"It's not an issue."

"Now why don't I believe you?"

"That's not my problem."

Lila groaned. "You fucked."

"Excuse me?"

"Your face. There's no love stuff but definitely sex stuff. I know the signs. It's happened a lot recently."

Margo pushed her hair out of her face. "We have history," she agreed.

"Which means you've had sex a few times. How recently?"

"That's none of your business."

"So, at the bar?"

"Ms. Shawcross—"

"Wow. It must have been good." She held up a hand. "Look, I know what Simon is. Don't get your panties in a twist. Whatever you two do after the show is none of my concern. Unless it becomes trouble for the show."

"This is not a done deal, Lila. I'm not one of the members of the band that you can railroad into doing your bidding."

Lila snorted. "Keeping these guys in check requires a firm hand, but it also is about knowing what they need. They are an awesome unit already, but since adding you to the stage, they've reached another level."

"I've only played with them a handful of times."

"Which is exactly why I want you to go to the rehearsals."

"Have you talked to the band about this?"

"No."

The decisive way she said it made Margo turn. "Why?"

Lila sighed. "Because they don't know what they need until they make the decisions for themselves."

"You know that doesn't make any sense, right?"

"It does for them. Nick would rather cut off his leg than bring a new person into the band, but even he was looking for ways to layer in the sound with his own. Deacon is our resident composer and he came to me asking if we could add you to the whole show for the Los Angeles performance, not just the three songs you were scheduled to do."

Margo lowered to a metal chair on the far side of the patio. "That was him?" She'd wondered why Deacon had been so adamant about getting her to learn the songs.

Not that she had to do much.

She'd been listening to them on a loop since she'd gotten an advanced copy of the album. She knew them all. "And Jazz and Gray?"

"They're mostly in the clutches of baby fever, but they are also most open to collaborations."

"Simon?"

"I think you can answer that question."

Margo laced her fingers together and sat forward. "The summer is when I make most of my money. Now, more than ever, that's an issue." She met Lila's direct gaze. "I'm not sure how you found out about the Philharmonic, but my current job situation also means that the studio work I'd miss out on would be detrimental to my livelihood."

Lila tipped her head and rattled off a number.

It was only because of years of training that Margo's jaw didn't drop.

"And that's per show."

"Per show?"

Lila nodded.

"When do I leave?"

Lila smiled. "Tomorrow."

Simon dropped onto the carpet of green grass and rolled onto his back, his chest heaving.

Deacon turned around, running in place. "C'mon, Simon. You're never going to survive the summer if you don't get some cardio training."

Simon waved him ahead. "I'm just gonna lay here and die. Nick can sing."

Deacon jogged over to where he was on the ground and ran circles around him. "You said you wanted to do this."

"Changed my mind." He pressed a hand to his sweat-slick belly. "You're a sadist."

"We've only done two miles."

Simon rolled onto his belly and buried his head in his stacked arms. "I'm good."

"You're going to cramp."

Simon lifted his foot and grabbed his sneaker to stretch out the back of his legs. "There."

"Don't come crying to me," Deacon said and jogged back to the path.

"Oh, I won't," Simon said more to himself than anything since Deacon was already gone.

Saratoga State Park butted up to the parking lot of the Saratoga Performing Arts Center and Deacon had found every damn path there was.

Just because Deacon felt the need to abuse his body with five to ten miles of running a day did not mean Simon did. Sure, he needed the cardio, but two fucking miles was more than anyone needed.

Add that in with the resistance training Deacon was forcing on all of them, and Simon was ready to kill him. If only the bastard wasn't so big, or so fast.

Day one of the rehearsals had gone well. They had most of stage set up and the soundboard was a dream. Nick, Gray, and Deacon still had hard-ons from that little tour.

Jazz and Harper were talking babies twenty-four-seven and he was fairly sure there would be a pair of really good wireless noise-canceling earbuds in his future.

All he needed to do was nod and smile, anyway. He might as well listen to good tunes while he was doing it.

"Fucking baby fever." Simon pushed himself up off the grass and stood. It was going to be a damn long walk back to the venue.

Or, he could run.

Because he was alone, he let himself whine a little before he picked up the pace. It was a gorgeous late May day. He brushed off the stray bits of grass from his chest and waved at the two girls playing golf.

He grinned when one completely missed her ball before twisting around to watch him run by. Okay, so the workouts for the last few weeks weren't all of the suck. He'd never work out like Deacon, but he had to admit he liked the six-pack he had going.

He was prone to skinny and only ripped because he was usually climbing on something. But he'd always been the skinny kind of ripped. Thanks to Deacon, he had a little more meat on his arms and shoulders.

And the fact that their bassist wouldn't let him sleep in anymore. Which sucked. But Simon needed to be in fighting shape for this tour. They weren't just doing a forty-five minute opening act anymore. The current setlist was reaching for two hours.

Slowing to a jog, Simon resisted the urge to grab his knees and pant like the bitch he was. He'd wait to do that on his bunk in the bus.

In privacy.

Where he could cry.

He didn't even know the name of the muscles that hurt. All of them?

He slowed to a walk as the huge gold and black bus came into view. "Home sweet home," he panted and grabbed the handle for the door.

He landed facedown on the loveseat at the front of the bus.

"You are a schmuck."

"Fuck off, Nicky."

The offending asshole dropped onto the longer couch next to him. "You're the one who decided it was a good idea to go running with marathon man."

"You did it yesterday."

"Yeah. But so did you. No need to run every day, idiot."

Actually, he did need to. Running on that stage and singing was going to kill him if he didn't find some way to train. Deacon had warned him earlier, but he'd never been the type that needed to exercise. When he was a kid, food wasn't exactly a commodity in his house.

He'd learned to go without a long time ago.

Nick moved over. "You smell like a fucking vodka bottle."

"Sweating out my sins, my friend."

"Lots of sins."

Simon grinned unrepentantly. "I believe you tried to hang with me last night, buddy boy. You didn't make it to midnight."

"That's because you're pickled." Nick rose and grabbed two bottles of water out of the fridge. "Here."

"Thanks." Simon took one and sucked it down. He rose to refill it from the filtered tap on the front of the fridge. The cold water felt awesome on his abused throat.

Landing facefirst in the grass wasn't his best move. He didn't have allergies like some people did, but he was a cement jungle guy — grass wasn't one of the staples in his life. The back of his throat was tickling like crazy.

"Lila's here with Donovan."

"Oh yeah?" Simon wiped his mouth with the back of his hand. "Did he see our sweet setup yet?"

"She's showing him around now. She wants us to meet her down there in an hour."

"Cool." He moved to the back of the bus for a shower. Now that it was just him and Nick on the bus, it was a helluva lot easier to take a shower. And the upgrade of the bus meant it didn't stink like chemicals.

He washed up and stepped into a pair of faded jeans. And because the big boss man of the label was there, he tugged on a Rebel Rage t-shirt instead of one with rude sayings.

He jammed his feet into socks and his motorcycle boots, and then grabbed a pair of sunglasses from his stash. A half-dozen brand name companies still sent freebies to him.

God bless America.

Nick had already left. The boy didn't know how to relax. The couch looked mighty comfortable, but he knew if he tried for a nap, he'd end up sleeping for four hours.

Even with enough vodka in his system to make his liver weep, he hadn't been able to sleep much more than a handful of hours.

They'd be officially doing their first rehearsal tonight. And of course Donovan had to be there. How the hell was he supposed to figure shit out if Mr. Suave was there to judge?

As if he hadn't been nervous enough.

He trudged through the gravel pit outside the bus to the stairs that lead to the underbelly of the stage. Half a dozen roadies were running around with huge trunks on wheels, unloading from the semi parked behind the building.

He climbed the back stairs to the stage and froze. Two forklifts with human sized baskets were on either end of the stage. A huge steel arch was being reinforced by two guys in welder faceplates.

Sparks spit and sprayed at each end.

"Holy shit."

"Impressive, huh?" Lila asked as she and Donovan came out from the side stage.

"Yeah. I didn't see this in the drawings."

"Well, since you continue to give me and my insurance people heart attacks during the shows, we figured we should give you something to climb on."

"Were you a gymnast in a former life, Simon?" Donovan asked.

Simon folded his arms, gripping his forearms, his eyes never leaving the archway. "I never knew when my old man was going to take a swing, so I got good at ducking and rolling. Just seemed to grow from there."

At Lila's shocked silence, Simon cleared his throat. "Anyway, I'm totally psyched to have something to climb on."

"Just don't split your head open, all right?"

He rubbed his hands together and finally looked away from the set-up. "Nice to see you again, Donovan."

The Englishman held his hand out. "I had to come out and see the build. It's impressive."

Simon shook his hand. "Yeah, I thought the ramps around the entire stage were rad, but *that*?" He shoved his hands into his pockets. "I want to get on it now."

"Wait until the welder is done with it, please."

Jazz and Gray walked up the front steps to the side of the stage. "Oh my God." She bounced with her arm hooked in Gray's. "This is ours?"

"Isn't it amazing?" Simon rushed forward and helped her up the last stair.

She tipped her head back and her dark hair flowed down her back with an arrow of blue at the tips. "Did they build us a jungle gym?"

"Looks like it, doesn't it?"

She dragged Gray to the back of the stage to the riser that was set up for her kit. Pipes were built out around the edges of the structure.

Lila moved around to the back and hit a switch.

Jazz yelped and hopped up and down. "I have my own neon?"

"LED actually, but the same effect without any of the chemicals."

Jazz cupped her growing bump and looked down at it. "Look at that, Aunt Lila taking care of you, kiddo."

Lila flushed and cleared her throat. "Yes, well, it's just good business."

"Of course," Jazz said solemnly and curled her fingers around Gray's.

Deacon and Harper came down from the back of the amphitheater and Nick met them halfway down. He'd been sitting in the middle of the second section of seats.

Hell, Simon hadn't even seen him.

Deacon helped Harper up the stairs, after Nick stopped at the bottom to let them go first. When he got on the stage, he crossed his arms and looked around, not saying a word.

He finally came to stand beside Simon. He nodded to Donovan, then Lila. "Nice."

Deacon tipped his head incredulously, then stepped forward. "It's amazing, Mr. Lewis. Thanks so much for taking such a chance on us."

Simon caught Nick making a face behind Deacon and practically sawed through his bottom lip so he wouldn't laugh.

If anyone could be a spokesperson for the band, it would be Deacon. He knew just what to say and how to play the game.

Simon didn't give two shits about games. He just wanted to play music.

Nick wanted not to give a shit, but was actually the worst offender. He cared far too much about every little aspect of the band. And the fact that Lila was the coordinator in almost every regard made him nuts.

Simon spotted his guitar in one of the open guitar trunks. "Man, I haven't seen Cherry in ages." He crossed to the tall trunk and unhooked his white Les Paul.

"With the expanded setlist, we figured you might want to play her now and again."

Simon smiled at Lila. "Yeah, you thought right."

"Donovan and I also had another idea."

Simon grinned. "Lay it on me. It's been a good day so far."

"Hey, everyone."

Simon turned to the voice and his shoes cemented to the stage for the second time that day.

Chapter 12

Margo twisted her fingers together as everyone stared at her.

The quick flash of pleasure in Simon's eyes melted away. His silvery blue eyes shuttered before he focused on the floor and dug his hands into his pockets.

"What the hell is this?" Nick asked.

Margo's gaze snapped to Lila. Yeah, this wasn't a good idea. What had she been thinking?

Lila folded her arms. "Have you checked your social media pages lately?"

Nick shrugged. "Me and Pix haven't been doing as many videos since the Baby Brigade has taken over all conversations."

"Just because I'm pregnant doesn't mean we can't do our videos," Jazz said with a sniff.

"I just said we haven't. Otherwise, why would I want to watch myself?"

"To see what's working and what isn't?" Lila pulled her iPad from her bag. She rattled off some numbers from the videos at the bar, from the release party, from some of the live radio spots.

"So, what, we're not good enough on our own? We need a violin addition to the band?" Nick glanced at Margo. "No offense."

She tucked her hands into her sleeves, but didn't say a word. What the hell could she say? There was no rhyme or reason to why they sounded so good together, but they did.

Lila lifted a slim brow. "Of course not. I'm thinking strictly from a business sense."

"You can take your business and sti—"

Donovan Lewis stood straighter and his shoulders stiffened.

Deacon held a hand up. "I think what she's saying is that it's just like any other tour that brings on another guitarist to layer in sound."

"We have two guitarists. For fuck's sake, we had three until we neutered Simon."

"Nick," Lila said in a warning tone.

"What? I don't give a shit if God himself is here." He glanced at Donovan. "I'll say what needs to be said."

Margo stepped forward, hiding her fisted hands in her sweater. "I can play a standup bass, a fiddle, the violin obviously, some piano, and the cello. I'm more than just a background player. It doesn't take away from your sound, just enhances it. You can't deny it, Nick."

"For a one-off special gig, sure. But every night?" He crossed his arms. "Why the hell do we need to change?"

"Why does it have to be one or the other?" Simon asked quietly.

Finally, he said something. She'd been wondering if he was actually going to talk or just walk.

"Are you so set to get in this chick's pants that you want her on tour with us?"

"Enough." Simon's eyes flashed. "You can be pissed off as much as you want about this, but for fuck's sake, she's standing right there. Don't be that much of a dick. She's a fucking artist same as we are."

Nick's mouth flattened into a line. "She's not the same."

Simon slashed his hand through the air. "She's exactly the same. Just because she uses a bow instead of a pick makes no difference. This isn't a done deal, right?" He swiveled his head to Lila.

"No. It's just an idea. Since you're in rehearsal, I thought it might be something different to try. If it doesn't work, then no harm."

"Exactly."

Surprised that Simon would go to bat for her, she relaxed her fingers.

Nick cracked his knuckles. "Are you thinking with your dick?"

Simon's nostrils flared. "For fuck's sake. Is that really all you think I am? A walking cock looking for pussy? This band is just as important to me as it is to everyone standing here." Simon glanced at Donovan. "Sorry."

"I'm not the English Rose you people think I am," Donovan said. "Look, take a few minutes and get acquainted with the sound system. Try it out with Margo. If it doesn't work, then all we've lost is a few hours."

"And what? She's free?" Nick tucked his thumb into the belt loop of his jeans.

"No. I'm a hired musician," Margo said.

"So now we're cutting into the money end."

Jazz stuck her hands on her hips. "Here we go with the money again."

"I get paid for each day I'm on the tour," Margo said. "Not a percentage. I'm not a member of the band."

"No fucking shit." Nick's voice was low and dangerous.

Margo stalked forward. "I can rip apart a song and learn it as fast as you can." She tilted her head. "Faster, I'd wager. I'm no amateur here. I've been playing the violin since before you got your first hair on your…" She looked down at him, then back to his arctic gaze. "Chin," she finally said. "I don't have to be here, but I thought we had something pretty amazing at the shows in New York and L.A. It's different and stands out from the crowd. But if you're too closed-minded to think out of the box when it comes to music, then you're going to sink fast, Nick Crandall."

He took a step back, his fists practically vibrating at his sides.

Margo's chest heaved but she stood her ground. Christ, she'd never pushed like that in her life. But she wanted this. Wanted to be a part of that amazing sound that had lived in her since the studio.

It was the first time she'd felt any fire for music in so long, she just wanted a little more time with it. Before she had to find another audition for another symphony. Until she had to go back to what she'd been trained for.

She wanted to try something different, dammit.

Hadn't known that was exactly what she wanted until it had been dangled in front of her.

Nick turned on his heel and tore down the stairs to the pavilion and to the back of the house before disappearing on the upper paths that led to the lawn seats.

Margo pushed her hair back and turned to the rest of the band. "I'm sorry."

"Don't be sorry." Jazz came forward and grabbed her hand under the sleeve and twisted her fingers around Margo's. "You really feel that way?"

Margo nodded.

Lila tucked her iPad back into her shoulder bag. "All right then. Get your gear situated. I need to go talk with Donovan for a few."

"Well, I'm excited," Jazz said. "This could be amazing." She let Margo's hand go and headed for her kit.

Gray smiled at Margo and hooked his arm around Jazz's shoulder.

Deacon rubbed his huge hands together. "Did you bring all those instruments with you?"

"I did."

"Awesome." He linked his fingers with Harper. "I'm going to go do some research and be back in a few."

And then there was Simon.

"Pretty passionate about joining a rock and roll band on tour there, Violin Girl."

She stuffed down her pride and her instinct to hold things inside her. "I love this album. From the first song, I knew it was something special. And if it's just those three songs that I'm a part of, I'm good with that. Disappointed at a lost opportunity, but proud of what I was a part of. But playing them live just…"

"I get it."

"I never did until now. I love music, but I haven't been in love with it for a very long time."

Simon dragged his knuckle down her forearm before he stepped back. "Then what are we waiting for?"

She tucked her hands into the opposite opening of each sleeve and gripped her wrists. "I won't stay if you're not good with this."

"Since when do you ask me?"

"Since this isn't just a one-time thing."

"Does that cover other aspects of what we do together?"

"Do you want it to?" God, her voice sounded shaky.

"Do we burn out or just fade away?" Simon asked with a smirk.

"I vote for burn out."

His blue eyes widened. "Is that right?"

Margo looked around but they were as alone as they'd ever be. "What if I said I want the full tour experience?"

His eyebrow winged up. "What exactly does your backstage pass include?"

"Everything."

"Oh, babe. You should never make that kind of blanket statement."

Margo's heart pounded in her ears, and in lower parts of her that only Simon seemed to engage. She swallowed. "An all-access pass. But when you're with me, it's just me, Simon."

His gaze drifted to her mouth. "With that kind of bountiful offer, why would I want anyone else?"

"Good."

His eyes bore into hers. "I hope you know what you're in for."

"No clue. That's the best part." She turned around before she could claw a new design into her forearms under her sweater. She had to go through her instruments and make sure they were tuned.

An hour later, she had a trunk for her gear set on the right side of the stage. Her latest acquisition, a Starfish cello, had been a gamble. As an instrument itself, it was gorgeous, but the electric cello wasn't exactly huge in the studio. It would sound amazing onstage, though, and Lila's advance had lured her into making a special request for it at one of the dealers she used.

She unlocked the case and pulled out the fragile-looking instrument. The open curves of the tulipwood frame made it much easier to manage than an acoustic cello.

The vibrant green and purple color was as edgy as a cello could look. It had been ordered by a band in Germany, but they'd defaulted on the payments. Their loss was her gain.

"Sweet shit. What is that?"

She looked down at Gray as he crouched in front of her.

"Electric cello."

"Seriously?"

"Same company that makes my violin. She's gorgeous, isn't she?"

"Fuck yeah." His storm cloud-colored eyes widened. "Sorry."

"I said pretty much the same in my head when I saw it."

He grinned. "That's gonna be so cool. Can you give me a little taste of the sound?"

She shook out a cord and plugged it into the amp she'd been assigned. She pulled out her long bow and tucked the cello against her shoulder. After a quick tune, she drew her bow over the strings until the deep tones echoed into the amphitheater.

She didn't look up. Didn't want to see if it was boredom or indifference on their faces.

She closed her eyes and let the instrument breathe. The notes resonated with sadness for a turn through an adapted opening of "Finally" from the new album.

Gray came in on the song and his flawless playing layered over her own.

Simon's whisper-soft voice took up where the verse should go.

As the song built, so did their sound. Jazz brought in the piano accompaniment.

"Again."

Margo opened her eyes. Nick was at the back of the bowl of seats, his arms crossed as he leaned against the railing that bisected the seats from the lawn.

She rolled her shoulders and cracked her neck. Taking it from the top, she put a little more grit into the song, shuttling her fingers down the neck of the bass.

Gray grinned and spun out the guitar so he matched. Deacon's bass complemented hers until she felt the sound in the middle of her chest.

But Simon's voice was the capper. The song was all longing and pain at the start until it built to anger and hopelessness, finally ending in a raging Foo Fighters-like climax. Everyone—including Jazz's drums—pounding out the loss of the narrator's last hope until it dialed down to the sad bassline, aching guitar, and her cello's reverberating tones.

Nick clapped slowly as he walked down the middle aisle and around the sound board. He didn't even look at Donovan and Lila. His eyes were for the stage.

He climbed the steps and reached for his Gibson. "Again," he said.

And they did.

Four more times until the song was nailed. Nick didn't say a damn word. He just moved on to another song.

With methodical calculation, he and Gray broke down guitar parts. Deacon did some rearrangements and she made a few suggestions.

The sun was low on the horizon line when Harper came onstage and demanded for them to eat and rest their throats.

Even without running around the stage, the guys' sweaty shirts were sticking to them. Jazz had stripped down to a tank and shorts.

Margo had lost her sweater on the third song, glad that she'd worn layers in deference to the temperatures of New York. May could mean cool and windy, or high seventies. And being from New England, she was used to the seasons here.

The California types were a little confused. One minute they wanted to peel off their clothes, the next Jazz was asking for a hoodie.

Margo followed them into the backstage area that Harper had set up with food, a mountain of watermelon, and a table full of drinks.

Margo frowned when everyone went to the table of watermelon first. Simon and Nick mowed through three pieces right at the buffet table before going to the cold cuts and salads.

Lila came up to her with a plate of cubed watermelon.

"Is this an initiation thing?"

Lila laughed. "No. It's a Harper thing."

She took the plate and popped one in her mouth. The sweet, juicy flavor flooded her tongue. Wasn't a bad way to start off lunch.

"Cures dehydration," Jazz said as she walked by with a bowl of melon and a plate of macaroni salad and two turkey sandwiches.

"Is that right?"

"Harper's a genius when it comes to taking care of the band's dietary needs." Lila selected a blush red cube and took an elegant bite. "How's it feel?"

"How does it sound?"

"You already know that, Margo."

"It sounds like nothing that's out there right now."

Lila nodded. "In a good way."

She chewed thoughtfully. "I think so. It's not different enough to make people scratch their heads."

"Good. I knew it was going to work." Lila lowered her voice. "Nick just needed to hear it for himself."

Her gaze found Simon at the edge of the group. She frowned. He was usually in the center of things. He drank a bottle of water between sandwiches and as soon as he'd cleared his plate, he thumbed off a candy or mint from a roll in his pocket.

Unsure if she should ask him if his throat was too raw, she stayed seated next to Jazz and Lila. Harper had finally joined the table to plow through her own plate of food.

Donovan came into the eating area. He held up his hand when Deacon started to stand. "Don't mind me. I just wanted to let you know how amazing I think you're sounding. These rehearsals were just what you needed to tighten up a few of the songs. Lila and I want you guys happy on this tour."

"We're getting an opener, aren't we?" Simon asked.

"I'm glad you mentioned it." Donovan dipped his hand into his pocket and checked his phone once before he settled it back without replying. "I've lined up two bands. One will follow you from the East Coast until Texas. About eight weeks, I'd say."

Nick pushed his plate away and crossed his arms on the table. "Better not be a douche."

"These ladies are not."

"Ladies?" Nick's head tipped back. "God."

"Have a little faith, Nick." Donovan opened his arms beseechingly. "I want this tour to be a success, remember?"

Deacon laughed. "You're going to say Brooklyn Dawn."

"Got it in one." Donovan tucked his hands into his pockets. "Jamie and Lindsey are rising stars. They're at the end of their run with their first album, but I want them to have some summer exposure. I think you're a good fit for each other. Definitely a similar sound."

Simon gave a thumbs up. "I'm down with some girls on tour."

"You would be, Super Slut."

Margo's belly tightened. She wasn't quite sure how she felt about that.

Simon escaped to the bathrooms as everyone said their goodbyes to Donovan. He'd have to do a little YouTube research on Brooklyn Dawn and see how they performed live.

Right now, he was more worried about his own performance. The damn pollen was going to choke him. His throat was on fire. No matter how much water he drank, it felt itchy.

He turned all the taps on full hot and prayed for a decent level of steam. He stood over one sink and breathed in the moist air.

His throat was damn happy about it. And the tickle he'd been fighting eased.

He was usually able to sing all damn day. How many times had they jammed well into the night on the last tour? And after a show, so it wasn't like the three hours he'd been singing should have taxed him.

Fucking allergies.

Knowing he was pushing his luck, he stretched it to ten minutes before he shut off the faucets and drained the three liters of water out of his fucking bladder.

He washed his hands and opened the door to find Margo in the hall-way. "Hello, Violin Girl."

She frowned. "Are you all right?"

"Fine. Just needed to open up the pipes a bit."

"Have Harper get you some ginger. Steep it in some hot water for a few hours. Tastes nasty, but my friend Siobhan swears by it."

The urge to snap at her itched at the back of his throat worse than the irritant he'd been living with. He didn't need her help. Nor did he want her to see him struggling.

"I'll tell her."

"Good."

She tried to slip by him, but Simon curled his hand around her hip. "Tonight, at the fountain."

Her dark eyes widened and the rosy blush under her cheeks hardened his dick. He wouldn't be happy until her cheeks were scarlet with exertion.

He brushed his thumb over her lower lip. "You want the experience, right? And nothing you've done before."

She nodded.

He lowered his head, keeping their gazes locked as he tugged on her lower lip. He bit hard enough that it instantly plumped and darkened to raspberry. "The fountain at eleven."

"What fountain?"

"You'll know it." He forced himself to walk down the hallway away from her. He wanted to suck on her lips until the hue was as deep as wine, but she already had too much control over his cock.

It was time to show her what would happen if she wanted the tour expe-rience. Then maybe he could finally fuck her out of his system and move on.

Because right now he couldn't see an end in sight to the want.

He climbed the stairs to the stage. Nick and Gray were in the middle of figuring out a longer guitar duel in "Ricochet". With the time to fill on the setlist, they could finally work with the songs and let them breathe.

Simon loved a perfect four minute song. It got the crowd engaged and didn't let them get bored. But sometimes the rest helped him with some of the grittier songs on the setlist. Letting Gray and Nick rock out to a three minute solo was welcome in the second hour.

As they hashed out the song, Simon moved out to the archway. It had been finished while they were having their lunch break. Tomorrow it would be sandblasted in cobalt blue and glitter-flecked silver.

He'd seen the designs, but the archway had originally been at the back of the stage. The fact that Lila had retooled it to be exactly what he needed warmed him and energized him.

He backed up and ran three steps before he vaulted up to the second tier of the arch. Hidden behind the artistry of their band name was a network of handholds for him.

Good goddamn, it was sturdy. It didn't even sway when he monkeyed his way up to the crossbars and pulled himself up to sit.

"Fuck yeah."

Nick and Gray moved under him. "Gonna be able to get down without help, asshole?" Nick asked.

"Yeah, but who would want to. I can see the whole damn pavilion." Simon spotted Margo at the end of the lower section. She was on her phone, pacing. "It's fucking gorgeous." He peered down at them. "It's going to be so goddamn awesome."

"How about you get down and sing?" Nick asked.

Simon dove forward, his fingers catching the bar just as he flipped around and hung for a few seconds. "Oh, yeah. Awesome."

"Just don't forget to sing while you're playing monkey, Pretty Boy," Deacon quipped.

"Har-har."

"Are you boys done with your solos?"

"Yeah, yeah," Gray muttered.

Margo jogged back down the main aisle and up the stairs. Her face wasn't quite as happy and open as it had been all day. A new tension seemed to gather between her brows.

But before he could mention something, it was gone and she was lifting her violin to join in on "Undertow".

Two hours later, Jazz begged for mercy because of swollen hands and feet.

"One more take of 'Renegade' and we'll be good for the day."

Jazz tipped her head back. "Thank God."

Simon burned through another bottle of water and shrugged out of his soaked T-shirt. He cupped his hands around his mic and felt the build in his belly.

The bridge needed a good long vibrato, so he tried to relax his throat even as he felt that tickle nagging at him.

The song built and he held the note. As the guitars increased, he heard the break. He left his head thrown back and hope to shit that no one heard it, but he knew they did.

"All right. We're all toast." Deacon raised his voice and the song died. "No need to push it. We'll need all that for the tour."

Simon hung his head and uncapped his water.

"Awesome job today, guys. We're getting somewhere and Margo is definitely an asset."

Nick crossed his arms. Instead of the sneer that had been his constant companion, he shrugged. "It doesn't suck."

Margo was smart enough to school her features, but Simon saw her fighting the smile. Winning over Nick was a trick in itself.

As everyone filed out, there was chatter about dinner and changing clothes. He was more than ready to wash off the sweat and steam out the dryness in his throat.

"Simon?"

He turned to Nick. "Yeah?"

"Everything cool?"

"Why wouldn't it be?"

Nick studied his face then mirrored his crossed arms and hip shot stance. "Everyone's tired. No big."

"You burning to say something, son?"

Nick rocked back on his heels. "You want to go there? I was just asking a question."

"You were dancing around a question."

"Don't get your panties in a twist, Pretty Boy. I'm just checking on you. We pushed your voice today."

"I'll be fine."

Nick held his hands up. "Enough said." He walked around him and to the stairs at the back of the stage. He stopped on the second stair down.

Simon braced himself, but Nick kept going. He rubbed the back of his neck. "Shit."

Instead of following the rest of the band, Simon headed out to the seats and the walkway above the pavilion. It was a serious hike to the railing that delineated from paid seats and the lawn. And fuck if the lawn didn't go on for forever.

It seemed as good a place to start the tour as any. The acoustics were certainly impressive. He couldn't wait to hear the difference with a theater full of people.

As long as he took care of his voice during the day, he could get through two hours easily. Five hours was asking a lot for even the most seasoned musician.

He walked until he cooled down and even then he didn't want to deal with anyone else. He circled the parking area and was rewarded with an empty bus.

Nick had already been there and gone. His dirty clothes were half in their laundry bin and half out, and there was a wet towel over the door.

His pocket buzzed.

What time?

Simple and to the point, that was Margo. He tapped the side of his phone. The park was a few miles off the beaten track. He and Deak had run around it on one of his marathon killer runs.

Fountain at the War Memorial. Midnight. No panties.

The text bubble started almost immediately.

If you get me arrested, there will be retribution.

He grinned.

Afraid?

She replied instantly again.

Fuck no.

He sprawled on the couch.

Oh, now you can swear?

She fired back a text in a moment

I'm learning that I might like a lot of things I never used to do. See you at the memorial.

Simon closed his hand around his phone and tapped the top against his forehead. The idea of facing the pitying looks of his bandmates was far too much to deal with. He drew his feet up on the couch and blinked out.

When he woke, the bus was pitch black. He swore when he read the time on his phone. He plugged it into the charger and stumbled to the shower.

Ten minutes later, he was tucking a faded black T-shirt into an old pair of black jeans. He stuffed his feet into boots and was out of the bus and halfway down the path before he realized he should have gone with his crosstrainers.

He was going to have to hoof it the last mile to where the memorial was in the city park. But at least for the first mile and a half, he could take one of the golf carts out to the edge of the venue.

When he got to the main road of Saratoga, he stashed the cart next to an ice cream shop and took a shortcut through the side streets.

Thank you, Deacon for making me run my ass off.

He slowed as he found the back entrance to Congress Park and ducked through the trees to avoid the security cameras.

Just like old times.

How many backyards and parking lots had he sneaked through as a kid? Christ, he'd lost track after the age of fourteen. Of course by then he'd discovered beer and things had gotten blurry for specifics.

When he spotted the fountain, he slowed his pace. Moonlight shimmered off the shallow pond and the burble of the water softened the night sounds.

She stood in the center of the monument. The octagonal shape seemed even larger and more imposing now that it was just them and the night. The ivory stone glowed in the half moon's light.

He slowly walked over the stone bridge and up the handful of stairs. Her hair was loose and rippled in the slight breeze. A dark skirt swished around her knees and a satiny blouse picked up the shafts of moonlight that teased through the columns.

So fucking beautiful.

On a night that was supposed to be about fucking, she looked like a cool, elegant dream. Something that would never belong to him.

The heat of anger bloomed in his belly. She didn't deserve it, but it was there. Actually, she *did* deserve it. She'd walked away from him so many times and now she wanted him to bend to her.

It was time for her to do the bending.

He stopped a foot in front of her. "Did you listen to my directions?"

She swiped her tongue over her lower lip and nodded.

"Show me."

Margo looked over her shoulder.

"Don't worry about anyone else. Only me."

She curled her fingers into the flowing skirt and inched it up over her knees, halting at her mid-thigh.

"Too much for you, Violin Girl?"

She lifted her chin and pressed her lips together as she raised it farther.

The shadow of her cleft left his dick as hard as the stone that surrounded them. "Higher."

Her chest rose and fell a little faster than it should and her nipples jutted against the shiny fabric. She liked it.

The white noise in his brain pushed out any sense of caution. Here, he had control and she was a willing playmate. Just how far could he push her?

She gathered the material to her middle and the low light highlighted her milky skin. A small triangle of dark hair ended above her slit.

"Are you wet?"

She nodded.

"Show me."

Her mouth worked, but nothing came out at first. "How?"

"Touch yourself."

Her fingers flexed on the material but she drew her right hand down and tentatively slipped a finger along her pussy lips.

"Two fingers. Around your clit, then deep inside until they're coated." His voice was raspy with recovery from singing all day.

"Simon, I…"

"This is what you want, right? The dirty side of sex. The kind that doesn't end with candles and five-hundred thread count sheets?"

She closed her eyes and tipped her head back. "I do."

"Then show me how wet you are."

The elegant line of her throat and the tease of cleavage under her blouse pulled a groan from him. "Like that. With your eyes closed. Tell me how wet you are."

"I thought you wanted to see."

"First tell me."

Her breath hitched. "Soft and warm." She moaned. "Sensitive."

He watched as she circled her clit. Was that how she pleasured herself? Under the covers in her bed where no one could see her? "Now deep inside, two fingers, Margo."

She tucked her forefinger and middle finger through her folds and pumped lightly.

"Fuck." His voice was little more than a whisper on the breeze.

With her head tilted and her hair flowing down between her shoulder blades, she sawed her teeth through her lower lip as her hips rotated lightly.

"Now take them out."

She sighed and withdrew. The moonlight caught on the silvery wetness.

"Come here."

She dropped her skirt and he took her hand when she was close enough. He watched her face as he drew her fingers up to his mouth.

Her lips parted and her tongue fluttered over her lower lip.

He sucked her damp fingers into his mouth and curled his tongue around each digit until he had every bit of her taste transferred from her skin to his greedy mouth. He pulled them free with a pop and painted the pads of her fingers across his lip before he bent to taste her. She drew in a shaky breath.

"Want to taste yourself?"

"I…" Her tongue touched her top lip and her thick lashes veiled whatever she was thinking or feeling.

"You taste like cool honey that needs to warm up on my tongue. The kind of taste that lingers and buzzes over taste buds." For fuck's sake, he hadn't even touched her yet and his dick was so hard he couldn't think around the wanting of her.

He touched the tip of his tongue to hers lightly before she sweetly sucked him inside her mouth. And that was where the sweetness ended. She went up on her toes to eat up the last few inches that separated them and the kiss went flame-hot.

Lips and tongues twined around each other even as their arms didn't. Chest and breasts brushed, knees bumped, but it was only their mouths that lost control. The cool night air urged him to drag her in, but he knew that was the quickest road to him pushing her over the thigh-high plaques that covered every space between the eight columns.

There would be time for that.

But this, here and now…he wanted to string it out. Wanted to control this one thing between them. Where they weren't screwing like rabbits without the ride up. Zero-to-sixty was too easy.

He cupped her jaw and turned her head to take him deeper. He felt her moan vibrate through his tongue, into his throat, and arrow to his cock. He tasted it, swallowed it, owned it.

Her nails scraped his wrist as he took everything. She fisted his shirt and held on as breath became a commodity in their kissing war. She tore her mouth away and panted against his neck and down to his breastbone.

"Go lower."

Her hand moved to his belly and scratched through the narrow line of hair to his buckle.

"Suck me."

When she paused, he wondered if he'd found her end. When the commands would be too much for his Violin Girl.

"God, yes," she said against his throat and sucked on his Adam's apple until his eyes crossed. Her tongue swirled around the shadow of a few days of beard that he hadn't bothered to scrape off.

When she did that to the head of his cock...

Fuck.

She lifted his shirt and trailed open-mouthed kisses along his ribs down to the flat muscle of his lower belly. She crouched in front of him and looked up, her face in shadow save for the thin slash across her cheek and lips. The clink of his buckle and slow tick of teeth separating as she peeled open his jeans were almost drowned out by the drumbeat in his head.

He honestly wasn't much of a blowjob guy. He liked the feel of a woman clenching around him, not just a warm mouth.

But the ultimate focus on her face as she pulled him free was enough to convert him. Even if it was the worst head he'd ever had, he'd gladly let her do whatever she wanted to him.

She dragged her tongue under the length of his shaft and hugged her lips around the head until she took him deep into her mouth, until the head of his cock bumped the back of her throat and then beyond.

"Jesus fuck."

Then she coasted back and focused on the head, with tongue and suction and a talent that went way past skill. It was as if she'd downloaded a blueprint from his brain on what he wanted.

He cupped her cheek to slow her down before he came by her sheer force of will. She looked up with her puffy lips holding his cock hostage.

The first sound out of his mouth was a strangled, ragged groan.

There was a knowledge in her eyes that brought him back to the moment and away from the path to a drooling idiot hellbent on coming. "Touch yourself."

Her eyes widened.

"I can't be the only one feeling this."

She widened her knees and slid her feet farther apart for purchase.

Under the cover of night and the black material, she could have been doing anything. He wanted to see, wanted to smell the arousal that waited for him.

"Lift the skirt, Margo. I want to see your fingers, see how you please yourself. I want the combination to all your locks."

She paused with her fingers hidden, her secrets still shielded from him. And again he wasn't entirely sure if she was going to follow his direction or exploit his weakness, which she held onto with a powerful jaw.

But she folded back the material and sidled her way to a larger beam of moonlight until her silver-kissed thighs revealed her raspberry red slit. Angry and flushed with arousal, it matched her lips.

He trailed his fingers down her neck to the buttons of her blouse. He flicked them open and found the half cup bra under the satin. Her breasts were too full for it, so he knew she'd worn it for him.

To please him.

And his balls tightened with the idea that she'd want him enough to dress for him, to come here in the dark. Whether she was reckless or searching out a new experience, he didn't really care.

Because tonight she was his.

He smoothed the blouse aside, tucked his finger under the cup of the bra and plucked and rolled her nipple until it was tight and moonlit-kissed.

She hummed around his cock until he inhaled deeply, praying for strength.

"Are you wet? Does it get you off to suck my cock?"

She groaned with a mouth full of him. She wasn't innocent, but did she know just how much she was pushing him?

She pulled back, bobbing over his head with her wicked tongue circling again and again. The teasing flutter along the underside was the last straw.

He drove his fingers into her hair and dragged her up against him. Her lips abused and so dark he couldn't concentrate on anything else.

He lifted her, wrapping her legs around his hips. The stone pillar was textured and scraped the shit out of his palm, but she wasn't going anywhere. He pinned her there with his hips and dug into his pocket for a condom.

"You want this? Here? Now."

She nodded, her eyes gleaming in dark. "So much."

"Hold onto me."

Her heels dug into his ass as he adjusted his loosened jeans.

"Sweet fuck," he muttered against her neck as he sank inside her never-ending heat. She rolled her hips with each of his thrusts, her heels and nails digging into him with equal measure. The sounds, though…that was what drove him to the edge.

Her heartfelt moan was a memory and a revelation. She took him stride for stride, thrust for thrust until there wasn't much left of him. His throat burned with the need to shout out his release, but he tamped it back.

This woman knew too much.

Saw too much.

Their lips fused as he took her cries and swallowed them down with his own. The night sounds disappeared, his pain faded away, and there was nothing left but her taking him so goddamn deep.

She tore her mouth away and pressed her cheek to his. He swiveled his hips as much as he could to get the friction she needed. She was there with him, but he could tell her release was just out of reach.

"Tell me."

Her voice was barely a whisper wrapped in a whimper. She gripped his hair, his shoulder, his back—always moving and changing in her restless search for something else. "I can't…"

He twisted with her in his arms and dropped to one of the huge stone blocks with the bronzed plaques. There was barely enough room to get her knees on either side of him, but it was what she needed.

"God, yes."

"Margo," he growled into her chest, nosing into her bra to suck on her breast as she slammed down on him. With her astride him, she took him even deeper. She arched back until he almost dropped her, but her hips kept never wavered. She never stopped slamming down against him.

He sucked harder, drilled deeper, held her closer. Watching her burn and sway above him held him at the peak. He couldn't let go. Not now. Not if it meant he'd miss this woman coming all over him.

She sobbed out his name and he gripped her hips, holding her down around him as he came viciously. The orgasm yanked out of him from his spine and out the top of his head.

The shout that tore from him left fire in his throat but it didn't matter. Nothing mattered but her shattering around him.

Chapter 13

Margo lost the will to move or even to bring her brain cells to the party. After that, what was she supposed to do?

He was still deep inside of her, as if her body couldn't bear the thought of letting him go.

She wanted an experience.

To finally have a moment of sexual awakening.

Simon had been more than willing. But somewhere in between the thrill of having Simon in her mouth as he teased pleasure out of her with words and the orgasm that blindsided her, she'd lost sight of her goal.

Just sex.

He was the ultimate fantasy. An outlet for pleasure with no strings. The perfect man for anything except a serious relationship.

All signs pointed to Simon. In theory. But if they kept this up, there would be a larger problem.

Because she felt the odd stirrings of infatuation. The need to watch him and figure him out to her advantage.

He wasn't a score to puzzle out. There was no staff full of notes to learn. She wasn't supposed to be making a playlist of Simon's greatest orgasms. She was supposed to be worried about her own.

And the fun.

Tonight hadn't been fun. It had been intense. It had been overwhelming.

It had been downright scary.

He shouldn't know her body that well.

And he sure as hell shouldn't have been able to lead her down that primrose path of destruction.

She didn't even know how to climb off him yet. How to let go of the perfection of his cock and return to the emptiness she'd never known was living inside her.

His music, she understood. It had been a long time since any music had spoken to her on such a fundamental level, but it was still a commodity she understood.

Simon, the man…she didn't understand him.

Didn't want to.

She didn't want these forays into his psyche through this connection that glowed so bright between them.

He slipped his hands under her skirt and around to her bottom. He soothed and massaged the muscles that still twitched from the aftermath. The tightness of the back of her thighs to the curve of her cheeks and in between.

Her heart stuttered when he lightly circled her rosette and she instinctively tensed. He didn't speak, didn't coerce, didn't have to ask permission.

Her body seemed to know how to accept his touches, even there where she'd never thought to touch. He reached around to the unbearable wetness between them and used it to dampen the sensitive skin.

He groaned as she tightened around his half hard cock with each progressive circle. When the pad of his middle finger pressed in the tiniest bit, she made a restless sound.

"I want to fuck you here, too. I want to take my time and open you up and fill you 'til you scream."

She hissed out a breath as he went back to the gentle circles and then left her altogether to use his thumbs along her lower spine. Finally, he curved his hands around her waist and simply held her restless hips until she quieted.

Until the night sounds intruded and the crisp breeze drifted over the water with a taste of the fountain spray.

"We should probably get back before someone catches us."

She nodded and scooted back a little, just enough until he withdrew from her, leaving her curiously numb inside.

She stepped off of him with a silent groan filling up her head. He took care of the condom, and she handed him a tissue from her pocket. They both buttoned up and walked silently across the bridge into the park.

At the first trash bin, Simon got rid of the condom, but there didn't seem to be words between them. They'd used them all up within the stone pillars.

It wasn't a loud silence, but not quite a companionable one, either. As usual, it was on the fine line of in-between where she wasn't quite sure how to act.

They followed the path around the park to Broadway. The shops were closed and the streetlights reminded her of gaslights in old paintings.

It was a quaint town full of one-of-a-kind shops and eateries. It was the perfect street for browsing tourists there for the races or the casino nightlife nearby.

"Where are you staying tonight?"

She glanced over at him. "With Lila at The Inn." She nodded up the street. "Probably why I made it to the park a little faster than you."

"Classy and elegant. I wouldn't expect any less for Lila."

Out of Nick's mouth that statement would have an acerbic edge, but with Simon, it was just a lazy drawl of fact.

"How did you get here?"

"Stole a golf cart and stashed it over near the Ben & Jerry's down that street."

She grinned and he stopped. "What?"

"I don't see you smile all that often, Violin Girl."

She brought her hand up to her mouth to cover the bigger laugh trying to bubble up. "I'm just picturing you in all black, curled over the wheel and zipping down the paths of SPAC."

"I'll have you know I'm a very good golf cart driver. Fastest on the block."

She curled her arm across her middle to hold in the giggle she felt building. "Simon Kagan, golf cart thief, tops off his night with a little stolen sex."

"Worth it."

Her laughter caved in on itself and she put it in the little drawer where she hid her few pleasures. "I'd have to agree."

"Good." He nodded across the street. "We need to cross."

"No, that's okay. You have to go down that way, don't you?"

"Know where your ice cream is, huh?"

"A Ben & Jerry's shop? Of course."

"Need I ask?"

She licked her top lip. "Ask what?"

"What's your flavor, Violin Girl?"

"Oh. Well…"

"If you tell me vanilla, I'm taking away that rockstar cello and not returning it. I will find a way to learn how to play it."

She laughed. "Hazed and Confused."

"I don't think I know that one."

"All sorts of hazelnut and caramel goodness."

He stepped closer to her. "So you like salty and sweet?"

Her heartbeat filled her head and pulsed between her thighs. She'd been studiously ignoring the fact that her inner thighs were still slick from before and she was deathly afraid a freak wind would blow her skirt up so her bare butt would be on display. But now with that question hanging between them, she was acutely aware of her body again.

It was a constant struggle around Simon. And now she wanted to go on tour with him? With *them*? In close quarters.

Masochist.

She stepped back. The way his eyes faded from intent and flirtatious back to indifferent sliced at her. Emotions didn't belong in their equation.

He moved to her side again, his hand hovering at the small of her back. "I'll walk you to the door."

"I'll be fine. The street's lit up like a Christmas tree."

"Don't want to be seen with me, Violin Girl?" With his distinct brow line, she couldn't read his eyes. They were hidden in shadow, but his mouth seemed hard. The usual smirk gone.

She cleared her throat and shook her hair back. "Lila figured us out from the start, but there's no need to throw it in her face."

"And when we tour?"

"I haven't been accepted yet."

"You will. Nick still has his back up like a pissed off cat, but he's already settling down."

She tipped her head to the side. "How do you know?"

"Besides the fact that I've known him since we were kids, I know his tells."

"Enlighten me."

"He came back after he walked off his mad. If he was really against it, he wouldn't have returned."

Her eyebrows shot up. "Really?"

Simon nodded. "He came back and he played. He came back because he knew how good it was at the release parties. He might play it off like he doesn't pay attention to the ins and outs of the business, but he watches and analyzes everything." He swiped his hand down his face. "He and Deacon started discussing arrangements long before you came to rehearsals. He was already looking for ways to layer in the guitars to mimic your violin."

Her belly jittered. God, could it be true? She didn't even want to voice how much she wanted this.

She stepped into the street and turned to him. "I guess we'll be figuring that out tomorrow."

He dipped his hands into his pockets. "I guess we will."

Simon dunked his head under the tap in the bathroom of the venue. Cold water sluiced around his neck to his jaw and dripped down his chin.

It was ass hot today and his fucking throat was on fire.

Allergies? Worse?

He didn't know and was afraid to know.

He'd brought down his voice a few octaves during rehearsals to the easier mid-registers and it helped. He had to save his voice for the real stage, in spite of Nick's perfectionist nature that normally required them to rehearse six, seven, eleven times for each song. His best friend would've bitched out loud except they'd actually gotten somewhere. The songs were tighter, and Margo's violin and cello were becoming part of their sound.

Her face as each song came together was enough to keep his dick hard all damn day.

It was the only thing that kept the panic out of his belly about his voice. No one seemed to notice. He usually tried to modulate it for rehearsals, anyway.

But fuck, he was struggling. He leaned against the tiled wall and sank to a crouch. With a shaking hand, he drew his phone out of his pocket and pulled up a search page.

The first search was for changing voice and that was way too broad. Voice cracking went into a terrifying territory that made him shut his phone off.

Vocal hemorrhage.

Nodes.

Polyps.

Cysts.

Fuck.

He swiped a hand down his face. He downed the water that was always next to him these days. With a grunt, he rose off the floor and tucked his phone away.

He just needed that fucking ginger shit that Margo mentioned. And to keep his goddamn mouth shut the rest of the time he wasn't singing.

Vocal rest.

All the interviews he had to do didn't help matters. *That* at least he could manage.

They had their first show in four days. He had to be ready. He slipped out of the bathroom and headed back to the kitchen that Harper had set up for the week.

"Harp?"

She looked up, her sunny blond hair in its typical braid. Was it him or did her hair seem even longer? Damn prenatal vitamins. He'd stolen Jazz's gummy ones for a while until his hair had grown out to his shoulders in two months. He didn't have time for that shit.

"Hi, Simon. Can I get you something?"

He looked at his feet, then jammed his hands in his pockets and rocked back on his heels. "It's kind of a weird request."

"I'm the queen of weird."

"Yeah you are. You married Deak."

"Har-har." She leaned against the counter and swiped at her brow with the back of her hand.

Jesus.

Simon's gaze crashed into her belly. She was due in two months, but it looked more like two days. Gigantor baby in there.

She looked down and rubbed the top of her belly. "I know. It's finally to the point that I couldn't hide it even with a satellite view."

He laughed. "Sure you don't need to sit down?"

"I'm fine. Moving around is good for my circulation."

"Right."

"Weird request?"

"Yeah. Nick's killing my throat with all this extra rehearsal. Margo mentioned steeping ginger in some hot water might help?"

"Huh. I wouldn't have thought of that. I use root ginger so that's no problem."

"You do?"

"I sneak in the healthy stuff when you guys aren't looking." She shrugged. "I'll do some research to see if I can make it taste a little better than just straight ginger. Because wow, awful."

"Your ginger chicken tastes awesome."

She smiled. "Well, thanks. But that's a lot of brown sugar in there, pal."

"Oh. Well, I'd appreciate it." He rubbed his triceps. He'd overdone it on the workout that morning, trying to get his head in the game. Stupid resistance bands didn't feel like they did much.

"Done." She tipped her head. "Is it just voice strain?"

"Yeah. I can jam it up for hours with the guys, but that's like once a week. Two days of five hours of singing—yeah, I'm just not used to it."

"Okay. I'll fix you right up."

"Thanks, Harper."

She flipped her braid over her shoulder and hefted a bowl. "Now shoo and tell everyone it's time for lunch."

"Want me to carry that?"

"I'm pregnant, not an invalid. Shoo."

"Will do."

He headed to the hallway that went up to the stage, but he didn't need to inform anyone. The scent of Harper's barbecue had brought everyone around.

Band and crew were clustered around the warming trays on the two buffet tables from Harper's truck. A cute little redhead was fussing with all the cutlery.

Well, shit. "Annie."

She looked up. "Hey, Simon." Her lips split into a wide, knowing grin.

He'd hooked up with her last tour. A few times. He winced when Margo stood in front of her and looked between them.

"Chicken, please."

Annie turned to her. "Sure. Just one?"

"Yes."

Simon pointed to the end of the line. "I'll just go get at the back of the horde."

"You're already here." Margo pulled him toward the table and handed him a plate.

"Right." The thought of the spicy pork that he so loved was enough to push him toward the milder chicken. He wondered if it was a bad idea to beg for ice cream.

Probably. Milk products never boded well for his voice. But man, it would probably feel good.

"Simon? No spicy pork? Are you all right?"

He laughed and wished the tickle would go the hell away. "Used too much Rooster on my eggs this morning."

Annie shrugged and put two pieces of chicken on his plate. He moved down the line behind Margo, but didn't say a word.

Vocal rest — thank you.

He sat with Nick and Margo moved on to sit with Lila. Before he could even pick up his fork, Nicky launched into his thoughts on "Lit" and making a bridge between "Ricochet" and "Monster" to make it one epic song.

Guess he didn't have to worry about not talking.

Especially when Deacon sat next to Nick and they started squabbling over which guitar to use where. All Simon could focus on was that "Ricochet" and "Monster" were both lower register songs.

"They'd be perfect in the second hour."

Nick pulled out the notebook that wasn't ever far from his hand and scribbled in a note. The page had scratch outs and some sort of shorthand that only Nick understood. "Yeah. Good point. Some headbanging to revive the crowd in the middle." Deacon and Nick put their heads together over the notebook.

Simon finished enough of his chicken to fill the hole in his gut to get through the rest of the day and tossed the rest.

While everyone was talking and laughing, he just needed to get out of the group and clear his head. He slipped out into the hall and up to the stage.

He thought about taking a run. But *that* much alone meant he needed his head examined.

Instead, he took his Taylor out of the trunk and settled down in the first row of seats with the familiar weight of his acoustic in his lap. Strumming usually calmed him down.

He picked out a few chords he'd had battering around in his brain. The urge to sing along with the words in his head was tough to ignore, but he kept singing them in his head.

The melody was perfect for his midrange voice. Is that what he'd need to do? Write songs in the midrange like some old rocker?

Fuck.

He stood and dumped his guitar on the stage with a hollow crash of sounds. He climbed over the orchestra pit seats and then up the middle aisle to the sunshine of the day.

He pulled his shades down and made his way across the bridge to the parking lot. Gravel and uneven pavement led to a grassy picnic area. He kept going until he found the main road and crossed to the gas station and liquor store he'd found the first night.

Anger and that tickle in his throat kicked up. All he could think about were ways to numb both.

He walked in, bought a flask-sized bottle of shit vodka and ran back across the street to the parking lot. Like the old days when he was a kid and he'd sneaked a bottle in and listened to bands from outside.

Only this time, it was his band playing.

His phone buzzed and he ignored it. He was sure Nicky was looking for him to start the afternoon process of picking apart songs.

He uncapped the vodka and flooded his throat. It stung like a bitch and tasted like ass, but the numbing had begun. He kept taking belts from the bottle until he didn't care.

When the first call came in, he finally headed back into the venue. He wasn't drunk, but the buzz was enough to get him through the day without tearing anyone's head off.

He jogged across the bridge and grabbed a water from the cooler Harper had set up at the back of the pavilion. He waved as he came down the main aisle. "Re-fucking-lax. I just needed a walk."

"You don't walk," Nick said with his hands on his hips, his Gibson hanging between his shoulder blades.

"Sure I do." Simon lifted his knees and marched his way to the stairs.

"Fuck off. This is serious, Simon."

"And I said I needed a fucking break."

"All right, that's enough."

Simon zeroed his gaze on Deacon. "No need to get all marriage coun-selor-like." He tripped on the last step and caught himself. "What are we singing?"

Jazz stood up at her kit. "Are you drunk?"

"What? No." He snorted and unhooked his mic from the stand.

"Did your *walk* include a trip to the liquor store, you shit?"

He shrugged. "Maybe."

"Save that for after rehearsals."

Simon walked over to Nick very slowly. "Since when did you become the boss?"

"Since you started half-assing the songs."

Simon swung before he could even think about it. Nick's head snapped back and he staggered back a step.

"What the fuck?"

"I don't half ass anything. I'm saving my voice just like I always do in rehearsals, you fuck."

"Really?" Nick lifted the strap over his head and put his guitar in the stand behind him. He wiped the blood from the corner of his mouth and advanced on Simon. "Because you haven't reached for one of the higher notes since yesterday. How do you know what the four other songs we're rehearsing are going to sound like?"

"It won't sound the same, anyway. It changes when the house is full of people and you know it."

Nick tongued the inside of his mouth and frowned. "What the hell is your problem?"

"You're pushing us for hours a day. I'm trying to make sure my voice isn't fucked before we even begin."

"That's never been a problem before."

"Yeah, well I don't usually sing for six hours a day and do interviews for half the night."

Nick frowned. "Oh."

"Yeah. So fucking cut me a break if I don't scream out a song to an empty room."

"Yeah." Nick scratched the back of his head. "Why didn't you just say that?"

"Not like you hear anyone these days, son." Simon threw up his hands. "You've got your nose stuck in that notebook and the rest of the time you're barking orders. We don't work for you, we're a band."

Nick turned to the others. "Is that right?"

Jazz plopped down on her seat. "I could use a few extra breaks. Kiddo is kicking me every song. My ribs are fucking killing me."

Deacon shrugged. "I'm fine."

"Of course you are. You're just as obsessed as he is."

"Some of us want this to be the best tour ever."

Simon widened his stance to stop the slight sway. "And like I don't?"

"I don't know, do you?"

"Fuck off."

Nick advanced on him and Simon lifted his chin in direct challenge. Maybe if he pounded on Nick, a little of the anger simmering under his skin would dissipate.

"All right, separate corners." Gray stepped forward. "We're all working hard, but we don't have to sing the whole time unlike Simon."

Nick's chest heaved as he clenched his hands into fists at his sides.

Simon crowded in on Nick until they were chest-to-chest. "C'mon, Nicky. Hit me. I can see you want to."

Nick's lip curled. "I should. You deserve it for that jab."

"Then what are you waiting for?"

"What? So you can go back to the bus and sulk after I kick your drunk ass? Nope." Nick took a step back, paused, and then Simon couldn't duck fast enough for the fist coming his way.

He went down on one knee at the pain exploding from his cheek.

Nick bent down to him. "Now we're even, asshole." He rose to his full height. "Let's take it from the top."

Simon blew out a breath. When he felt a hand at his elbow, he shrank back.

"Stop being a prick," Gray said and helped him to his feet. He slapped a water bottle against Simon's middle. "Hydrate up."

Simon took the water and because his damn throat felt like there was a bee stinging the fuck out of his vocal chords, he finished that bottle and the one he'd dropped on the way up the stairs.

The rest of the afternoon was a slog of songs he couldn't even remember. The heat and the liter of vodka put him into the ground.

He knew every word because that was how he was built. Lyrics stuck in his brain. Singing them a million times in the studio helped, of course, but it was the same for any song he heard on the radio or at a show.

The way they sounded—*that* he had no clue. And right now he didn't care.

When dinner was called, Simon staggered back to the bus. He didn't need any more band time today. He wanted to just crash and start over tomorrow. He'd slept like shit the night before. Head full of Margo and the monument in different incarnations.

All of them were full of her heated moans and then leaving him in the octagon alone.

"Simon."

He paused at the rear panel of the bus. "What is it, Violin Girl? As you can see, I'm not exactly in an accommodating mood."

"Are you okay?"

"I'm always okay."

"I don't believe you."

"I don't fucking care if you do or not." He flattened his hand over the gold and black swirls of the trunk and stared at the gravel until it solidified.

She ducked under his arm and he pressed her back against the bus.

"What?" He locked his gaze with her. "You want to see how fucked up I am today? Want it up close and personal?" He curled his fingers around the back of her neck, twisting them into her hair. "I don't think you want any part of me tonight, Violin Girl."

"I'm not here for that. I'm just…"

"Just *what?* You give a shit about me?" He slid his hand down her back and to her ass, dragging her to his dick that was hard no matter his mood.

Because she was there.

Because she fucking breathed.

Because she was within thirty feet of him.

"All you care about is my dick and how it makes you feel. Whatever entertainment I can provide before you get off and disappear."

"Is that what you think?"

"It's what I know." He ground his pelvis into her. "I see it in your eyes right now." He pulled down the front of her shirt until the tops of her breasts showed over the wide, round neckline. "Here in your tight as a diamond nipples." He flicked open the button of her black shorts. "If I pushed my hands into your panties, I'd find you dripping for me."

She lifted her chin. "Do it then. Use me. Put that anger to some good use."

"Fuck, Margo."

She slid her hand under his shirt and tugged on his nipple ring until he hissed. "I want it."

"What if I don't want to give it to you?"

"Is that what your hard cock says?"

His belly jumped at her words. She rarely swore, and she sure as shit didn't call his dick a cock on a normal day. "It doesn't matter if I'm pissed off or happy, my dick always wants inside your hot pussy."

If he was crass and cruel, maybe she'd walk away. He wasn't entirely sure he could handle a fuck-and-run from Margo today. Not when he was already so goddamn raw.

But she was right.

He wouldn't say no.

He wanted her even as his anger collided with the leftover vodka in his veins. And he was fairly positive he'd leave marks on her. He wanted to brand her.

He didn't care that he could still hear staff moving around, or that daylight was still peeking in between the dense trees back near the busses.

She moved down his chest and belly to fumble at his zipper, then her hand was inside and he bowed his head as she circled the base of his cock.

He pushed her hand away and turned her around. He reached in front of her to cup her breasts and pushed them out of the top of her bra to get a hold of one as he shoved his hand down her pants. "Is this what you want?"

"Yes."

"Hands up against the bus." When she did so, his voice went darker and lower with the aftereffects of singing that day. He'd reached for the high notes and hit a few of them if his throat was any indication. "Hang on."

She trembled for him and he crouched down behind her, peeling her shorts down enough for him to get to her ass. He slipped his hand between her thighs from the back and she wasn't just wet. She was soaked.

He pressed open her thighs as far as they would go with the shorts on and tongued her. Her scent filled his head and her taste exploded in his mouth.

He used his fingers from the front and the back until he was crowding inside of her, spreading her open to get every groan and shudder out of her.

Relentless fingers on her clit from the front, two fingers from the back and he pressed his thumb against her rosette.

He owned them all right now.

Choked moans were followed by her trembling thighs. And he didn't stop. He took all the liquid heat from the front of her and spread it to her back until he could breach her with the pad of his thumb.

Her thigh shook so bad, he had to hold her still with his arm. He rimmed her with his tongue as her taste and her scent filtered into his vodka-soaked brain. He held her there at the edge, not letting her go over. He needed to hold onto that for his cock.

Had to have her spasm around him until there was nothing left of him.

When her gasps turned to whimpers, he let her go and stood. He suited up and fit himself against her swollen lips. "This is what you want?"

She reached back and he grabbed her hand to put it back on the bus. "Don't move."

He slipped his shaft along her lips and bumped his head under the hood along the front until he brushed her clit again and again.

She pressed her forehead against her hands and rose on her toes. "Simon," she said with a begging tone.

He reached between them and tucked his head inside her. The grasping warmth seared through the condom as he slowly slid inside.

She pushed back on him, lifting onto her toes to get him closer.

He crowded in on her and flattened his hands against the bus above hers and he snapped his hips against her ass.

"Yes." Her voice was low as she repeated the word again and again as he plowed into her. He didn't let up, didn't gentle, didn't allow himself to worry about her pleasure.

He took.

And he took.

And when she vised around his cock with a moan flavored scream that traveled through her back into his chest, he threw his head back and came.

He came so hard lightning filled his head and shorted out his brain. He came so hard that his spine went numb.

She was shaking and curling in on herself when he came back to himself. He wanted to hold her, wanted to curl around her and promise her everything, but he just pulled out and tied off the condom.

"Hope you got what you wanted." He zipped up and backed away from her.

The anger was back tenfold.

That kind of fucking should end with his arms around her to calm down. But the thought of her wiggling out of his hold and walking away burned his ass and fried his brain.

So he walked away first. He went straight to the door of the bus and to the showers to get her off him.

Because what he really wanted, she wasn't offering.

Chapter 14

Simon pulled his shades down over his face and settled back into the folding chair in the orchestra pit. It had been a much better day for rehearsals. They tried out the setlist as a whole and timed the show at an hour and thirty-five minutes.

With the commentary he ran through and the nights that things went long, it was looking like they would give people a good show. That didn't include their covers and whatever crazy songs ended up on the docket thanks to their legion of Twitter followers.

Jazz and Nick were upping the ante for the YouTube channel by doing interviews with the fans once a week.

Part of him was jealous. Those are the things he used to do, but now the thought of spending even ten more minutes in interviews was enough to make him cranky.

Hell, Jazz was getting endless amounts of name suggestions for her baby on Twitter. It was one kid, man. He couldn't figure out what all the fuss was about.

Deacon and Harper were much more private about their impending parenthood, and Simon was glad he didn't have to hear their baby crap all day long in Twitter-land, too.

Lila came onto the stage. "Thanks for coming in, guys. I know you're fried from practice, but I thought you might like a little treat." She nodded to someone at the soundboard behind them. A huge screen came down and the logo for the local NBC channel filled the screen.

"Now that is a theater setup," Nick said and kicked out his feet in front of him. Their little blowup from the day before had been forgotten by morning, as usual.

Hell, they'd come to bloody blows and ended up laughing through a drink within the same hour. It was just their way. They'd been scrapping since before they were legal to drive.

Deacon sat behind him, his arm curled around Harper's shoulders, Jazz and Gray in a similar clutch. The marrieds and the other.

That's what they'd become. At least the magic on stage hadn't changed, even if the smug married people had different plans after rehearsal or a show. Those plans usually included rubbing pregnant feet.

Ugh.

Margo sat on the other side of him, her face impassive. She hadn't really talked to him today, but she hadn't *not* talked to him, either. She was a cagey one on a good day.

"Two things," Lila said as she walked across the stage. "We're going to do a special fan club only show on Thursday night to get some reactions, see if we need to do any tweaks."

Jazz clapped behind him. "That was me and Nicky's idea. That way if something doesn't work, then we still have a day to replace a song."

Yay.

Christ, he hoped his voice held out. Most of the rest of the tour was staggered so he had a night off at least every three days. Now, the first week would be five nights in a row.

Fucking phenomenal.

"And now…" Lila glanced over her shoulder. "*Music Life* had so much left over from the release party that they teamed up with NBC to do a primetime special with you guys. The fact that 'Lit' is still in the top ten doesn't hurt, either."

Nick punched him in the arm. "Dude, everyone will see this."

Simon smiled wide for the first time in two days. As Kim Forrester's face filled the screen, the house speakers went live. She talked about their humble beginnings, the YouTube song that had changed their lives, and the fight for a contract between two different music labels.

The way Kim told it, they'd been in more of a bidding war than what had really happened. She made them sound so altruistic for choosing the smaller label and how it had worked out for them.

No one would know the real story. Not unless one of them actually coughed up the info. Simon hated to remember those days. The way that Trident had played them, turned them on the rest of the band.

The way Jackson Miller had worked the contract until it sounded like they'd been protecting Oblivion. That the numbers wouldn't matter for the one album. And he and Nick would have controlling interest in the band for a year.

It had sounded so safe, so doable. After the train wreck the band had become after Snake was ejected, he and Nick had been looking for any way to protect the band.

Every part of it had been a bad idea.

And the only reason they still had their shirts, or even their songs, was because Deacon had questioned every piece of the contract.

He'd saved their ass.

And they'd never spoken of it again. Because those dark days had showed he and Nicky had been lacking in the trust department—in a big way. And listening to Kim Forrester make it sound like they'd been so brave to try a smaller label made his stomach turn.

Beside him, Nick had his arms crossed over his middle, his face impassive. He must have been thinking back on their shitty decisions, as well.

But in the next segment she talked of "The Becoming" and their use of a string section to create an epic song experience for the soundtrack.

It had shot them to the top of the charts and had brought the EP into their lap. Once they'd gotten out from under Trident's thumb, they'd found out that they were a great band in the studio.

Everything that had been a chore and a slog in Trident's studio space had become magic and intimate with Ripper Records. Donovan Lewis understood what artists needed.

To an uncanny degree, to be honest.

Simon didn't give two shits about how the guy knew, but he was grateful for it. By the time *Music Life* showed footage from their release party he was willing to buy an album.

She'd spun it so they seemed like the next Rolling Stones, for fuck's sake. And her take on adding a violinist to the band made them sound like geniuses.

Kim's huge bluebell eyes filled the screen. "In our last segment, we're going to get a little insider information on how the band came to be."

Simon turned to Nick and they both frowned. "Did you talk to her?"

Nick shook his head. "Not since the release party."

He twisted in his chair. "You guys?"

Deacon, Gray, and Jazz all shook their heads.

Nick folded his hands behind his head. "I hope to shit they don't talk to one of your road skanks, Simon."

"Fuck off." Simon swiped his hand over his face and glanced at Margo. She was sheet-white. "Hey. Are you all right?"

She tucked her hair behind her ear with trembling fingers. "I wish I'd known they were going to include me."

Simon lowered his eyebrows. "Ashamed that you're slumming it with a rock band, Violin Girl?"

"No, of course not. But now I'm going to have to do some explaining."

"Mommy dearest doesn't want to know that her daughter has any interests outside of chamber music."

"Fuck off, Simon."

He laughed without an ounce of humor. "I didn't know you had such language living inside your head, let alone that it could come out of that mouth."

"You don't have to live with the repercussions of this."

"You're right. My old man hasn't cared what I do since I was twelve."

Margo's mouth dropped open, but before she could say anything else, the commercials ended and the screen was filled with Snake's face.

The entire pavilion went silent in shock.

"We're here with William Scotsman, best known as Snake from the original lineup of Oblivion."

"Would you prefer Snake or William?"

"Snake, definitely."

"You were the original drummer for Oblivion, correct?"

"That's right. Me and Nicky and Simon started the band when we were in high school then we added Deacon in a little later."

"So why did you leave?"

"I didn't."

Kim sat forward in her chair. "They asked you to leave?"

"No. More like I was shoved out. I had some problems and had to go away to rehab, but we were always really tight. They were only supposed to get a temporary drummer for when I was away."

"And did you feel betrayed?"

"Of course. That band had been our dream first and then that girl came in and ruined it all. She almost tore the band apart."

"You're talking about Jazz Edwards?"

"Yeah. She blindsided Nick."

"What the fuck?" Nick sat up straight.

"Shhh," Simon said. He was very interested in hearing just what kind of lies Snake was going to weave together.

He'd been one of his best friends for years, but the band had never been a priority for Snake. It had been a means to score dope and girls. When he'd come to see them during the *Burn* tour, that had been very apparent. He wanted them to go back to their club roots and never move on from that.

"That's why a girl should never be in a band with dudes. When sex is involved, and it always is, there's no checks and balances. The chick has all the power."

"You do realize how sexist that sounds?"

Snake shrugged. "I speak truth. Jazz has two dudes in that band wrapped. She married one and got knock—"

"Okay, let's change gears," Kim interrupted.

Jazz clattered to her feet. "He's going to start up all those rumors again."

Simon turned around. "C'mon, Pix. We'll rip him apart after."

She sat down and leaned into Gray, a protective hand over her baby bump. "When you got out of rehab, did they inform you of your place in the band?"

"My lack of one? Oh yeah. I got informed."

"You sound bitter," Kim said with that sweet voice that could get anyone to talk.

"I started that band. I helped write those songs. Songs they still sing."

Nick sat up. "Bullshit." He turned to Simon, his face pinched and red. "Fucking bullshit. We wrote all the songs."

Simon searched the stage for Lila, but she was off to the side with a man in a suit. Simon stood for a better look as Snake ranted on their screen about the injustice and disloyalty of the band.

Lila was reading something on a clipboard and finally signed it before accepting the large white envelope.

"Are you just coming forward now because of Oblivion's commercial success?"

Snake's arms tensed on the chair arms in the interview. "I went to them during the last tour and was kindly turned away from the bassist, Deacon

McCoy. And advised I was not wanted."

"Was it true?"

"No. When I went backstage later that night, Nicky and Simon were thrilled to see me. I was excited to see my boys again. We partied up—"

"Even though you'd just been in rehab?" Kim asked.

"Nah, man. Not that kind of partied. Just some brews. I don't touch the hard stuff anymore."

"I've heard that alcohol is a slow slide back."

"Unless you've ever had a needle sticking out of your arm, then you don't know, lady."

Simon heard the belligerent edge and now that he wasn't seething, he watched how Snake's gaze never landed on Kim. Just kept bouncing around the room.

"Fucker is using again."

"Yeah he is," Nick said darkly.

Simon's gaze drifted to Lila again. She had papers out of the envelope and she was walking toward the side door with her phone.

That probably wasn't good.

"Is there anything you want to say to the band that you haven't gotten the opportunity to say?"

"Yeah." Snake looked at the camera. "You made a huge mistake pushing me out of the band."

Simon stood and went after Lila as Kim wrapped up the interview and tried to push some hard-hitting questions to the fans.

The only people that would ever have known about Snake were some club rats at the Blue Rhino. Christ, they'd barely gotten a blip of recognition before Gray and Jazz had been added to the group.

Nick caught up to him and grabbed his arm. "Where are you going? To get drunk again?"

"Fuck, no. Well, maybe later. What the fuck, man. Rats coming out to get their piece of cheese now that we have some status. Even when Snake did come out to the show, he was going on about club days, not the stuff we've been doing."

"No. He wanted the good old days where he had to drum for forty minutes then booze the night away with whatever girls actually gave a shit enough to stay after the show."

"Exactly."

"So what? You just need to walk it off?"

"No. Someone came and gave something to Lila in the middle of that interview. I got a bad feeling, man." Simon raked his hands through his hair. "Really bad feeling."

They got out the side door to find Lila pacing. "I don't give a shit, Robert. I need to talk to Donovan. Unless he's in with the President of the United States, he's going to want to take this goddamn call."

Simon's eyebrows skyrocketed. Yeah. Not good.

"What the hell?" Nick asked under his breath.

"Yes, I'll hold." Her voice was part seething, part Dragon Lady. She looked over at them. "I have to talk to Donovan first. Why don't you guys go back in?"

Simon crossed his arms. "We're thinking *that* has something to do with that lovely broadcast."

She pinched the bridge of her nose. "It does, but I don't want you to get bent out of shape unless it's absolutely necessary. You have a show to worry about in two days."

"What we're making up in our heads is going to be far worse," Nick said.

"Probably not."

"Oh, honey, you don't know what I can come up with."

She held up a finger. "Yes, I'm here. Hi, Donovan." She sighed. "You got one, too." She made a noncommittal sound and resumed her pacing. "Is there any strength in the claim?"

"What claim?" Simon tipped his head back. "Oh, shit."

"He wouldn't." Nick curled his fingers into fists. "That fuck. He's never written a lyric in his goddamn life."

Lila turned around to him and held her phone out. "Donovan, can you hear me?"

"Yes." The British voice came across the speakers of her iPhone.

"Never?" she asked.

"No." Nick raised his voice. "In the beginning, Simon and I wrote the songs and Deak did the composition at the end. Snake just showed up for skins. Even the one demo we did, I did the drums because he was too wrecked."

Lila's slim golden brow rose. "Good. That's good."

"I'll have my lawyers look this over and contact you in a few hours."

"Thanks, Donovan."

"Guys? Don't get riled up. This happens. The moment any artist gains momentum, there's always someone in their past that tries to come up and make trouble. They always want their payday."

"Jesus fuck," Simon muttered.

"Accurately offensive," Donovan said smoothly. "I'll be in touch."

Lila tucked her phone back into her blazer pocket. "Donovan's right. We just have to get ahead of this."

"Ahead of what exactly?"

"William—"

"Snake," they both corrected.

She rolled her eyes. "How am I supposed to call anyone by that name?"

Nick shrugged. "Evidently there was good reason for the nickname."

"Oh God." Her nose wrinkled.

"Yes, that was yelled out a few times," Simon said.

She rubbed two fingers between her brows. "Look, Snake is trying to get a payday on three of the songs that were recorded on the *Burn* EP."

"He really is high," Nick said, wonder in his voice.

"He probably doesn't have a leg to stand on if what you say is true."

"Of course it is," Nick snapped.

She held up a hand. "Nicholas, please. I'm sure you're correct, but when it comes to songs things can get tricky. Did you guys ever copyright your lyrics?"

"Lila, we could barely afford Spaghetti-O's when we were first starting out."

She nodded. "All right. Donovan is going to check into the claim and see if it has a chance in court. If so, we might have to settle—"

"No goddamn way," Nick said. "He's got no claim on our songs."

"Singing a bit of a different tune now, aren't you? Weren't you the one that wanted Snake back in the band?"

"There's a difference between loyalty and fact. We loved that idiot and he was our boy for a long damn time. But when he went away for mandatory rehab, things fell apart. I just didn't want to see it then."

"*We* didn't want to see it," Simon agreed. "We had no idea what a real band was until Gray and Jazz joined up."

"Is that true?"

Simon and Nick both turned around at Jazz's voice. Nick grunted as Jazz flew into his arms and knocked him back a step.

He sighed. "Yeah, Pix. You're stuck with us."

Jazz looped her arms around Nick's waist and looked up at him. "Okay, you're forgiven."

"Forgiven for what?"

"For that bullshit you pulled last year. You're forgiven." Fat tears dripped down her cheeks.

"Aw, man. Don't turn on the waterworks, Jazz." Nick tried to step out of her hug, but she held on tighter and pressed her cheek to his chest.

Nick patted her arm helplessly, giving Simon a look of panic. Nicky hated pure emotion coming at him. He didn't know what to do with it.

"All right, Pix," Simon said. "Let's get you back inside."

"What's going on?"

"Lila's taking care of it."

"That's not an answer," she said and stepped back from Nick.

"Snake's trying to get money out of us."

"No freaking way."

"Not if we have anything to say about it," Nick said.

Lila held out an arm. "Everybody back inside. I'll tell everyone what I know."

Simon followed everyone back in until he spotted Margo heading to the bus.

Margo hiked up the hill to the path that lead to the far side of the park. She needed to walk. It wasn't like she'd specifically kept the news of her work with Oblivion a secret, but she definitely hadn't gone around screaming it.

But a national news show? There was no hiding it now.

Her pocket vibrated, but she ignored it. She was definitely not prepared to talk to anyone. Being swept up into the fun and intensity of a summer tour was one thing, but actually having to explain that to her parents was another thing entirely.

And they didn't even know about that. It was unspoken that she was staying on, but the minute she did the fan club show, it would be common knowledge.

If her parents wanted to know, they'd know.

Hell, Juliet was probably the one texting or calling her right now. She didn't want to share this. Everything about this was just for her. From the unbelievable money to the tingles under her skin when she was up there with these people — that was just for her.

No one, not even her judgmental mother, could take that away.

"Violin Girl, wait up."

She crossed her arms. "Not now, Simon."

She definitely didn't have it in her to figure out what was going on between her and Simon. Whenever she got near him, she lost her damn mind.

What had she been thinking yesterday? She'd seen just how wound up he was, how the alcohol had made him volatile.

And she'd gone after him.

And it had been amazing.

Her insides still throbbed and each move on stage reminded her just how hard he'd fucked her. There was no other word for what they'd done. The ache between her thighs was the proof.

And he'd been the one to walk away that time.

The intensity aside, she was still reeling from the loss of him. Because every other time had felt like she was connecting with someone for the first time, but *that*...

Against the bus had been animalistic and amazing, but had left her so empty.

She wasn't sure what to do about the empty. That didn't seem to fit what they were to each other.

"Damn long legs," he muttered from behind her.

"What do you want? Looking for another angry bang?"

He caught her arm and turned her around. "You were the one who came at me for that one, sweetheart. I warned you that I was in no mood for anyone touching me, even you." He drew her closer. "You were the one who pushed me." His gaze dipped to her mouth then back to her eyes.

"So, what? A repeat performance because of Snake?"

"No." He let her go and stepped back. "Of course not. You seemed upset, so I was checking on you." He held up his hands. "Heaven forbid we have a conversation that doesn't surround us both coming our brains out. Fuck ya later, Violin Girl." He made it halfway down the hill before she called his name. He turned back around, his silvery blue eyes blazing.

She stared at her ballerina flats. "I wasn't expecting to be included in the special."

He climbed the hill again until they were face-to-face. "Is that a problem?"

She shrugged. "Not exactly." She blew out a shaky breath. "My parents aren't exactly welcoming of anything that isn't under their purview of acceptable projects."

"And their baby girl working for a rock band is probably not under that purview."

"No."

"And you care about what they think that much?"

Did she? Or was it just easier to fall in line? The idea of examining that dynamic right now was too daunting.

He rubbed her arms then cupped her jaw to bring her eyes to his. "I don't get the parent thing. I wish I did, but I don't. My old man didn't care. Unless I didn't bring beer home to him at night. Then it was usually a belt to the ribs."

Horrified, she unlocked her arms and laid a hand on his chest.

"Don't feel sorry for me. It is what it is. He didn't want to have anything to do with me so I got out. Music saved me, Margo."

She pressed her cheek into his hand. It had saved her, too. Once upon a time, it had been Vivaldi and Beethoven to keep her happy and whole. But everything was changing now.

Collaborating with Deacon and Gray, and even Nick to a certain extent, had made music exciting again. The fact that she had a say in arrangements and changes to a song was heady.

She'd never allowed herself to think about composing, but now her head was full of it at all times.

"And if I'm reading that beautiful face correctly, *this* is what's making you happy. We can't live for our parents. Then everyone's doomed to disappointment."

"You're pretty intuitive for a—"

His eyebrow winged up. "A…"

"Man."

"Uh-huh."

And because it felt right, she stepped into his arms and laid her cheek against his chest. He froze, then his arms came up around her shoulders until she was completely surrounded.

She waited for the claustrophobic sensations she usually had when anyone hugged her, but they never came. She wasn't sure how long they stayed like that. Her heartbeat synced to his, birds chirped around them, and the breeze ruffled her hair.

When her phone buzzed for the third time, she finally had to break their hold. She sighed and checked the readout. "It's my sister."

"You have a sister?"

She sighed. "Yes."

"Lesser of the two evils?"

She huffed out a laugh. "You could say that."

He traced the back of his knuckles down the center of her neck. "I'll find you later."

She nodded and fought back a shiver. She tapped call back on the missed call, waiting for her sister to pick up as she watched Simon lope down the hill to Deacon and Nick at the top of the pavilion.

"Did you know that was going to be on television, Margo Elizabeth?"

She winced. "Honestly, Jules." When her sister didn't reply, she looked at her phone to make sure the call hadn't dropped. "Juliet?"

Her sister cleared her throat. "I…you just haven't called me that in a really long time, Go-Go."

Margo teared up a little before blinking them away. She and her sister had been so close before she'd joined the Boston Philharmonic. Then it had been nothing but practice and the merry-go-round of auditions for studio work.

"Has Mother said anything?"

"She's currently in her room with the door bolted."

"Really?"

"There may be Xanax involved."

"Great." Margo pinched the bridge of her nose. She had tried to call during the middle of the show, but Margo had ignored the call. And the subsequent two since it ended.

For someone that was as proper as a nun, her mother's dramatics were legendary. She did not miss them in the least.

"Then she should really love the next bit of news. I'm playing with them for the summer leg of the *Rise* tour."

"You're what?"

Margo pulled the phone away from her ear so she didn't hear the rest of the tirade. "Are you done?"

"You can't. I'm sorry, Go-Go, you are not cool enough to tour with a rock band. It...there—just no."

"You should see the purple and green electric cello I got for the tour."

"You what?"

"Is there a parrot in Boston?"

Juliet huffed out an exasperated breath. "How?"

"The money's really good. It's triple what I would make on the studio work I usually get offered."

"And that's all? I've seen you on stage. You love it."

She did. Saying it out loud to Simon had been scary enough. There was no way she could give that kind of information to her sister.

She just couldn't.

As much as she loved Juliet, her sister was not above a little emotional blackmail. Especially since she had so many issues with their mother. Juliet had been in just as many gifted programs as Margo, except her sister got bored and burned bridges in the process.

And not just a little fire that her parents had to put out, more like a nuclear power plant meltdown.

Margo had been the one to follow the right path in her mother's mind. And that was one of the reasons she and Juliet had so many issues.

Her mother's favorite way to start a conversation was, 'Why can't you be more like Margo.'

"It's some of the most interesting work I've done since I was in the Philharmonic."

"Understatement."

"It's a job, Jules."

"You are delusional. You're on stage with all those delicious men, especially Simon Kagan, and you're calling it a job? You're a damn liar."

If only her sister knew just how in deep she was with Simon. Juliet would have a conniption and then hold it over her head for...oh, ever.

"It's exciting. And will bump up my resume for studio work now that I'm not in the BPO."

"You still haven't told Mom about that."

"No. And I won't be. I'll be going on auditions by the end of this tour."

"And being dismissed by Renard isn't going to hurt you there?"

"Has that gotten out yet?" Margo dropped her chin to her chest. Her sister's on-again, off-again boyfriend hated her and had gleefully taken her chair. "Tomas needs to keep his damn mouth closed."

"You know how he is. Vindictive to the end."

"Again, why did you ever date him?"

"His asshole gene came with a certain perk, but even a big dick and twice blessed hips to go with it only goes so far."

"Nice."

"Oh, it is — well, was. I kinda crashed his Ducati into the fountain at the Piazza Navona. Not sure he's going to forgive me for that one. Me and his truly amazing cock may have parted ways for good this time." She paused. "Hmm, I wonder if that's why he ignored Renard's directive."

"You think?"

"Right." Juliet sighed. "Sorry about that."

Margo rolled her eyes heavenward. She didn't sound sorry in the least. And now she'd have to dodge her parents' calls for the foreseeable future. Wonderful.

"Oh, c'mon, Go-Go, you understand, right? Tomas just gets under my skin. I didn't mean to smash his ride but it was so fast and then the wrong side of the road thing. I panicked."

"Juliet, you could have been killed."

"Nah. I was in full gear. I do miss the sex, though. That was legit."

The fact that Margo could legitimately understand the draw of sex for the first time in her twenty-five years was the only thing that kept her from screaming into the phone.

"Was there a purpose in your call or…"

"Wow. A little more chill in that tone and you could sound just like Mother."

"You take that back."

"No. It was the truth."

Horrified, Margo dropped onto the bench near her on the path.

"Dammit. I'm sorry." Juliet rushed on before Margo could answer her. "I didn't mean it. You just make me nutso sometimes. I wanted to know how you wanted to play it. I can run interference."

"And why would you do that?"

"I'm hurt that you would ask that."

Yeah. Sure she was. "What do you want, Jules?"

Her sister huffed out an exaggerated sigh. "I might have mouthed off on my Periscope account that I could get an interview with Simon Kagan."

"Oh, Jules."

"You guys are tight, right? You could get him to do that when you guys are at The Greek."

"And why would you be at that show?"

"I might be staying with my friend Steph for the summer."

"Explain to me how you'd be helping me out with Mother if you're in California?"

"Well, I would be the one answering the phone, of course. And explain that you can't. You know, for work."

Margo groaned. "That's weak."

"And what would your plan be? Just never answering?"

"Yes."

"Lame." Juliet huffed out an exaggerated breath. "At least when I do it I can come up with a decent story. You suck at lying."

"Normally, this isn't a problem."

"No, but under these circumstances, you need me. My version of spin is exceptional and you know it."

"Mother doesn't believe a word out of your lips."

"Yes, but she never calls me on it."

"Your argument is invalid, Jules. And more than lame," she said, throwing her sister's words back at her.

"C'mon, Go-Go! This is a defining moment in our sisterhood here."

Her idea of a defining moment and her sister's were about as far apart as California and New York.

"Does Mom know about the Philharmonic?"

"Yes."

"Perfect." Margo leaned back on the bench.

"I'll let her know about the cattiness in Boston and that you're looking to aim higher."

Except she wasn't. At least not from her mother's point of view. She liked what she was doing—loved it, actually.

"Okay, do that, please. I have to go. Band meeting."

"You're in those?" Jules asked.

"Yes. We're finishing up rehearsals."

"I don't think I can convey just how jealous I am."

"Goodbye, Juliet."

"You suck." And her sister hung up.

Margo pressed her fingers against her throbbing eye. She was officially going to go mad.

Chapter 15

Simon choked down the steeped ginger water with a healthy squeeze of honey in it. It definitely helped. He'd hit all the high notes for the night.

The fan club filled the middle of the arena and Donovan had even arranged to have one-hundred fans from California flown out. The fans paid a pretty penny for the adventure, which Simon still couldn't believe.

He loved music. But these people ponied up over four-hundred dollars for front row seats at the fan club show. Not even a regular show.

They were pretty much playing their playlist for the following night—a practice run of sorts. And honestly, only two songs of the fourteen needed to be rethought. "Torn to Pieces" was a ballad that had Margo in the spotlight, but they'd slowed it down too much. Added too much "Careless Whisper" flavor to it. Awesome for George Michael, but a little too smooth for him.

In fact...

"Hey, Nicky."

"Yeah?" Nick swiped at his sweat-soaked hair with a towel.

"What do you think about doing 'Careless Whisper' before 'The Becoming'?"

Nick tipped his head back and laughed. "So, what, you're George Michael now?"

Simon finished the mug of his heated miracle drug. "No. But come on, that's some sexy shit. We can do it like Seether did. All rocked out. We've done it a million times when we're fucking around with guitars."

"Gray," Nick shouted.

Gray shook off a cup of ice water that he'd poured around his neck and jogged over. "Whew. It is fucking hot."

"Yeah. Goddamn New York," Simon said and lifted his cup. "The grass is going to end me."

"You're killing it, though. So whatever Harper put in there, you need to mainline that shit."

Simon shook his head at the drug reference. Gray made them all the damn time and there was always a little sparkle in his eye about it. Fucker. "No shit, man."

Nick nodded to him. "This guy wants to do 'Careless Whisper' before 'The Becoming'."

Gray draped his wet towel over his neck. "Really?"

"The Seether version."

"Oh." Gray stretched his hand above his head and rolled his shoulder. "That could work."

"I have a cello piece for that."

Simon turned to Margo. "Yeah?"

"If I did it all classy and low and then Nick or Gray came in with the huge guitar opener—I think that would punch it up even more."

"I like it." Simon waved at Deacon. "Big D, Pix—c'mere."

Jazz tucked herself under Gray's arm and stole his towel. She had a babydoll top made from a bra and sparkly sheer material over her belly and hot pink bike shorts. How she made that work, Simon would never know, but it did. Her outfits always did. Give Pix enough time and she'd have a maternity wear clothing line made up, for fuck's sake.

They argued over the opening and closing of the song for two minutes then they were all rushing up the stairs to do the encore.

The sun was setting along the skyline through the trees and people were screaming for them. On their feet and losing their minds as they all got to their places.

The stage went dark and Margo stood in the diffused light, drawing her bow over her cello in an eerie rendition of the sax parts from the iconic Wham song. Their spot guy, Randy—Harper's brother—was the most intuitive guy he'd ever seen.

The moody blue lights softened to white at the end before he blinked over to Simon. He kept the opening verse of the song soft and smooth like the original and then Nick and Gray both came up and powerhoused the guitars, Jazz joining in on the drums until the entire arena was screaming.

Simon followed Deacon as he always did. He turned his voice into a growl and forced himself not to tense. The ginger had done its job and relaxed the tickle in his throat.

He stalked across the stage and dropped to his knees in front of the first row as the song ended and they did a medley into "The Becoming".

By the time they'd finished that song and ended on "The Boys are Back in Town", the pavilion was completely off their feet and every bit of rehearsal had been worth it.

"Fuck, yeah!" Simon yelled and they all came forward for the bows.

That was the way to do it. They all waved and scattered for backstage. Part of the fan package was a meet and greet afterward. There was a pile of records waiting for everyone that had come.

All three hundred of them would get a signed copy and picture with the band.

Simon ran for the showers and steamed up the whole house. His skin was still slick from sweat and he didn't want to think about how much bug juice was on him from all the fuckers he'd swatted at.

But he needed it.

And as his vocal chords opened, he breathed a sigh of relief. He was getting the hang of this professional singer shit.

Maybe, just maybe he'd have it all figured out.

He met everyone back at the room they'd corded off to control the crowd. Six huge boxes were lined up behind them. A flag version of his jungle gym archway was tacked up on a huge accordion-style divider.

Lila, being Lila, had a professional photographer there with equipment. And another videographer was following around Jazz.

She'd upgraded from an iPhone to a little handheld camera that indie directors used, for God's sake. It was unreal how different it was to go from opening act to headliner.

Margo was off to the side, her huge dark eyes taking in everything. So much a part of them and still so separate. At first, he'd pushed to include her, but she seemed to like to be on the fringes.

She wore a sheer long skirted dress that reminded him of a ballerina with tight leggings under it. And over it was a scarlet bit of nothing that matched her fuckable mouth.

Christ.

He forced his eyes away from her.

She was already so different from the woman he'd met in the studio that long ago summer. She smiled more, her shoulders didn't look so tense, and goddamn if she wasn't the sexiest thing he'd ever seen.

Lila clapped. "All right, guys. You ready for the first wave?"

"Are we allowed to say no?" Nick asked.

"Um…no."

Nick gave a gusty sigh. "Then let the games begin."

The first group of twenty poured in, definitely averaging high on vaginas, but he was glad to see some dudes.

They wrote their songs to cover both sexes, but women were the ones that usually wanted the backstage packages.

He shook out his bracelets and rolled his shoulders as a pair of Barbie dolls headed his way. Ready for vapid squeeing, he was surprised to get a natural smile from the unbelievably pretty sisters.

Maybe it wasn't going to be such a long night, after all.

"Hi, ladies."

"That show was so amazing. I can't believe you guys did that for the fan club. We're so freaking excited."

"Well, get in here and get that excitement all over me," he said with a waggle of eyebrows.

By the time he'd smiled and hugged his last set of fans, he was ready for another shower, and his head was pounding from the mix of perfumes and colognes.

Simon fell into the leather couch they'd stashed against the wall. "Jesus fuck, how many people was that?"

"Three-hundred-and-eight," Gray answered from across the room.

"How do you do that?"

Gray shrugged. "Just can, man." Jazz was sitting across from him on the other couch and he was rubbing her feet.

"I've got a little something for you guys." Harper pushed a cart in. "I know the singing types aren't supposed to do dairy, but they didn't say anything about Sno-cones."

Simon laughed as their resident chef scooped shaved ice into little cups and wielded a rainbow of flavors.

Exactly what they needed after the heat of the day and night, he decided as he stood behind Nick and scooped out a handful of ice.

Margo hid behind the couch that had been pushed into the center of the room like a bunker. She looked over her shoulder to make sure no one was going to ambush her from behind.

She reached her hand into her bra to scoop out ice. Deacon had already dive-bombed her from above. Damn giant.

She shook her cup but her weapons were low…and melty. A trip to the basin of ice was in order, but Jazz and Gray had teamed up to guard that.

They were ninjas.

"Nick, where are you?" she called out.

"Your six."

She turned around and saw the ice ball coming her way and ducked just as it slapped into the couch. "And here I was going to play Black Widow to your Hawkeye."

Nick peeked up from his hiding spot. "Really? Do I get to know what happened in Budapest?"

She aimed and caught him in the neck. "You wish." She kept her face expressionless as Lila came up behind him.

"You little…" Nick scooted forward to get to the next hiding spot. "I need reinforcements."

"Nope." Lila poured a five gallon bucket of water over Nick's head.

"Cheater," Nick roared.

"Absolutely," Margo said and crossed to high five an equally drenched Lila.

"Cheaters never win," Simon and Deacon shouted and the entire pan of leftover ice came their way.

She and Lila shrieked and crouched.

"Holy shit," Lila said with chattering teeth. "And to think I was crying about how hot I was an hour ago."

Margo sluiced water off her face and flipped back her hair. "There will be retribution, boys."

"Bring it."

Harper came in with three mops and a bucket. "Enough! I bring you people treats and this is the thanks I get."

Deacon headed her way with a cup of ice behind his back.

"And if you think that ice is going down your pregnant wife's back, you will be sleeping alone!"

"Aww, c'mon," Deacon said.

She pushed a mop into his hands. Turned to Simon and Nick with the other two.

"This is sexist," Simon said.

"No. This is your mess to clean up. You started it, Simon."

"I did not."

Harper's eyebrow rose. "You were the one who dropped a handful down Nick's shirt. I saw it. You were the instigator."

"Dammit."

"Gray take Pix to get her cleaned up."

"How come they don't have to clean up?"

"Because, Pretty Boy, Jazz has been on her feet too long. I got to sit while you guys were doing photo-ops."

Simon growled.

"Chop, chop." Harper turned toward the kitchen. She held a finger up. "If I come back in here and you guys left the room a mess, you will never live through my retribution."

"Would she really be that bad?" Simon asked.

"You don't even know," Deacon answered.

Margo helped Lila push the furniture back to where it belonged and collect the leftover fan club memorabilia. "You guys are kind of amazing."

Lila shook out her wet hair. "We do all right. These guys are still excited about everything. It helps for all the fan stuff."

"True."

"So, you're going to stay with the tour?"

Margo looked up. "I want to. If they'll have me," she said on a low voice.

Lila smiled. "No need to whisper. They're excited. The thing is you have to decide if you're going to stay with me at the hotel—which I don't mind—or take the bus with the guys."

"With Simon and Nick?"

"I doubt you want to take the baby central bus."

"Um, no."

Lila grinned. "Didn't think so."

The idea of being on the same bus as Simon had her stomach swirling and her head spinning. "Can I take a look at it first?"

"Sure."

Margo glanced at the three guys mopping. "They look like they actually know what they're doing."

"Bars. Lots and lots of bars."

"That makes sense."

"Doesn't it?" Lila nodded to the doorway. "Let's go take a look at testosterone express."

"I'm probably asking too much for an ounce of privacy."

"You are correct." Lila laughed and took the stairs to the side of the venue where the busses were parked. "But it's a lot nicer than their first bus."

Margo followed Lila onto the bus. It was huge. The front was fashioned with a chair that she was sure bus drivers in the city would drool over. Then there was a rather large common area that had couches on either side beneath the tinted windows.

Lila pressed in a knob at the front of the bus and revealed a guitar holder and shelving units full of notebooks and pens. There was another holder on the door for another guitar, or maybe one of her violins.

"They do a lot of writing on the road. Passes the time." She nodded to the bottom shelf. "Simon is forever drawing so be careful if you have your own notebook. He's a thief."

Margo laughed. "I'll remember that."

"The couches convert to a larger mattress." She pulled down a hidden handle and slid the couch cushion out like a trundle bed. "I try not to think about what they could possibly do on those things, but it's usually reserved for extra guests on the bus. A family member coming to visit, that sort of deal."

Margo's eyes widened. A groupie banging station. Well, that was a different way to look at things.

Lila rolled her eyes. "Yeah. As I said, don't think about it too much or you will end up carrying around a can of Lysol."

"Too late."

"Kitchenette and microwave." She opened slim cupboards that were remarkably deep. "Just let me know what kind of thing you want." She reached up to the top. "This one is a freezer, so you can get little dinners for the long rides."

"You think of everything."

"My job." Lila kept moving. "And back here are the bunks. This bus was outfitted for four, so you can pick up or down."

"They didn't spread out?"

Lila shrugged. "They have their rituals."

She peeked into the bunk. It was plenty big enough to sleep in and long enough for her height. That was something new.

"Bathroom there."

Margo opened the door, expecting a closet but found a huge glass shower, a commode, and a sink. "Holy crap."

"Yeah, all the guys ever asked for was a better bathroom, so we went with really nice."

"I think that's bigger than my second bathroom in my house."

Lila laughed. "So there you have it. You can stay with me or with the heathens."

The idea of rooming with Lila had merit. They got along well and both tended toward the quiet. But if she was on the bus with Simon and Nick, she might be able to see how they wrote together.

Watch the build of a song from the ground up.

She also got the dirty socks and unfortunate bodily functions of males in the con column.

But to be surrounded by music again? A different kind of music?

"I can see it on your face."

"The music thing."

Lila nodded. "You've got the bug. I can see it. Nick can be a little peckish about sharing when it comes to music, but I bet you can get around him. Simon…he is always scribbling. He had no problem collaborating."

"It seems like it could be amazing."

"The only thing I will tell you is…being a woman and knowing what's going on because I have eyes."

Margo crossed her arms over her chest.

"Drop the defensive act. We all know you and Simon are…" She waved her hand. "Doing stuff."

"Great."

"It's no big deal. I would just recommend that you keep it off the bus. Things can get hairy and this should be a safe haven for you and for everyone."

Margo relaxed. "That's a good idea, actually."

"I have them."

"That you do."

"Okay, let's go get your stuff from my hotel room and get you settled."

"Good deal."

They turned and Simon stood in the doorway. "Ladies."

"You have a new roommate."

Simon's eyes fired then did that slumberous *I-just-got-out-of-bed* thing and Margo's skin prickled with goosebumps. Definitely keeping sex off the bus.

"Welcome aboard, Violin Girl."

"Thanks," she said quietly.

"Hurry back, now. I love bedtime stories."

"Simon," Lila warned.

"What?" He grinned.

Keeping sex off the bus was going to require Herculean strength.

Definitely.

DESTROYED

Chapter 16

Simon blew on his mug of ginger honey tea and stared out the window. The lush green crept out from the median and along the sides of the highway. With them heading across the country, he wasn't sure how much longer they'd have green and vibrant instead of brown from lack of rain.

He grinned as the Brooklyn Dawn bus passed them with a yawning Jamie sitting in the sun. They didn't have the super-tinted windows that Oblivion's bus did and were probably dying. The sun had been ruthless for the last few days. It was mid-June and they were entering the fourth week of the tour.

As much as the thick heat of Georgia hurt to think about, he'd appreciated the heavy moisture. His throat did, especially. His vocal cords had actually felt well-lubricated.

The outdoor amphitheaters were dry as dust in most towns. Of course the Midwest was having a record-breaking heat wave, and that's where they were headed next.

"Morning."

Simon's gaze swiveled to Margo and he swallowed a groan. The heat meant Margo wore a helluva lot less than she usually did. Like the boxer shorts and racerback tank top she habitually wore to sleep.

God help him.

They'd both agreed to keep sex off the bus. Well, mostly he'd gotten the directive from Margo, but knowing it was only Nick on the bus with them gave him the heebs.

No need to step into that arena with him. Things had been different a few years ago. The women he'd hooked up with had been transient. This was a whole different kind of...thing.

It wasn't a relationship. It was more like frenetic sex in any and all available places. Last night had been in the stairwell between the venue and the locker room.

Christ, she'd tried to blow the top of his head off when she'd pushed him against the wall and sucked him off in three minutes flat. Then walked away with a flick of her tongue at the corner of her mouth.

His cum.

There, on the edge of her mouth. And she'd neatly licked her lips clean and went about her business.

Now she would sit across from him on the bus in her all purple night clothes and he wasn't supposed to jump her.

How had his life come to this?

"Sleep all right?"

She nodded and unwound the braid she always wore to bed. Her eyes were heavy and her cheeks rosy with fresh creases on them from her pillow.

She was fucking beautiful without a lick of makeup on.

It was disgusting.

"How long until we arrive, Joe?" Margo asked.

"You've got a good six hours, Miss Margo."

She tipped her head back. "Ugh. I should have slept longer." With a disgusted groan, she stood and rummaged through the coffee cupboard. "What are you working on?"

"Nothing." Simon looked down at his notebook. He'd been scribbling lyrics in the margins, but none of them went together. A verse, then a bridge of another song and a chorus of yet another.

None of them were good either.

In the middle was an owl that looked more like a dragon in disguise. He was pretty fucked up. Probably because he'd started it in his bunk last night when he'd had too much wine.

Damn Lila for bringing wine onto the tour. He was enjoying it more than booze lately. There had to be something wrong with him.

"Doesn't look like nothing." She tipped her head. "Looks like one of the little guys from *How to Train Your Dragon.*"

"Yes. Thank you. I couldn't figure out how I'd come up with it."

"We were on a cartoon kick last week."

"Yes, you made us watch *Tangled* four times."

She smirked over her shoulder as she added milk to her coffee. "You know you liked it."

He and Nick had watched it a fifth time without her, but she didn't need to know that. "More like we were thinking up ways she could use her hair for more than its healing properties."

"Perv."

"Indeed."

She picked up the remote. "Want to watch *Charmed*?"

Simon stretched out his legs on the couch. "I do love me some Piper Halliwell."

"Really? I thought you liked Phoebe."

"Nah, I like the one who can blow up shit."

"Huh." She curled onto her couch and hit play on their Netflix account. "You surprise me sometimes."

"Yeah, well, you surprise me every day."

She turned her attention to him and gave him her half frown, half smile thing. It was so cute because it made her freckly nose scrunch up.

They passed the time watching the three witch sisters blow up shit, discover Phoebe's boyfriend was a demon, and help random idiots in every episode.

Somehow scintillating stuff.

Nick came out during hour two and watched with them.

"Okay boys and girl. T-minus thirty."

Margo jumped up off the couch and sprinted for the showers.

Nick stood. "No...dammit." The door slammed and the snick of the lock made him groan. "Every time."

"I'm getting to like cold showers."

Nick snorted. "You need them for a whole different reason."

Simon turned in his seat, spreading his arms across the length of the couch. "It's hard being me."

"Oh yeah, hardship of the ages."

"You don't know."

Nick rolled his eyes. "You want to take the interview for the radio station or me?"

"I'll get the one after the show."

Nick nodded. "Sounds good."

By the time they pulled into Alpharetta, he and Nick had a game plan and a setlist.

"So, no on 'Lit' and 'Taste of Candy'?"

Simon shrugged. "Not feeling 'Lit' lately. If you want to do a 'Taste of Candy/Sugar Kiss' medley, that's cool."

"Hmm. Maybe." Nick scribbled in the little Moleskin notebook he kept in his pocket at all times. It had every setlist from the start of the tour in it. And his off the wall grading system, as well.

Margo scooted across the narrow passage between the bathroom and her bunk, flashing a lot of leg.

Christ. Damp Margo did not need to be in his head today.

He stood and grabbed a baseball cap from the overhead bin. "I'll grab a shower later. I'm going to sweat as soon as I walk out that door."

Nick nodded. "I'll see you in there."

He slapped Joe on the shoulder on his way by. "You are the man."

Joe grunted which made Simon grin. They traded off between Joe and the new driver, Bobby. He knew Joe preferred to drive the baby bus. Mostly because he was in love with Pix, like an indulgent father with an impending grandbaby. The man was fiercely loyal to Jazz and to a lesser extent, Harper.

He hopped off the last stair and caught sight of Jamie and David from Brooklyn Dawn. "Hey guys."

Jamison DuCaine pushed her jet black and red-streaked hair over her shoulder. "You're up before noon. What's wrong, forgot to go to bed?"

"I should ask the same. You were drinking me glass for glass of that California white last night, DuCaine."

"Yeah, well it was a cool one hundred degrees on the bus. I couldn't sleep." She tugged her sunglasses down her nose. "Besides, wine is for pussies. May as well be drinking grape juice."

Simon barked out a laugh. "Nice. It worked for me."

Jamie put her shades back on. "That's because you pickled your liver with vodka, man. You can't hang with the big kids anymore."

"I'm literally two years older than you."

"I know, so old."

Simon shook his head. "You are a cruel, cruel woman."

"You have no idea, Pretty Boy."

Simon sagged his shoulders. "I'm going to kill whoever told you that nickname."

"You'd have to kill quite a few of your bandmates. They all call you that."

"Bastards, all of you." Simon called out to the group standing near the side entrance to the venue.

The two pregnant ladies just wiggled their butts at him.

"Nice."

They were wearing matching denim overalls with tank tops, Harper in red and Jazz in screaming yellow. He hated to admit that they were adorable. As long as they weren't in his bus they were adorable, anyway.

Simon climbed the stairs to the backstage area and paused when he saw Lila and Donovan both there. Well, that wasn't good.

"What's up, guys?" Simon asked as he met with the rest of the group. "Where Nicholas?"

Really not good. Simon tipped back his hat. "He was getting dressed."

Lila pulled out her phone and typed before slipping it back in her pocket. "All right. As soon as he gets here, we're going to talk."

"Is there something wrong?" Jazz wound her arm around Gray's.

"The whole band should be here for this," Lila said. She looked up at Donovan. "There's a small room over there we can use."

Jamie pushed her sunglasses onto her head as she walked by with a frown.

"Why do I feel like I'm going to the principal's office?" Deacon asked.

Simon snorted. "Like you were ever in detention, St. Deacon."

"That's what you think."

Simon's eyebrows shot up. "Well, well. Looks like I might have to ply you with shots tonight, Big D."

"Unlikely."

Simon made a face at his back. He followed everyone in and sprawled in a folding chair.

Nick came in five minutes later with his wet blond hair slicked back. "Oh, shit," he said and stared at Donovan. He sat down next to Simon. "What's the suit doing here?" he whispered.

Simon shrugged.

Donovan nodded to Nick and dipped his hand into his pocket. "As you know the lawsuit with William—I'm sorry, Snake—has been a beastly bit of business. I know he used to be a mate, but at this point, we'll have to cut off any talks with him."

Nick shrank down in his chair.

Simon nudged him. "You haven't."

"He's texted me a few times."

"Christ, Nicky."

"What was I supposed to do?"

"Mr. Crandall?"

Nick sat up. "Yes?"

"If this goes to trial, you're on the list for the plaintiff."

"I'm not great with the legal-speak, but did you just say I'm on Snake's side?"

Donovan tapped his steepled fingers together. "No. But whatever they have to bring to court on this will hinge on your testimony."

Nick stood. "I didn't do anything."

Lila held up a hand. "He's not saying that. But whatever Snake has up his sleeve will have something to do with something you said."

"That sure sounds like I did something."

Donovan touched her arm. "I don't like where this is going. I'm still convinced he doesn't have enough to win, but a sob story and a tough jury in a civil suit don't always go together. I think we should settle."

"Fuck that." Nick swiped his hand through the air. "I felt bad that we replaced him with Jazz, but last year we saw just how little he cared about the actual band. He wanted us to go back to the old days when we played clubs and partied, not the actual work that goes into this shit."

Donovan's eyebrow arched.

Simon swallowed a snort.

"Okay, it's not shit, but you know what I mean."

"Yes, Nick, I know what you mean," Donovan said. "But even that statement right there could be twisted in a few different ways if he has a good lawyer. And he's got a bit of a shark who's always looking to make headlines."

"Awesome," Nick muttered and dropped back into his seat.

"We just have to be smart. Is it worth the legal fees and getting dragged through court or do we give him the seventy-five thousand dollars he's asking for?"

"The—" Simon sat forward. "How much?"

"It's not a lot of money compared to what you're making on the tour and his lawyer knows this. Sales of the albums are pennies compared to what goes on here with the tour. And we've just added another ten dates."

Simon swallowed down against the tickle that was forever plaguing him these days. He probably peed ginger and honey with how much he drank it, for fuck's sake.

And now ten more dates?

He rested his elbows on his knees and stared at the floor as everyone started talking.

"There is no way in hell we're settling or giving him a damn dime," Nick said above everyone.

"Okay, okay. Just calm down. We were hoping to keep this from becoming any bigger, but I get it. We get it," Lila said and waved a finger between herself and Donovan.

Nick doubled his fists. "If he had any part in writing it, I wouldn't be such a dick, but he didn't."

"Then we'll fight it," Donovan said.

Nick's shoulders and fingers relaxed. Simon sat back in his chair in reaction to his best friend calming down. The idea that everyone in this room had something to lose because of Snake — again — was just insane.

When was their past going to stop biting them on the ass?

"Now for the good news." Donovan pulled envelopes out of his suit jacket.

"Pink slips?" Nick quipped.

"No. I think you'll find that this is much more to your liking, Mr. Crandall."

Donovan walked around the room and handed everyone a sealed envelope. "I don't usually do this sort of thing with all this ceremony, but we've come a long way from that tense meeting a year ago."

Understatement. Simon stared at the envelope, unsure if he really wanted to know what was inside. It felt bigger than just a check or a contract.

"Well, go on. Open it up."

The sound of paper tearing and unfolding was the only noise for about three seconds.

"Holy shit," Jazz shrieked and bounced to her feet for a step before plowing into Gray and strangling him.

"Okay, babe, one sec. I didn't even — well, shit." Gray's voice was half whisper, half shout. Something that only he could pull off.

Simon flipped open the corner of his envelope and tore off the end. He pulled out two pieces of paper. The first one was a series of numbers with a fuckton of zeroes and then on page two they were all added together with a bank account number.

A metric fuckton of zeroes.

He was pretty sure his gut just liquefied.

"As you can see, the tour is going well, which is why we added the dates." Donovan turned his attention to Jazz. "That's if you can manage it, of course."

Jazz patted her belly. "Is this extending the tour?"

"No, just within the end dates we've established."

"Then it's fine. I don't need to rehearse as much as everyone else since Margo has taken the piano pieces this past week. And the kiddo loves when Mommy drums for two hours a night."

"Excellent. Any of the video things you can't handle just let Lila know and we'll make other arrangements. Simon and Nick do well with the interviews."

Simon drew in a slow breath and let it out. *Awesome.* Then he looked down at the bank statement in his hands and couldn't even complain in his head.

Fuck. Ton. Of. Zeroes.

"I set up accounts for you and if you go the route of an accountant or financial advisor, which I recommend you look into, then it can be transferred anywhere you wish. But with that kind of money, it needs to be protected."

That kind of money didn't even compute. Being on tour they didn't really worry about money. Harper took care of their feeding and the bus was for sleeping. Booze seemed to appear upon request.

It wasn't real life, but he sure as shit had gotten used to it fast. Especially since he'd been used to having next to nothing all his life.

He looked over at Nick, who was the only one not chattering excitedly. He had the paper trapped against his chest with his arms folded.

Simon slapped him in the arm. "You know that piece of paper was good news, right? Not that you owed that total. *Paid,* son."

Nick swallowed, and blew out a breath. His mouth tipped up at the corner. "Yeah. I can't even…that number doesn't even look real." He stood up and slipped out the door as everyone else talked over one another.

Simon caught Lila's worried gaze and he waved her off. He followed after him. "Nicky, don't get all…Nicky."

"I'm not. I just—it's happening really fast, man."

Simon leaned a shoulder against the wall. "Not really. We've been scrimping and hoping for a long time. This is a good thing."

Nick tapped the paper. "I know. I know."

"Then don't get all upset about it. This is cause for a celebration. And a car."

Nick laughed. "Two cars."

"A house."

"Fuck. I don't even know what to think about that. I don't want to leave the Hills, man."

"So, don't."

"What are you going to do with your money?"

Simon took off his hat and scrubbed at his hair. "I don't even know what a financial advisor does besides gamble with your money."

"We suck at gambling."

Simon laughed. "No shit. But man, imagine going into some badass casino like Bond and putting down one of those million dollar chips?"

"Fuck yeah," Nick said on a laugh.

Simon slapped him on the back of his neck and steered him down the hall. "This requires day drinking."

"So much day drinking."

Margo dragged her shredded bow over the strings of her Starfish. She had so much fiber blowing around her wrists, she was probably going to have to get it restrung.

But she didn't let up. Her arm screamed and her fingers were numb from trying to keep up with Nick's guitar. Bent at the waist and as tense as her strings, she spit out heat and passion from every note.

She stared him down as he lowered to meet her gaze. The crowd was screaming and the sweat coated her from neck to ankle in the Georgia heat.

Simon skidded onto his knees between them and bowed back, his chest slick with sweat. His abs quivered with each bounce.

Jesus.

He held the note. The long cry of "Torn to Pieces" last verse emptied her out and his vibrato was flawless. Her eyes widened and then he popped up, his chest heaving.

She blinked out of the surprise and shredded another length of her bow as Nick waggled his eyebrows and stood tall.

Out of breath and so turned on she couldn't even stand herself, she staggered back and caught her heel on the cord behind her.

Simon rose off his knees and scooped her up. He dropped the mic into her lap and she juggled it with her violin and bow as he brought her to the front of the stage. He lowered his mouth to her chest. "And I rescue damsels, too."

"You wish."

Delighted, she clapped as the deafening roar of the crowd surged and the people on the lawn stood. Okay, so it was cute, but not that funny. She looked over her shoulder and Deacon stood behind her.

"Is this man bothering you?"

She laughed and wrapped her arm around Simon's neck in a mock clingy damsel reaction. "He's my hero," she said in her best Marilyn voice.

Jazz beat the shit out of her skins and Nick picked out the first notes of "Holding Out For a Hero."

Gray leaned into the mic and sang the opening verse in a surprisingly husky, deep voice.

Simon put her down and turned around with his hands on his hips. "Hold up, hold up." He waved. "Excuse me, sir." The crowd screamed from behind him.

Gray cleared his throat. "Yes?"

"I don't believe we allowed such nonsense. I'm the singer, boyo."

Gray peered around Simon. "Is it okay if I sing?" He looked back at Simon. "I think they like it."

Suddenly the piano tones of the song started. Margo twisted around and Lindsey York from Brooklyn Dawn was on the keys.

Simon stalked around the stage in a fake temper and the crowd went insane. Margo fit her violin to chin and twisted her pins to loosen the strings slightly. She bounced her bow against the strings until it made a similar sound to an old eighties tone.

By the end of the song, they'd all dissolved into a fit of hysterics and Simon was hanging off the archway by the knees with his arms crossed, fake sleeping.

Lindsey waved as the song ended and she ran backstage. Simon snorted into the mic. "Oh, are you done now? Do I get to sing again?"

The crowd screamed back a resounding *yes*, and they finished the show with every single person in the pavilion on their feet and half the lawn crowding the railing.

The reaction was so strong that they actually ended up doing a second encore. By the third song in the encore, Simon was pulling away from the microphone and coughing into his elbow.

He covered it up as laughter at Nick climbing all over Jazz's drum kit to get to the ramp behind her.

But she saw his eyes.

The flash of pain and the crack at the end of "Summer of '69" made even her throat hurt. They finally took their bows and all hugged like drunk puppies.

Simon slid his forefinger through the frown of her brows and hung his arm around her neck as he dragged her off the stage with the rest of the band.

The backstage was in an uproar and Lila was fielding a phone call and shaking her head at them as they all filed into the after show room that Harper had set up.

She went right for the watermelon, completely a convert of Harper's hydration system. She was dizzy from exhaustion and sweating out eighteen buckets of fluid.

The whole band fell on the melon and water like wolves, moving onto food as they excitedly recapped the show.

"Good thing the ticket sales were good enough to cover that fine I just had to pay," Lila said loudly.

Nick had switched out from water to beer. "Oops?"

"Yeah, *oops*. You went well over the midnight curfew for the park, kids."

Gray looked down at his phone. "Shit, three hours?"

"Yes, three hours."

No wonder she was still sucking down bottles of water to recover. Margo held a hand over her middle and laughed with everyone.

Poor Simon had dealt with three nights of long shows. By some slice of a miracle he'd still sounded good—well, until the very end.

She looked around, but he was gone. He'd been quiet, but after the shows he tended to be. Not because he was depressed, but lately Simon had turned into a watcher after the main event was over.

Watching everyone, taking everything in. Watching *her*. Always watching her.

She tried to ignore it. Ignore him. Some nights she had to disappear for her own general well-being. Because when they got into the same sphere, there was too much between them. They required the buffer of the rest of the band. Or she required it.

She just wasn't sure anymore.

But he was hurting tonight. She could feel it in her bones like she felt a song, like she lived a melody on stage.

She passed the lockers, but the room was empty. Sometimes he escaped to steam his vocal chords. She knew he didn't want her to know that. Didn't want anyone to know it.

Everyone was still too euphoric about the success of the tour to notice the little flubs here and there. But she saw the signs. Hell, she knew them better than anyone. Her friend Siobhan was a jazz singer and had been through three bouts of complete vocal rest when she'd toured too hard.

"Margo?"

She jumped. "Geeze." For someone who habitually wore stilettos, Lila could be surprisingly stealthy. "Don't sneak up on a girl."

Lila leaned against the wall in the hallway. "I didn't realize we were being sneaky."

"No. I'm not."

"Is it booty time?"

Margo scrunched her eyes closed. "Really?"

"Am I lying?"

Margo crossed her arms over her chest and sighed. "No."

"About which?"

"I'm not being sneaky and I'm not looking to bag some naked Simon time."

Lila's eyebrows shot up. "You have been hanging out with these guys too much. You're starting to sound like them."

She straightened. "I do?"

"Yeah, you do."

"That's bad."

"Eh. Depends on your point of view. You smile and laugh a lot more these days."

"Oh."

Lila smirked and rolled her eyes. "What are you doing?"

"I'm looking for Simon." She held up her hand. "Not for what you think." At her skeptical look, Margo rushed on. "He pushed it tonight and after two long shows, I think he's…"

Lila stood up straight and her blue eyes went laser-sharp. "He's what?"

Margo tapped her middle finger to her thumbnail. "His voice cracked."

"Is that all? That happens all the time with singers."

"Not Simon."

"What makes him so special?" Lila asked with a bored look.

"Look, I work with the orchestra and a lot of different vocalists. Simon's a natural. No training, at least I'm pretty sure no training."

"Not that I know of."

"Instinctively, he just finds the right notes to any song. It's pretty genius, actually." Margo held up a finger. "If you tell him that, I'll break the heel off your pink Jimmy Choos."

"Wow. Don't hate on my Jimmys."

"Anyway. He's definitely straining. He rocked out tonight. Totally rocked out. I've never heard his vibrato so well-timed since the first week of the tour."

"That's a good thing."

"Yeah, it is. But he got a little cocky on stage when they were having so much fun. We all did. I swear my triceps are still crying from all the high speed playing I did tonight." She rubbed her arm as the ache came to the surface at the mention.

"So, he needs to relax tonight."

"No. I think he needs more than that."

"We have a show in Indianapolis tomorrow."

"Right, but maybe you should let him sit out on interviews tomorrow."

Lila sighed and pulled out her phone. "I don't know if I can. The radio stations want him and they have an acoustic set in the park."

Margo shut her eyes.

"I'm fine, Violin Girl."

Margo's shoulders instantly tightened. "Simon, I…"

"I appreciate it. I do. It's been a big week, but I'll be fine." His voice was as rough as sandpaper and he barely spoke above a whisper.

Lila frowned. "Are you sure?"

"Yeah. I asked Harper to steep me a pot of my tea and I'm going to go back to the bus and sleep."

"I can shuffle a few things—"

"No. It's fine. I'm fine." He swung his gaze to Margo. "I just won't be talking tonight or tomorrow until the radio show."

Lila nodded. "Right. Okay. I'm going to…go."

Margo folded her arms. "I'm sorry."

Simon seemed relaxed and tired, but he wouldn't look at her. And she was learning he was a better actor than she thought.

He shrugged. "Just watching out for me."

She stepped forward and curled her fingers around his hand. "You were amazing tonight. You didn't hear me say that part."

"No, just the part where I sucked."

She jammed her molars together and forced down a growl. "Nothing about your performance tonight sucked."

"Except that last part, right?" he whispered. He cleared his throat and swallowed, his eyes still not meeting hers.

She lifted her hand to his chest and he held up his hands. "Not now." He headed down the hall.

She stomped her foot, unable to help her reaction. God, he frustrated her. "Simon, wait."

He looked at his feet, but he stopped.

She hurried after him and stood in front of him, lowering her knees until she could catch his gaze, but he wouldn't look at her. "I just don't want you to overdo it." She cupped his jaw and shook him a little.

His fierce winter blue gaze crashed into hers.

"I care, Simon." She tipped her head up and rose onto her toes. He didn't close his eyes as she brushed her lips over his. His fingers tightened on her hip, but he simply watched her as she lightly touched his mouth. She stroked his lower lip with the tip of her tongue, and then nipped his upper lip lightly.

"I wouldn't have told Lila except she's overscheduling you to compensate for Jazz. But no one's thinking about you," she said lightly against his mouth.

"And you are?"

She nodded and swiped her tongue in between his lips until he sucked her deeper, until his arms came up around her and squashed her against his chest.

He went from stillness to intense in the space of a heartbeat. He pushed her down the hallway and across the hall to the lockers.

He slammed the door and snicked the lock closed. No corridor this time, just tiles and the echo of their harsh breathing as he attacked her neck, his teeth clicking against the rose and filigree leaves of her ear cuff.

She groaned as he swiped his tongue over the space behind her ear, then over her fluttering pulse. The tiny nip of his teeth made her shudder.

The mark would be small. The tiniest star-sized bruise. But she had three there, for three nights that she'd taken him like this.

In secret, in hidden spaces around the venues they'd been at every evening.

He pushed at the short A-line skirt she wore and groaned when he found the crotchless hose she was wearing. He crouched down in front of her and breathed over the three inches of skin that showed between the top of the garter-style hose and the band around her thigh.

He dug the tip of his tongue through the see-through lace she wore. "Fuck."

It wasn't a whisper, it was a sharp, hard *K* that she heard over everything else.

The rasp of his tongue at her clit made her squirm. Just that. All it took was his breath on her and she was as wet as if they'd spent an hour in foreplay.

He rose and stared into her eyes as he pushed the scrap of panties aside and slipped his two middle fingers inside her. She wanted to close her eyes, to lose herself in the moment and the pleasure, but she couldn't.

She watched his intense face as he thrust those fingers inside her again and again. The way his shoulder muscles flexed, the way his Adam's apple bobbed with each swallow, and the sounds.

She whimpered at the sounds echoing around the tile. Her needy sounds that made her cringe warred with the way her body opened and soaked his fingers. Always for him.

As if he was the single key to her lock.

She did close her eyes at that thought. He twisted his fingers so that his thumb came up and circled her clit until the little sounds turned to a sob.

With his other hand, he struggled with his zipper.

And finally, when she got her hands to work, she went for his button and found a button fly, not a zipper. The satisfying rending of buttons through their respective holes revved her higher.

"Inside me. Please."

He palmed one of the condoms he always had on him from his pocket and stuck it between his teeth. He lifted one eyebrow and she stole it, jerking the plastic open.

"Shit." She'd never actually had to put one on before.

His lips spread into a smirk. "Trampoline," he whispered.

She looked down and flipped it, holding the tip as she firmly and slowly pushed it down his length. His face went from smirky to serious as she circled the base of his cock tightly.

"Inside," she said.

He withdrew his fingers and pulled her knee up on his hip. These were the perfect moments when she loved her height. When they lined up like this.

He bent his knees enough to drag the head of his cock along her slit, rocking it up and over her clit in a wide, slick circle before he tucked himself inside her and lifted her onto her toes with the force of the thrust.

"God, yes."

She gripped his shoulders and took each punishing slam of his hips, each dragging stroke as he found that spot deep inside and exploited it. Nothing else existed but the sounds of slapping skin and his harsh breaths against her neck.

She held on through the storm and pressed her cheek against his collarbone, following the tremor of pleasure until her thighs quaked and her insides trembled.

She scraped her nails up the nape of his neck and along the top of his head, gasping his name as she came. He didn't stop, never stopped.

Never let up until she heard the tiniest moan through his chest as it crawled into her and she shook through the aftershocks of his release and a second one of her own.

She couldn't let go. She cursed herself, but her arms wouldn't unwind. She needed to breathe in his mint and ginger scent a little while longer.

All the ginger and honey tea he'd been drinking had changed how he smelled, even the taste of his skin. It infused her with the new Simon that the tour had created.

The open wounds she felt getting just a little bit bigger as each week passed. She tried to hold him together as much as she could in these small moments when words were lost to her.

To them.

Where his heartbeat and hers knew how to communicate, when the rest of them didn't.

DESTROYED

Chapter 17

Simon pulled the towel over his head and crouched over the sink. His pores were completely blown out from the steam of the day, the steam in the goddamn room, and the hot tea he had to drink.

On a ninety-seven degree day. Sweet fuck.

He'd joked his way through the acoustic show, keeping to the midtones that didn't tax his voice, but the talking did him in. Like it always did.

He tried to stay quiet, to let everyone else do the heavy lifting, but every single freaking question was for him. Hell, he waited for the band to grouse and bitch that everyone wanted to talk to him, but the round robin snark and sarcasm that came after whatever comment he made fueled the fire.

And then there was nothing but laughter. And the joy of it was there, staring at him, surrounding him. This was what the tour was supposed to be about. These little fun moments between everyone.

He wanted to participate. He knew he'd pay for it every damn time, but he wanted it—couldn't fucking shut up. And now he was steaming his throat to moisten it and hope to shit the tickle would settle back.

The click of someone putting down his metal pot on the next sink made his heart plummet.

"You can hide under that little steam tent you've made yourself, but you'll still have to talk to me before you go on stage."

He dug out his phone.

Talking is the problem.

Lila sighed. "You're an ass, but this is fine. I don't care if you answer me in text."

Good, because that's what you're getting.

"Is it that bad?"
He thumbed back a quick answer, then erased it and started over.

Definitely not doing a double encore tonight, Dragon Lady.

"I'm glad you can still joke. Hope you will tomorrow too when you see Dr. West."
Simon flipped off the towel and met her impassive gaze.

I don't need a doctor.

"Oh, I beg to differ, singer boy. If you're having trouble, you should get checked out before it gets worse."
He blew out a breath. It was smart, but for fuck's sake, he didn't want to know. He just wanted to keep doing what he was doing. It was working.
For now.
Simon ignored the little voice and poured a cup of his tea, wincing at the first shot of ginger taste before the honey chased it down to a semi-decent flavor. He replied to Lila.

Who is he?

"He's an Ears, Nose, and Throat doctor. They specialize in this kind of thing. And he comes highly recommended."
Just the thought of scopes and lights down his already abused throat was enough to kill whatever buzz he was feeling earlier. He wanted a drink, but he'd done some reading and alcohol made things worse when

it came to vocal problems.

And then he'd closed every goddamn window on his browser because everything else was terrifying.

Nodes. Polyps. Hemorrhages.

WebMD was the goddamn devil. But all he had was a tickle in his throat. Everything else seemed so huge. It couldn't be what he had.

Maybe we can look at getting me a coach?

A little of the tension eased around her eyes. "Yeah, definitely. That's a great idea. I'll get on that, all right?"

He nodded. A coach he could deal with. He'd always sucked at school and having someone tell him what to do, but this was important. This was his career.

He just needed to get through this show and then he had two whole days that he could just shut up and rest. Maybe he could even get away from everyone and hole up.

That idea was both exhilarating and horrible. He hated to be alone. But he didn't want everyone staring at him with sympathetic eyes, either. That was one step away from pity.

Lesser of two evils was to disappear for a bit.

Nick slapped the doorjamb. "Ready, Prima Donna? On in five."

Simon nodded and flipped him off.

"You wish," Nick shot back.

He stared into the mirror and groaned. He looked like hammered shit. He slapped the palm plate on one of the hand driers and flipped the vent up to blow the wet out of his hair.

It wouldn't last long on stage, but at least he'd have a few songs and the tour photographer had a few minutes to catch him looking almost decent.

As long as they didn't look too closely.

Simon ran to his spot with seconds to spare. Deacon's low thrumming bass set off the mood and Margo had traded violin for cello.

Simon looked over his shoulder and had to breathe deep before he swallowed his tongue and fucking choked on it.

Jesus fuck.

She was in head-to-toe black—sheer black thigh-highs that stopped an inch from her ultra-short dress that hugged every curve. She had on stilettos that made her legs seem miles long and that ridiculously sexy cello against her shoulder. Her hair was up to show off her long, elegant neck and she had blood red lips that made his cock harden.

He wanted between those lips, to watch them stretch open and take him.

Starting a concert with a boner. Awesome.

The crowd lost their collective minds as the shroud dropped from the front of the arch. Because they were into late June, the days were long enough that the sun didn't set until well into their set.

They couldn't play with the lights for effect until later in the night. And because the crowd was as hot as the Indiana temperature, he jumped into the archway and sat cross-legged on the metal pieces to get a look at everyone.

The crowd was open to his antics and he used every one of them to let the guys do the heavy lifting on singing. He crawled along the arch and hung down into the side pit of people from the fan club.

And because he was feeling daring, he dropped into the pit and let them grope him. He played it up as if he was fighting to get out of the pit and back onstage.

Laying on the ramp, he peeled off his white t-shirt and hung it off Nick's mic stand. "I give up."

Nick flipped off his shirt and faux stomped on his ribs. "Get moving, Pretty Boy."

Simon gasped and reached for his mic. He whispered for some help with the first verse of "Lit" and was rejuvenated with the sing-along song.

By the middle of the show, he was pretty sure he was going to make it without incident. The tickle lingered, but didn't made a nuisance of itself.

He even pulled a lower register vibrato out of his ass for "The Becoming" at the end of the night.

When he ran around the ramps that circled the stage for the cover song of the night, he finally felt the first moment of panic.

As he opened his mouth for the last verse of "In the Still of the Night", his voice shattered. Not broke, not cracked, it absolutely shredded itself in two.

Enough that Deacon came up and met him on the ledge of the stage, and Nick and Gray scooted to either side of him to sing the end a Capella.

For the first time in his entire life, he lip synced. Had no fucking choice.

His face must have been as pale as he thought it was when Nick swiped his thumb over the corner of his lower lip and Simon automatically did the same.

And found blood on his thumb.

The house lights went down and he found Margo's hand laced in his as she led him off the stage.

Shouts and scrambling roadies started the breakdown of the set like usual. The house music started and "The Final Countdown" was piped through the pavilion.

Christ, that was an ominous song.

A bottle of water was pushed into his hand and he was funneled into the backstage area and deposited onto a faux leather couch in the corner.

Lila was on her phone and pacing the length of the room. Food was piled up and the watermelon station went unheeded.

Everyone was crowded around him.

"Stop," Simon said on a raspy voice. "I just overdid it all week. I'll be fine."

Lila whipped out an arm and pointed at him and made a shut-your-mouth gesture with her fingers and continued talking to the person on the phone.

Had to be a doctor.

He glugged down the water and the metallic aftertaste made him wince.

Lila's voice raised. "I don't care what his after-hours visit cost is. Get him here now."

"Remind me never to cross her," Nick said.

"Right," Jazz said with a snort.

Simon curled his arm across his belly and stared at the wall as his friends all teased and taunted Nick and alternately tried to console him.

He didn't want to hear it.

He wanted them all gone.

All he wanted to do was escape and drink himself into stupor where there was no pain. Drink until he blacked out and then he wouldn't be able to speak for sure.

Then he could hide in the darkness and erase the looks on each of his friends' faces. The ones that were too earnest, too concerned, and then even worse, the ones between each other when they thought he wasn't paying attention.

He stood and broke through the love and support that felt too much like lead-lined blankets. He bounced against the wall like a pinball in fatigue and dehydration until he got to the bus.

The screams from those that had gotten beyond the ropes or around security reverberated in his head. He didn't even turn around.

His sole focus was the stairs and the quiet. The bus was dark save for the running board lights and he left it that way.

He tripped his way into the showers and soaped off the grime and sweat of the show. He wanted to clear his throat, but even the thought of it made his eyes cross. No matter how much steam he used, he couldn't fight down the tickle.

The only thing that battled it back at all was the cold water or hot tea. How much liquid could the human body hold?

It seemed like such a small problem, but the constant itch at the back of his throat was slowly driving him mad. And now, he'd fucked up a song. What if that had been in the middle of the show and not the end?

What if it didn't get better?

He pressed his forehead to the shower tiles. The sound of the glass door opening and closing made him jump.

Margo's arms came around his belly and her cheek pressed against his back.

"I thought there was no naked on the bus," he whispered.

"Shh."

He wasn't sure how long they stood like that. The water ran from hot to cool and his head felt like an overcooked lobster.

She didn't say another word, just climbed out and left him alone. He finally turned off the taps and climbed out. Surprisingly, he felt steadier and was afraid to examine that too closely.

When he dried off and came out of the bathroom, Lila was there on the couch with a strange man. He was wearing a polo shirt and shorts and reminded him of a TV dad.

He didn't look at all happy to be there.

That made them even, because he wasn't at all happy to have him there.

Simon sawed his thumbs through the sides of his favorite torn t-shirt.

The familiar softness and age of the cotton weirdly felt like a coat of armor.

The dad-doc stood. "Hello Mr. Kagan, I'm Dr. West."

Simon opened his mouth and the doctor waved him off.

"Let's take a look in there before you talk. See how much damage you did."

He sighed and clenched his jaw. He looked around the bus, but Margo was gone. He glanced at Lila and she sat across from him on the edge of the couch with her hands folded.

With no other choice but to sit down, he let the doctor lead him to the small table where they ate breakfast. It had the most light.

"I'm going to just do a visual exam to start and see where we are, all right?"

Simon shrugged.

Dr. West set a bag on the table and pulled out a thin, bendy tool with a light at the end and something that looked like a dentist's mirror.

"Now relax. I know you want to cough. I can see how irritated your throat is already. I'm not going to go all the way down with the guide, just shine a light into your vocal chords."

Simon hid his hands under the table and fisted them on his lap as he opened his mouth. The guy mumbled a few things into his cell phone and then wrote down a few other things.

He put the instruments into a plastic bag and tucked them all back into his case. "Not awful. You're young and fit and you don't smoke, right?"

Simon shook his head. That had never been one of his vices.

"You've strained your chords and the tissues are definitely engorged. You need full vocal rest for a minimum of three days. I'd be more comfortable with two weeks to be honest, but I know you're on tour."

Lila leaned forward. "What are we talking here, Doctor?"

"I'll need to do a more thorough exam, but you mentioned you're heading to California, so I'll give you some names of specialists there."

"Thank you." She stood and put her hand on Simon's shoulder. "Three days?"

"Yes. No talking, no singing, obviously no shouting."

Simon's shoulders tensed. They only had two days off. The third day was The Greek in Berkley. It was in their backyard, goddammit.

"The ginger tea is good to keep the irritation down so you don't cough, but it also can numb it so you think you can push harder than you should. That's why they're so inflamed." The doctor held up his two forefingers and moved them close together, but not quite touching. "When you sing, they move closer together to make the individual sounds you need. Yours are so big that they're vibrating against each other and making little inflammation pockets. Could be nodes or cysts forming. I won't know without a full exam."

Simon tipped back his head. Those were words he didn't want to hear. He'd seen them when he'd gone online.

"Does that mean he's a surgical candidate?"

Evidently, Lila had gone onto the same scary sites.

"I'm not sure it's that far, but again, this is just a visual. He's too swollen right now to get a good read on it. I need them to shrink down a bit."

"Okay. Thanks for coming out tonight. I know it's late."

"I'd rather come out late than find out he had a hemorrhage." He shook Lila's hand then turned back to Simon. "No talking. Use your phone or a whiteboard to communicate, all right?"

Simon put his hand out for a shake and nodded. As soon as the doctor left the bus he dropped his forehead to the table with two bounces for good measure.

When he raised his head, the front of the bus was full of the band. Jazz was cradling her stomach as she did nearly all the time now, her other arm wrapped around Gray's bicep. Harper stood with Deacon behind her, hands on her shoulders, but it was Nick that had on the blank mask. Everyone else just looked worried.

Margo peeked from the stairs, her teeth buried in her lower lip.

"Well, I guess this means I don't have to call a band meeting," Lila said, all business as usual. If he didn't look too closely at the lines of tension shadowing her eyes.

Simon raked his fingers through his hair and stared at the ceiling.

"How bad is it?" Nick asked.

"Not that bad. Simon needs three days of vocal rest and then we'll see what's what. He's just strained it, so you'll have to take the interviews, Nicholas, and—"

"I can do interviews." Jazz bounced a little, her eyelashes starred with wetness.

Fuck.

He didn't want Pix upset. Of course at this point, she just needed to get pancakes instead of waffles on a breakfast order and the waterworks could start.

"Thank you, Jasmine. Do what you can. I don't want you to overdo, either. I don't want two of you to be on bed rest."

Simon scribbled in the notebook in front of him and slapped the table. When Lila turned around, he held it up.

"I know you're not an invalid. You just have to rest. I know it's a new and outrageous topic, but that's what we need to do."

"We have a show in two days. What are we going to do with that?"

"I'm going to look into rescheduling, but our timeline is very tight. I don't know if we'll have time to swing around before you finish the first leg."

"Then we cancel." Nick folded his arms.

"I don't advise cancelling. The tickets have been bought and returns are a nightmare. Not to mention the contract with the venue. They can sue you for lost revenue."

"What?" Jazz let go of Gray and came forward. "They can't do that."

"Sure they can."

"But I've heard of shows getting cancelled."

Lila nodded. "And they pay through the nose for that. Do you all want to pay about, oh…one hundred grand each?"

"What?" Jazz's eyes went huge.

"It's an expensive endeavor, Jasmine. If we could reschedule it, that would be one thing. But with you and Harper ready to pop in the next few months, we're kind of in a bind."

"I'm sorry."

Lila sighed. "Do not start with the waterworks, I'm just saying this plain. It's no one's fault. It's not even Simon's fault. This happens to singers and this is as much my fault as anyone."

"What can we do?" Deacon asked in his reasonable voice. The voice that made Simon want to walk over there and deck him for being so calm.

Harper twisted her fingers. "I know I'm not in the band, but…"

"You're part of the family," Jazz said. She moved over to her and tipped her head against her shoulder. "What's your idea?"

"Well, when you guys were fooling around the other night, Gray sang."

"Wait," Gray began.

"Oh." Jazz turned around to face everyone. "That's a great idea. Gray has fronted groups before."

"Yeah, when I was a teenager, babe."

"It's okay for one night, right? Just to fill in? Then Super Slut will be back to his operatic self. We have another day between The Greek and The Hollywood Bowl. So that will give him almost four full days off."

Simon crossed his arms over his chest, his phone in his hand. He thumbed out a text and sent it to Nick.

Nick's phone buzzed. He pulled it out and read the message, then looked at him. "Are you sure?"

Simon shrugged. No, he wasn't fucking sure, but it was the best option they had.

"It's not like Simon can't be on stage. He can run around and get everyone crazy." Lila pulled out her iPad. "We'll play it up that he needs a nurse to make him feel better, maybe?"

Awesome. He could just be the guy that was the mime cheerleader. That sounded like more fun than an acid wash for his nuts.

Fuck.

Nick cracked his first smile. "Do we know any strippers that could put on nurse outfits?"

Simon did a two thumbs up. There was nothing wrong with that scenario. He texted Nick.

Make sure he sings "Bad Medicine".

Nick snorted and flashed his phone at Gray.

Gray swung his gaze to Simon. "Oh hell no. I'm not singing Bon Jovi."

"C'mon," Simon mouthed.

"Absolutely not."

If he had to stay on the sidelines, at least he could have some damn fun with it.

"All right, everyone. Time to pack it in. Joe and Bobby have to take off with the busses to make it to California in a reasonable time. You have lots of press on your home turf."

"Who the hell scheduled us in Indianapolis then to California?" Nick asked with a groan.

"We have to work around the venue schedules. You guys asked for The

Greek, so we got you what you wanted."

"My bad," Nick said.

"Shoo, pregnant people and dads. Off we go." Lila herded people off the bus.

Jazz ducked under Lila's arm and came at him. Her sweet watermelon scent wrapped around him as she curled her arms around his neck. "Feel better, Super Slut."

He rested his cheek against hers for a minute and swallowed down the lump.

Had to be bad if Jazz was voluntarily hugging him. He patted her ass to make sure she knew he was still the same old Simon. And when she punched him in the arm, he was able to find a smile.

It lasted until everyone left.

And then there were three.

Margo was quiet. She picked at the dark nail polish on her thumbnail. Nick sat next to her and neither of them would look at him.

It was going to be a long damn drive of silences.

Simon stood and stretched with a yawn. He texted to Nick that he was going to hit his bunk. He really couldn't stand the stares, or in this case, the avoiding stares.

He was so very done with the day.

Maybe he could sleep twenty-four hours straight and save himself the muzzle.

Chapter 18

"Up and at 'em, Simon. We're pulling in." Nick's voice boomed into the silence.

Or it had been silent.

Simon covered his eyes with his arm. His head was pounding. He'd watched Netflix on his tablet for about twelve hours straight. He just hadn't been able to face anyone.

Margo left him a pot of tea every few hours. She'd attempted to pull back the curtain once, but then had let it swing closed again.

Her honeysuckle scent teased him every time she moved around the back of the bus, but neither of them seemed to know how to approach the other.

Sleep and nocturnal raids on their freezer when everyone else was sleeping covered the rest of the hours on the road. He knew it was cowardly, but he just didn't give a shit.

If he wasn't allowed to speak for three goddamn days, that was the perfect time to watch every episode of *Daredevil*.

Matt Murdock beating the ever-loving shit out of every bad guy in Hell's Kitchen was enough to keep his rage in check.

He lived vicariously through the character.

And no one else had tried to bother him. The few times he'd pulled out his earbuds, he'd heard Margo and Nick working on a song or watching *Charmed*.

He didn't have it in him to play nice. Not when he'd have to for the next thirty-six hours. He rolled out of his bunk and because he was rank, he closeted himself in the bathroom for a hot shower.

He knotted a towel at his waist and looked out the window. The spire of the University of California's bell tower came into view as Bobby pulled around to The Greek Theater.

They'd played the smaller venue of the same name on the Rebel Rage tour. Los Angeles was, and would always be, home turf. That had given him a boner for days, but this park...

This was bigger and was fast becoming the place to play. The mere fact that Lila had gotten them in with only a request from him and Nick was just out of control.

And he couldn't fucking sing.

He flattened his hand on the window. Before he could do something stupid like smash his fist into the glass, he stepped back. The overhead compartment came into his eyeline and he flipped it open.

Hello old friend.

He pulled down one of the Crystal Skull bottles. He downed a bottle of water, ripped off the label, and refilled it with the crystal clear vodka.

That would be one way to get through the day.

He took a hit from the eerily smiling skull and tucked it back on the shelf. "You're alive."

Simon swallowed down a sound that was half groan and half seething sigh. He turned to her and lifted his eyebrows in answer. Christ, she was fresh-faced and beautiful.

Onstage, she had perfected the vamp look with her all black outfits and screaming-colored electric violin and cello. She'd taken to the rockstar skin as if she'd been born for it.

But here, she was short white shorts and tanned legs. A striped T-shirt showcased her tiny waist and amazing tits.

All he wanted to do was haul her into his arms and wrap that lush body around him. He wanted to forget that his voice sucked, that the world sucked, that his life sucked.

But he didn't.

Because that luscious mouth of hers was pinched with worry, and her dark eyes were searching for a way to ask him if he was okay.

He wasn't fucking okay. And he didn't even want her to make the pretense of asking him.

As if she somehow read his mind, she rose onto her scarlet-painted toes and nipped his lower lip. "We have the whole evening to escape this bus. Since you can't do the interviews and they're going to play up the sick card instead of the voice card, you're mine." She palmed his dick through the towel then snaked her hand under the flap. "Tell me, do you think you can play college co-ed with me today?"

He resisted the urge to groan and tipped his head back as she stroked down his shaft and slipped her thumb around the crown of his cock.

She nibbled his Adam's apple and he jerked away. Instead of looking repentant, she smiled and released him. "Get dressed."

He grabbed the bottle and slid on his oldest pair of jeans under his towel. The knee was ripped out on one leg and there was a huge hole in the thigh of the other. An equally abused Ozzy shirt finished his college look. Half hipster douche, half irony. Sunglasses and an Angels' baseball cap hid his overlong hair and eyes.

"That's quite the ensemble."

He pulled his phone out and texted.

Hey, I showered. More than most college kids.

She shook her head and looped a wide canvas purse over her head and settled it cross-body. "Want me to hold your water?"

He shook his head.

"Okay, ready?"

He gave her a thumbs up with his most sarcastic smile.

"Look at that. You don't even need a voice to convey asshole."

He sighed.

"We will have fun. It's an amazing word and we shall find the true meaning today. Then tonight we'll meet up with everyone and you can stop pouting." She held up her hand. "Don't even deny it. I let you pout for a day and a half. That's all you get."

He tipped his head back and looked at the ceiling.

"Such a tough life. Okay, let's go."

They got off the bus and escaped down an alleyway to the main campus. Trees and reddish walkways offset all the light-colored buildings. They fell into step with students as they wandered through a huge quad with a circular fountain at its center.

A huge patinated archway lead to food vendors. Simon sipped his way through the bottle of vodka during their lazy stroll through campus and knew he needed to drink actual water or something before he stank like vodka through his pores.

It was ridiculously hot.

Feeling better with two hotdogs in his belly and a large fresh lemonade, he finally relaxed. The sun was bleeding through the trees when they finally circled around to the back end of the campus where the stage was located.

They dropped onto the stone stairs where there was finally some shade. Margo took a long drink from the tall bottle of water she'd refilled a few times.

"I can't believe this campus. It's so different from Boston."

He hadn't even thought about the novelty of a new campus for her. She was an East coast girl. Sure, she did some studio work in Los Angeles, but that was a far cry from this slice of collegiate life.

He pulled his phone out and texted her.

"Yeah, I went to college. I have a Master's in music theory and a minor in business from Brown."

His eyebrows shot up. Well that was certainly a far cry from his own high school diploma.

"Holy shit!"

Simon hunched up his shoulders. His half-assed disguise had worked all day. He really didn't want to have to fend off fans. Especially when he couldn't charm his way out of it like he usually did.

"Crap, you probably don't remember me. I look a little different."

Simon slid his sunglasses down and looked her over. Ass-hugging denim shorts and a bright red top initially distracted him, but her face started pulling at a memory.

He was pretty sure he hadn't slept with her, but couldn't be absolutely sure.

"Simon, it's Tori."

He frowned. That name definitely niggled.

Margo held out her hand. "I'm Margo. Simon has laryngitis, so he can't talk."

"Oh. Oh, wow." Tori pulled her hair over her shoulder and twisted it into a coil.

Simon snapped his fingers. He dug out his phone and texted Margo.

She looked down at her phone then gave him a deadpan stare. "I'm not saying that."

"Can I see?"

"It's rude."

Tori laughed. "I bet it is."

Margo sighed and turned her phone around.

Tori snorted. "Yep. That would be me."

Nick's blowjob girl from the first tour had turned into a little bit more than just a fun flirtation. She'd gelled with Nick more than any other girl Simon had seen on tour.

Ultimately, the tour was just too much of a force and Tori had gone on to greener pastures. Yet whenever they had a show in California, Nick seemed to hook up with her.

Looked like this one might not be any different.

"I was hoping to find Nick somehow with the show tomorrow night. He gave me an all-access pass to whatever show I could get to."

Margo tilted her head in that way that made his cock harden. So curious. "Nick doesn't really do the backstage scene all that often. You must be something special."

"I like to think so." Tori flipped her dark hair over her shoulder. "He's always so damn serious. I like to shake him up a little."

"He…" Margo trailed off.

Simon nudged her with his shoulder.

She rolled her eyes. "I don't want to sound bitchy."

"Oh, girl. Nicky can be an absolute asshole. That's why I love him so much."

"Well yeah." Margo tapped her middle finger against her nail. "He needs to get laid."

Simon tipped his head back and clapped. Oh man. If only Nick could hear what she said. And it was so very true. Nick wasn't exactly a saint on tour, but he wasn't hooking up in every town, either.

Hell, not even every fifth town.

The boy needed to get out of his own way when it came to pleasures of the flesh. He kind of satiated himself with the pre-game warmup, but rarely sealed the deal after a show.

At least from what Simon could tell.

Tori grinned. "Now that is one thing we always excelled at."

"Well, you should definitely come back with us. We're not doing anything much tonight with the big show tomorrow."

Simon's shoulders tightened at the reminder. The show where he would still be on stage, but not able to sing a goddamn note.

"Are you sure it's okay?"

Simon nodded.

Margo grinned. "See? Perfect."

The girls chattered about the tour, about Tori's major, and Nick. By the time they found the bus again, dusk was falling.

Nick was coming down the stairs from the bus when they walked up. "Jesus, where have you guys been?"

Tori hid behind Simon, her fingers twisting into his belt loop.

"We just walked around. Figured I'd cheer up Grumpy Cat."

Nick snorted. "Good. He needs it."

"How'd the interviews go?"

"Same old, same old. Did a question-and-answer session with the students. I swear they ask some of the smartest and dumbest shit."

"Ahh, college life," Margo said with a little wistfulness in her tone. "Speaking of college life, we found you a little something."

Nick peered around Simon. "I see you have a third person."

"Not just any third person," Tori said.

Nick frowned and circled Simon. "Well, fuck."

"Yes, yes, we have," Tori said with a happy laugh.

Nick scooped her up off the pavement. "Well hey there, stranger."

Tori wound her arms around his neck. "I tried to text you when I saw the tour dates, but you changed your number."

Nick laughed. "Yeah. I left my phone at one of the interviews for the new album. Someone found it and holy shit, they blew up my phone. Posted the number on Twitter."

Tori giggled. "Oh, I missed that one."

"How many dirty texts did you get?"

"That number is classified," Nick said.

"I bet I can get it out of you."

Margo looked over at Simon, then back to Nick. "So, she really is a longtime friend."

"I told you," Tori said. "So, do I actually get to finally see the bus?"

Nick grinned and opened the door. "This one is far more impressive than the last one."

Tori climbed the stairs and dragged Nick after her. He gave them a happy grin and let her lead him into the bus.

Well, maybe things weren't going to be too boring, after all.

Simon held his arm out for Margo to go ahead of him. He went up the stairs behind her, palming her ass as he crowded into her.

Instead of the usual admonishing look, she grabbed him by the neck of his T-shirt when she got to the top stair and dragged him in for a kiss.

Her tongue was wild, stroking his until she could suck it into her mouth. He stopped her on the stairs, not willing to go inside just yet in case she changed her mind about touching him within the confines of the windows and walls.

She nipped his lower lip and backed up. "I'm thirsty." Margo reached for the overhead compartment that she'd commandeered. She pulled down a bottle of Silver Cabo tequila. "I think a little celebration is in order."

Where the hell did she get the tequila?

His eyebrow winged up and Margo grinned. "I stole it from Jazz's bus. Not like anyone over there was going to put it to use."

Simon snorted and she waggled her finger. "Uh uh, no sounds."

He rolled his eyes and went to the lower drawer and pulled out four shot glasses.

Tori rolled onto her knees on the couch. "Count me in on the tequila."

Nick got up off the couch and held up a finger. He grabbed for the handle and pulled out the cushion until it was double the size.

Tori laughed and fell on her butt. "Man. Do I want to know how many times this thing has been used?"

Nick laughed. "There's a surprising lack of sex on this bus."

"That I do not believe."

Margo laughed. "He's right. We tend to have sex in the more inspirational areas of a venue or park."

Tori's eyes rounded. "You and…" She pointed to Nick.

Margo shook her head. "No." She gave a head nod in Simon's direction. "I'm partial to this guy. Don't ask me why."

Simon glared at her, but she just laughed and belted a shot. "Everyone drink up."

Margo picked up the half-gone bottle of tequila. Tori had hooked up a playlist that piped through the bus's speakers. The bass heavy Sixx AM song curled low in her belly.

She'd been introduced to a lot of different musicians since she'd started touring with Oblivion. The guys had an eclectic mix of current music, classic rock, and traditional classic rock from the seventies.

They loved their covers and had inspired her to get creative with her strings accompaniment. In fact, she was creating a list of her own to surprise them with.

She and Nick had spent the previous day vetting new songs since Simon had closed himself off from them. It felt weird.

She and Nick had gone from standoffish to an easy truce, but the hours on the bus had cracked the outer layer of his shields. Margo didn't believe she'd gotten much deeper than the surface, but she felt and responded to the genius living inside him.

All her life, she'd been surrounded by classically trained artists, but this band—these men and woman—was full of natural and instinctive talent that called to her on a deeper level.

And now, yet again, she was seeing a different side to Nick and Simon as a unit. She stepped in front of Nick and her knee brushed his denim-clad thigh as she poured his shot.

He slid his leg out farther until the folds in his jeans teased the back of her knee. Her belly flipped and the odd sensation fluttered through her middle and washed over her skin.

His golden eyes were so very different from Simon's. They should be warm, but the golden brown was more like amber. A frozen shard of sun in the dark.

He watched, assessed, and she was pretty sure he thought too much. But with the tequila warming her veins, she wasn't sure if it was just her being fanciful.

She moved onto Simon and his winter blue gaze. He'd gone shot for shot with her, but didn't seem to be affected by the liquor. His fingers dangled along the edges of the couch. He was settled in what at first seemed like a lazy sprawl, but he was ever watchful, and his fingers tensed on the small ledge under the cushion.

Margo refilled his shot glass and tipped it into her mouth, but instead of swallowing the alcohol, she licked into his mouth and transferred it to him.

His eyes flashed and his tongue tangled with hers as the fire chased from her tastebuds to his and then echoed again like an afterburn. Just the barest sliver of silver blue glowed from his heavy lids and full lashes.

Watching.

Always watching.

She backed away from him, nipples tight and clit throbbing. But she wasn't paying attention and bumped into Tori. Her arm came around Margo's waist to steady her.

Both Nick and Simon's eyes widened as Tori's hand flattened on her middle.

Curious in a way that only tequila could allow, she swayed with Tori. The song had changed to a sultry, digital-heavy song with a female singer.

It spoke of watching, echoed in flavor to what was there in front of her. Two intense men who weren't ashamed to show both of the women in the room that they were attractive.

Her gaze trailed down over Simon's rock-hard belly to the worn denim that molded to the steadily growing bulge between his legs.

She glanced over her shoulder at Tori. Her eyes were a little out of focus, but she wasn't so far gone that Margo was worried about the consequences of the moment.

A curiosity that could be sated without drama.

She tilted her head and waited to see if Tori would reciprocate or if she backed away. She was fine with both, but couldn't deny that she wondered if a girl kissed differently than a man.

Her nose brushed Tori's and their lips hovered on the cusp of a kiss, but neither of them seemed to want to take that extra step.

The intent was enough. The heat between them as their hips swayed to the rhythm. Margo's hand fell to Tori's waist, and they matched each other beat for beat.

Finally Margo broke the tension between them. Well, between her and Tori, anyway. Margo sucked in a breath and she closed her eyes against the warmth invading her belly.

Tori's chin brushed along her shoulder as they both looked forward. Simon's gaze scorched down her neck, then from her breasts to her hips. She and Tori let the song pull the strings and the heat in their men's gazes brought them full circle.

Simon gripped the couch and his Adam's apple bounced with a heavy swallow. Margo watched it bob and his throat work another shot glass full of tequila.

She wanted to taste it off his lips again.

She wanted him to lick it off her skin.

God, her breasts felt heavy. Not for Tori's touch, but for Simon's.

They slid away from each other with one last fleeting brush of fingertips. Hers along Tori's hip and Tori's along Margo's belly.

Tori sauntered to Nick, her hips rolling with each step until she pressed one knee into the cushion between his legs. His hands came up to cup her ass and stroked up to her hips then back again.

Simon sat forward on his end of the couch. Margo slipped her fingers into his raven wing's black hair and shuddered as he drew the tip of his tongue across her belly where Tori had lingered. Her shirt had ridden up and he took full advantage.

He watched her as he lapped at her skin and scraped his nails over her flesh as if he could erase Tori's touch.

Her nipples tightened as he used his nose to push the hem of her shirt higher so he could trail up her belly to the underwire of her bra.

She glanced at Tori and Nick and her breath shuddered out as Tori tucked her hand into the front of Nick's jeans.

The song changed to a dark Nine Inch Nails song that urged her hips to move against Simon's touch. He licked along the scallop of lace that hugged over wire and gripped her ribs.

It was a shell of a camisole that molded to her breasts, holding her in. Simon pulled the stretchy lace up with his teeth and breathed over the deep dip of her bra. The fullness of her breasts required her to be creative to keep the lines of her shirts smooth.

And in a moment Simon turned her body against her. The out of control curve of her breasts spilled out and he opened his mouth to taste every inch.

She closed her eyes against the sensation, overwhelmed by the way he made her forget herself. That she was right next to Nick and Tori. It was so easy for her to get lost in his touch.

Her eyes fluttered open to find Tori's hand stroking over Nick's hard length as the two of them watched her and Simon.

Bold with the moment and her body's haywire reactions to the situation, she tore open the buttons on Simon's jeans. He hissed as she slipped her hand into the fly and found his cock digging into his belly.

She slid her thumb along the head and spread the moisture at the tip around and under to the tight skin at the ridge where his shaft met the curves there.

The deliciously sensitive ridge. She rubbed there again and again, the same place she would have cupped him with her tongue.

Nick watched them as he stroked his tongue along the underside of Tori's jaw to her ear. Tori pumped him harder and his moan carried over to Margo.

Simon's attention finally skidded away from their friends and back to Margo. Solely on her. He brushed his stubble-coated jaw against her belly and slid his hands up into her shorts from the bottom. He cupped her backside then tucked his fingertips between her thighs and against her panties. A moan rumbled in his chest.

She was soaked. She'd known it from the way her hips kept rolling at the gnawing restlessness building inside her.

Simon looked up at her and she was torn between watching his reaction and the show beside them.

Tori licked the palm of her hand and increased her grip and the pressure on Nick's cock until his hips were lifting to meet each stroke.

Simon nosed the cup of her bra aside enough to get to her nipple. He tongued her, flicking over the tip as he watched their neighbors. Simon's gaze bounced from watching her watch them to simply observing Nick and Tori. And the whole time he sucked on her nipple until it stung. Until it ached.

Finally Simon lifted her up and stood. "Enough," he whispered against her neck. "I can't share you any longer."

His raspy voice knocked her off her axis and stole the tenuous control she had over the insane situation. He strode down the length of the bus to her bunk and tore back the curtain.

His eyes were fierce and possessive, his touch almost rough as he stripped her shirt off, flipped her bra cups up and fell onto her breasts.

She'd never felt Simon cover her before. Pin her against walls, against tile, a bus, but never the delicious pressure of his pelvis fitting into the bowl of her hips. He opened her legs until he fit against her tighter.

His jeans still on, her shorts still buttoned, but he didn't seem to care about that quite yet. His sole focus was her breasts.

He laced their fingers and brought them over her head until the backs of her hands were pinned against the carpeted surface. He went from one to the other, sucking and biting until she bucked under him.

Still, he didn't stop.

She was at his mercy, her breasts thrust high. The heavy curve of the underside was on display because she was spread out like she was on a rack of his own creation.

"Is it wrong that I want to see silver through these?" he asked with a sandpaper whisper.

She shuddered at the thought of his nipple rings. God, she couldn't stop herself from touching them. Except now, when he'd caged her hands.

"Do they hurt?"

"Sore," he said on a breath of air. "So sensitive, though." He released one of her hands and flipped his T-shirt off. He hovered over her, his chest above her mouth.

She lifted off the pillow and traced the ring then tucked her tongue in and tugged it away from his body. His groan was hurtful to her own ears, but the ecstasy on his face made her tug it again.

He shivered above her and as he lowered she coasted her mouth over his chest to his shoulder and sunk her teeth into the muscles there.

"Mark me," he whispered. "I'm yours as much as you're mine." He laved and sucked along her neck and found her pulse as he always did.

Unerringly.

Lovingly.

The sting of his tiny bite zipped through her like lightning and ended at her clit. It pounded with each rasp of his tongue and the ceaseless undulation of his hips into hers.

But everything felt bigger here in this tiny space. As if she couldn't get away from him, or more importantly that she didn't want to.

She squeezed his fingers. "Simon, I need…"

"You need what?"

She was so empty.

The thought of telling him that was so huge and so scary that she shut it down.

She didn't own him. Had never owned him, she was only borrowing. "I'm yours."

Her eyes flew open and he gazed at her without fear and without a lick of hesitancy.

"I've always been yours, Violin Girl. I've just been hoping you would take me."

Too huge.

Too much.

She buried her face in his neck as he brought one hand down to his fly. She could hear the metal buttons clicking against each other as he tipped to his side just enough to get himself free.

The snap of latex and then he was rocking into her, his pelvis tilting against her. He watched as she took him inside her body.

She curled her free arm around his neck and they met forehead to forehead as he drove into her. Friction. Heat. So much of both. He swiveled his hips and the control she clung to dissipate like fog in sunlight.

He canted his hips until the stroke was so overwhelming and so deep that he touched every part of her. She squeezed her eyes shut against the waves of pleasure that swallowed her.

"No. Open those eyes. See this, see us."

Her vision wavered, but she managed to stay locked into him as her orgasm started in the center of her and radiated out like starlight, like the spotlights that blinded her some nights, like a note that resonated through her skin and became part of her.

"I love you, Margo."

She tore her hand out from under his and cupped the back of his head with both hands. She couldn't find the words, couldn't even trap the words that tried to form in her throat. They completely failed her.

She'd never given them before.

Her body shuddered under him and she turned her face into his neck.

Oh God. What had she done?

Chapter 19

Simon's shoulders heaved as he held onto her. She'd gone from tense and wrapped around him to pliant and quiet.

Watching her in the main part of the bus, the curiosity glowing in her dark eyes as she danced with Tori, when she almost let it be more…

Fuck. He'd never seen anything more beautiful in his life. The awakening of her confidence, the sway of her hips as she let the music and the moment take her over.

But then Tori had dared to touch her.

Where that would have been a dream come true a year ago, the thought of someone else touching her, of Nick watching her — he'd held on as long as he could. He'd wanted to celebrate that bloom of sexual awareness she'd found.

But he couldn't.

Determination and the blush of alcohol on her cheeks combined into a force that could only be called Margo. It was the only reason he'd lasted as long as he had.

Her hands on his body, the music, the need to stamp himself over her, inside of her — to make her his. He'd lost it.

And now in the crashing aftermath, he'd gone too fast. He hadn't even realized the words were bubbling inside of him. Denial had been his friend for too many months.

He couldn't breathe around the stupidity.

The only reason he hadn't stumbled out of her bunk was because of the gentle glide of her fingertips along his back. She hadn't spoken, but she hadn't pushed him away, either.

He pressed his forehead into her shoulder, inhaled their combined scents and her more prevalent honeysuckle, and just let himself own the words. Even as his belly quivered with nerves and fear, he held them close.

In the silence of the moment, the slap of skin and the sounds of Nick and

Tori intruded. His body reacted to the sounds and his constant need for her.

He rolled to the side of her bunk, the insulating material at his back as he tucked her ass against his front. He licked along her neck and dragged his nose through her hair to the nape of her neck.

He stroked his hand down over her heavy breasts, plucked at her nipples until she rocked back against him. He tried to put himself back into the box she'd owned since the release party.

The need to give her pleasure, to take her pleasure. To smooth over the huge words that had changed this thing between them. Words that should never have been uttered — both because he was ordered into silence, and because he knew she wasn't ready to hear him.

Maybe she would never be ready.

He fell back on the things that did make sense. The utter destruction that they raced for each time they got their hands on one another.

The noises outside taunted him.

Nick was making up for lost time, for his self-imposed dry spells that Simon never understood. If he was single, then why would he deny himself?

Each moan from the neighboring bunk seemed to make Margo more fitful. The rustle of sheets, the moans, the slap of flesh. Imagination was a far better aphrodisiac sometimes.

Gauging the culmination of sounds from outside and how they were syncing up in the heated space between them, he knew it wouldn't take much to bring Margo over.

Maybe that would even overshadow his words for a moment.

He wouldn't deny them, couldn't now. Once they were out of the secret spaces inside of him, he couldn't shove them back. But he wouldn't use them as a weapon.

They were precious, because he honestly hadn't thought he had the capacity for them. He'd never known softness. A belt, a backhand, a fist — those were things he understood. The occasional slap on the back from his friends had sustained him for so long.

He hadn't realized how greedy he was for something bigger than that. Something more.

She was restless against him, her belly and hips undulating to bring his fingers lower. He knew once he touched her silky liquid he'd be done.

He was only a man and the real live sexcapades outside the curtain had pushed him further than he realized.

Margo fumbled above her head and he covered her hand, realizing she was looking for the hidden pocket along the bunk walls. There were no headphones, no iPod, no stash of mints in her hideaway. No, it was far more important.

His fingers found the plastic wrappers of condoms and palmed one. He ripped and fumbled to cover his dick. His one focus had become delving into her warmth. He wanted to hold on to this moment. One that wasn't taking place in some stairwell or against the wall or acting as a quick fix.

He reached around her and brought her knees up against her body, groaning into her ear as she clung to his arms, her breathing shallow in readiness.

He tucked the head of his cock into her waiting body, hovered there at the precipice of her fisting around him. Knowing that the instant he drove inside he'd be gone, he held them there.

The small, keening noise that escaped her and ended in his name was the catalyst. He thrust inside of her, holding her tight against him as his hips took over. Sweat and the ache of overused abs and thigh muscles frayed the pain centers of his system, but the intense pleasure trumped all of that.

He curled his fingers between them to find the slick, stiff clit that crowned over their joined bodies. Her pussy so swollen and sensitive that she tried to twist away.

He hushed her as memories of their first time together and her struggle against the pleasure made him hold her tighter. She shook and nearly hyperventilated, but he held her and fought against the blackness that was creeping around his brain and threatening to end this moment.

He wasn't ready to come yet.

He wanted to ride this release that she was fighting against. Her sob turned into a hiccuping moan of his name and then she trembled.

He buried himself deep and let go. The soul-destroying pleasure wrapped around him, shredded him, then reformed him into something else entirely.

A man who loved this woman.

Completely.

When he woke, he didn't quite know how the night had ended. They'd been so drained—literally—that they'd both just slipped into sleep.

He was facedown in the bunk, Margo's chest plastered to his back, one leg between his and the rest of her curled around his side.

He could happily wake like that for the rest of his life. And that was too serious to think about first thing in the morning.

Simon dug under their tangled bodies to find his phone in his pocket. The battery was on its last fifteen percent, but it was enough to check in. He tucked his chin onto his arm and scrolled through the messages on the one huge band chat thread.

He smiled at the argument between Gray and Deacon on what was the finer foot pedal brand. That was as individual as a pair of shoes.

He wandered over to the itinerary for the day and the list of interviews that he was actually free from for once.

The fact that relief warred with jealousy showed just how fucked up his life was. He was growing to hate interviews with his last breath, but now that he wasn't included, he itched to sit in on them.

He'd be bored in about three minutes, but he still hated being excluded.

Margo stirred against his back. Sleeping with her was new. He liked how she sort of just dropped like a doll that had lost its animation. She wasn't restless, wasn't a snorer, wasn't even overly clingy. She was just completely out.

She rubbed her cheek against his back and stretched then jumped a little.

He turned his head and gave her an easy smile. Her eyes were wary, but she relaxed against him again.

"Anything doing in Oblivion world?"

He flicked the screen so her itinerary got larger and passed his phone over to her. She groaned and slid off him.

He rolled until they were face to face.

"I'm going to be gone all day."

He took his phone back and flicked to his note application.

She snorted. "Oh yeah, I bet you're going to hate not being on the second student panel."

Since the venue was on a college campus and they'd been on the front lines of using social media to build their image, they'd been asked to answer questions.

Pix and Nick would just love to be in the center of that. Well, Pix would, but Nick would probably rather scoop out his own eye.

She folded her hands under her cheek. "Are you going to be okay today?"

He nodded. It was going to suck, but he'd live through it.

Margo fluttered her fingers through his hair then climbed over him. He halted her escape, dragging her astride him. He pushed up her T-shirt—she'd lost the bra long ago—and tongued around her nipple, sucking it until he was sure her eyes were on the verge of rolling back in her head.

He smiled around her hot raspberry flesh and let it pop free. Then he dropped back onto the pillow and stacked his arms behind his head.

He wanted her to think about him, but he wasn't going to give her a morning orgasm. He wanted her to remember how hard he'd sucked and plucked at her and when she moved, she'd remember.

And she'd want more later.

"That smug smile doesn't impress me."

He just smiled wider and waggled his eyebrows. She climbed off him with a disgusted grunt and let the curtain fall back.

Because the thought of being awake and alert with a side of quiet was questionable for his sanity, he plugged his phone into her charging station in the bunk, rolled over, and went back to sleep.

When he woke again, his stomach demanded food and his throat was dry as dust. With showtime less than an hour away, he wandered out to the trucks where Harper's crew would be with his white board under his arm.

Annie was taking care of most of the cooking since Harper's reach was similar to a turtle's. She was all of the pregnant and cranky with it.

He waved at the redhead.

"Hey, Simon. Chicken, beef tips, or turkey burgers are on today's menu."

He walked over to the steno stations and filled a plate, plowed through it, then a pot of his tea and finally felt human.

Jazz and Gray laughed on their way into the eating area.

"Hey, Super Slut. You finally decided to join us?"

He made a fishing rod windup action with one hand and a slow middle finger raise with the other.

"Nice."

He scribbled onto his marker board and flipped it around.

"Rehearsal went great. Gray knows all the songs. Tonight will be great."

He nodded and tried not to let the fact that Gray was essentially replacing him tonight matter too much. He didn't want it to be easy, dammit.

"All right, people. It's time to get on stage. They're ready for you."

Jamie and Lindsey, from their opening band, came in looking like a couple of college girls themselves. Jamie in a ripped shirt and cutoffs that were an inch away from indecent, Lindsey in one of her girly dresses.

Lindsey hooked her arm through Jamie's. "I don't think we've ever played such a cool stage. You're going to love it out there, Simon."

Jamie elbowed her in the side and Lindsey's huge blue eyes went even rounder. "Oh shit."

Simon waved her off and gave her a thumbs up.

Fucking coolest venue ever and he was a mute. Fantastic.

He followed the sounds of the crowd, his gut clenching and unclenching in nerves he'd never had going on stage.

Excitement, sure — that was a given in his world. Nerves? No, there'd never been nerves in the mix.

He shook out his jangle of silver bracelets, cracked his neck, and tugged his Red Cross shirt into smooth lines. As he was going up the stairs, he stalled.

A roll of silver duct tape was on a trunk. Destination names were always marked on the equipment for protection.

Knowing he was about as likely to stay quiet now as he'd been while balls deep in Margo, he ripped off a strip and slapped it on his mouth.

Maybe that would help.

He charged onto the stage. Didn't let himself think about the fact that he was just a face tonight. If he was going to be a clown or a fucking monkey, he was going to be an amazing one.

As he skidded into the center of the massive stage, he lost his breath. The crowd was like a neverending bowl of faces. The stage was endless and they were almost insignificant to the perfection of the treeline and tradition of the campus.

Holy shitballs.

Deacon, Nick, and Gray came forward and Simon grabbed his box mic. As they surrounded him, he let the cord out until his mic dangled down between his legs. He looked down at it as it swayed then looked at Deacon, then at Nick, then back at the mic.

The crowd laughed and screamed.

Simon tapped his throat, then his taped mouth.

"See, this is the only way we can make him keep his mouth shut. Simon's lost his voice because he doesn't know how to shut up."

Simon gave Nick a side eye glance and put his mic into the stand before setting his hands on his hips with a huge sigh.

"So, do you think it would be all right if this guy sang tonight?" Deacon asked in his super deep voice.

Gray stepped forward and zipped his fingertips along the brim of the Fedora he wore most nights—at least for the first few songs until it grew too fucking hot. He peered up from the shadows of the hat and gave a shy smile.

The crowd lost it.

Simon's belly jittered at the reaction. Jealousy gurgled like a geyser ready to blow. Forcing it down, he went behind Gray and clamped his hands on his shoulders, giving him a shake.

Jazz jumped off her kit, ran forward and gave Gray a kiss on the cheek, then handed Simon his marker board.

Simon looked down at the board and scrawled out three words. He looked around for the camera that followed them around for the big screens and held it up for the lens.

Don't fuck up.

The words filled the screen and the crowd ate it up. Gray bent at the waist and curled his fingers around the head of a regular mic. Not Simon's mic. That one thing would not be allowed.

"No pressure," Gray said in a low voice.

Simon shrugged and leaped into the archway above them as they went into the opening song. He climbed, he ran, he sweated under the lights.

He played the monkey.

He played the clown.

He died a little inside as Gray handled song after song.

Natural talent shone through the long, lean lines of him. Gray didn't quite know how to handle singing instead of playing lead guitar. Nick had to pull extra solos and Margo was all over the stage with her cello or her violin.

She even pulled out her acoustic violin for the ballad "Finally" that suited Gray's smooth voice. The utter quiet of the crowd as Gray sang his words, the ones he'd written and molded to fit Margo's strings, drove him mad.

When they started the Renegade and Monster combo piece, Simon lost it. He launched himself into the general admission pit in the front.

The leap of faith left his heart exploding in his chest. They passed him back and forth from one end to the other. Security scrambled and he caught Lila's shriek of outrage as she came off the side stage.

He waved at the band on stage. Jazz was standing at her kit, her eyes huge. Margo's hand fell to her side with her bow dangling from her fingertips.

Then she lifted her violin and slid back into the song, but her eyes never left him. Three burly security guys came to the edge of the pit and helped him down. Simon ran up the stairs and waved at Lila as he bulleted to the middle of the stage and back up on his perch.

He shaded his eyes and looked out on all the perfection, hating that he couldn't add his voice to the slice of history.

This place that showed just how far they'd come from the tiny clubs on The Strip to sold-out shows. This venue should be in the palm of *his* hand. Not Gray's. It was his job to bring this all home.

The lights went down as everyone scrambled for instruments and towels, water and sports drinks. Anything to soak up energy for the encore.

They didn't bother going down off the stage. Instead they all congregated into the center around him and dragged him into their circle.

This band.

This moment.

His life.

His dreams right here.

They waved and the night curled around him as they all went back to their stations. Simon ripped off his tape and switched on his mic.

Deacon's moody bass flowed out and the cue taunted him. *His* cue.

The song that had been his since the studio. The one that had given him Margo.

The one that had taken her away.

Now, here in this perfect night, he opened his mouth and let instinct take him.

Gray and Nick looked between them. Nick ran to the side and snagged his other guitar. The layered and guitar-heavy song sounded exactly the way it was supposed to.

Nick and Gray passing back and forth between rhythm and lead, Deacon's bass, Margo's strings, and Jazz's beat.

And his voice.

He kept it steady and didn't go for the high notes, controlled it and felt his way through the verses and chorus, fought his way through the bridge, but he owned it.

As the epic end rushed forward, he followed it. And then something burst.

His throat. Everything going tight. The pain. Jesus Christ.

The flood of blood choked him and he hit his knees.

He tried to breathe, tried to find his way through it as the silence descended and the crowd surged forward. He coughed and the splatter down his white shirt made him waver. Was that his blood? So much.

And then the stage came rushing for him.

His cheek hit the floor and he jerked as everything fuzzed out at the corners and became a narrow path.

A girl in the front with her hands up over her eyes, the horrified screams. And then the whole stage went black, the shriek of his name was the last thing he heard.

DESTROYED

Chapter 20

Margo rushed forward. Had she shouted his name? Was she shouting or was it everyone else? When he'd started to sing, she wanted to shut him down, but he'd sounded fine.

Until he didn't.

The blood. God. Someone pulled her back and she fought.

"They're helping him."

Security surrounded him. And because it was a general admission show, there was a paramedic on the campus.

Thank God.

He handled Simon. The white latex scarlet-tipped as the paramedic rolled him and cleared his airway. Blood puddled on the stage, splashed over Simon's shirt, and streaked across his cheek.

She swayed.

"No you don't. C'mon, you're not that girl, right?"

Margo looked over her shoulder at Jamie DuCaine from Brooklyn Dawn. They were eye to eye, both of them tall compared to the other women on the tour.

Margo shook her head and swiveled to watch them again. A plastic tube flashed and she watched in horror as the medic forced it down his throat.

Simon thrashed and she tried to go to him again.

No.

Simon.

Didn't they know they could be doing more damage? But at that point it was only oxygen that mattered. Then he was on a stretcher and whisked across the stage.

Lila reached through the crowd and grabbed her hand.

Margo tried to turn around to thank Jamie, but the crowd on stage swallowed her and she was on the move. Lila dragged her over cords, through trunks, and to the backstage side door where a car was waiting.

"Get in."

Lila's assistant jumped out from the driver side. "Do you want me to drive so you can do the phone thing?"

Lila nodded. "Good thinking."

Margo climbed into the back of the silver Camry and they spit gravel as they fishtailed out of the side parking lot.

Traffic was murder, but Lila's assistant had to have been an Indy driver in a former life. He jumped the curb, sped along the sidewalk, and then out to the main road. "Find me a side street to go around this."

Lila turned to Margo and she caught the cell phone that Lila shot back at her. With trembling fingers, she found the map program and directed.

The hospital felt like it was a million miles away. California traffic was cruel and capricious, but this was home turf for the band. Once they were off the campus, Lila's assistant knew where to go and what streets to take.

Lila was talking so fast that Margo couldn't keep up. A call to Donovan, the hospital, the specialist that they'd already looked into.

Everything went so fast.

They pulled up to the hospital. She and Lila jumped out and their driver peeled away from the curb before security shooed them away from the loading area.

They rushed the ER. They didn't want to give Lila any information, but since Simon didn't have any family and Lila pulled out some paper, they were pushed ahead.

"What was that?"

"What?"

Margo swallowed. "What was that magic piece of paper that let us in?"

"Power of attorney, baby. In an emergency, I have it for those who don't have family."

She didn't want to examine why that hurt her on a basic level. All she could focus on was getting inside and getting to Simon's bedside.

Lila swore at what awaited them. The waiting room was full of people. Some were for their own emergency needs, but the bulk of the crowd was clearly reporters.

Margo gasped as even Kim Forrester from *Music Life* was there. How the hell had they gotten there so fast?

Kim spotted Lila and advanced on them like a tsunami on the coast. Margo stumbled back as two other reporters with cameras zeroed in on them.

"Is it true Simon Kagan collapsed onstage at the end of a sold-out show?"

"We were advised that it was laryngitis, but it seems far more serious than that."

"Was it drug related?"

"Was he stabbed?"

Margo pushed her way out of the crush. What the hell? She understood it was big news, but not to this level. Oblivion was one of the largest bands around right now, and especially here on their home turf, but they weren't quite the Beatles.

Not yet.

"Did he collapse because of the news of Snake's death?"

Margo whirled around. Kim's intelligent and gleefully bright gaze met hers, then moved onto Lila.

Lila stopped moving. "What did you say?"

Kim Forrester was the center of attention now. "William Scotsman was found dead this afternoon, an apparent accidental drowning. Or suicide."

The reporters doubled their efforts and Lila grabbed Margo's hand again. A small anchor in the center of insanity.

Nick and Deacon pushed their way through. Seeing fresh blood, Kim arrowed her microphone and her camera at Nick.

"Did Simon collapse at the news of William Scotsman's death?"

Nick's gold eyes widened as he advanced on the reporter. "What did you say?"

"William Scotsman, otherwise known as Snake, was found dead at the Santa Monica Pier this morning. He'd washed up with the afternoon tide. It's unclear if it was a suicide or accidental."

At Nick's horrified face, Kim's gleeful eyes lost a little of their sparkle.

Deacon pushed Nick through the throng of reporters and gawkers. Lila hooked her arm through Nick's and they powered their way to the back of the waiting room.

Security muscled into the room and shouts of first amendment rights were drowned out by the swift and precise orders of very large orderlies and three officers.

Margo was jostled into a hallway and an eerie silence fell around her. People were rushing around a glassed-in room. She couldn't stop herself from walking toward it.

Somehow she knew it was him.

Three men in lab coats and a woman with red hair and surgical scrubs surrounded Simon. His concert clothes had been removed and the cotton johnny coat sagged around his shoulders.

The redheaded doctor was shouting, but Margo couldn't hear her above the white noise filling her head. The woman jerked the gurney away from the wall and shoved at one of the men in the lab coats.

Two nurses and the doctor in scrubs wheeled him into the hallway and Margo finally snapped out of it.

"Move!" The redheaded doctor's blue eyes blazed.

"Please, he's my…" Margo swallowed. What was he to her?

Just hers.

Mine.

He was so pale and that tube down his throat made her ache. She reached over the side railing and ghosted her fingers through his dark hair.

"We have to go, Miss."

Margo blew out a breath. "You take care of him."

The doctor nodded. "I'm the best."

Then they were gone and the elevator doors closed after him.

FIND OUT WHAT HAPPENS TO SIMON — AND THE REST OF OBLIVION —
IN CONSUMED.

CONSUMED

Is it better to burn out or fade away…

Oblivion lead singer Simon Kagan is used to being in the spotlight for his model good looks and his voice, not because of the epic ending to Oblivion's last show on their home turf in California. That unforgettable night rocked Oblivion in more ways than one, and now the journey back seems almost impossible.

The only bright spot is Margo. Margo, the one woman he'd been sure would never be more than a hot ride in the dark. Margo, who would never be his.

Except she is…for now. But taking one dream and trading it for another isn't supposed to hurt this much.

As long as Margo never realizes the man she fell for no longer exists, maybe he won't lose everything that matters due to just one all-consuming night.

Lost In Oblivion

the Series

SEDUCED (intro)
ROCKED (book #1)
ROCK, RATTLE & ROLL (book #1.5)
TWISTED (book #2)
UNTWISTED (book #2.5)
DESTROYED (book #3)
* * *
Coming soon
CONSUMED (book #3.5)
SHATTERED (book #4)
FUSED (book $4.5)

IF YOU'D LIKE MORE INFORMATION ABOUT THE SERIES & EXTRAS,
PLEASE VISIT WWW.LOSTINOBLIVION.COM.

ANYTHING BUT MINE

WHEN YOU'RE GONE TRILOGY
BOOK ONE

by Taryn Elliott

Rock star Logan King has come home to Winchester Falls for the annual Summer Festival. Only this time he's hauling a helluva lot more baggage than a few suitcases and vintage guitars. His closet contains more than the usual skeletons…and if he doesn't keep the door firmly locked, someone might get harmed. The specter of what haunts him forces him to turn away from anything more than one-night-stands.

Until Izzy and her topaz eyes finally give him a reason to try again.

Since moving to town Isabella Grace has found friends and a place to belong for the first time in her life. Running the Summer Festival is the perfect way to show how important her new community is. She just never planned on a whirlwind fling with a man too used to saying goodbye. Or to fall for a guy who has as many secrets as he does hit songs.

Logan is used to protecting himself, but protecting Izzy is all new territory. With everything that matters to him at risk, he refuses to let her get hurt—even if that means he has to walk away. For her own good.

SHADOWBOXER

TAPPED OUT series
BOOK ONE

by Cari Quinn

She's in for the fight of her life…with the man who only wants to be her lover.

Fighter Mia Anderson has faced the dark side of life and survived. But just getting by is no longer enough. To fund her new life with her baby sister, she's determined to beat the reigning king of the male fighters in New York's underground MMA circuit, Tray "Fox" Knox.

Tray refuses to fight a woman, until he learns Mia's tougher than anyone he has ever known. He soon realizes he wants more from her than blows and blood, and he's willing to hit below the belt to get it. He'll fight her, but if he wins, she spends the night in his bed. All night long, his rules. No tapping out.

Mia agrees, certain that he'll lose. What she doesn't realize is that Tray loves to fight *dirty*…and that this match may end up being the most important one of their lives.

About the Authors

USA Today BESTSELLING AUTHOR *Cari Quinn* likes music and men, so she figured why not write about both? When she's not writing, she's screaming at men's college basketball games on TV, playing her music too loud or causing trouble. Sometimes simultaneously.

NATIONAL BESTSELLING AUTHOR *Taryn Elliott* is obsessed with rock stars, men, and her unending playlists—maximizing these things seemed like a very good idea. When she's not writing, she's losing hours to hot men on TV, and/or a graphic design project. Multitasking is her middle name.

They decided to combine forces and found that hey...this writing deal is even more awesome when you collaborate with your best friend.

AND SO LOST IN OBLIVION WAS BORN.

www.ingramcontent.com/pod-product-compliance
Lightning Source LLC
Chambersburg PA
CBHW061950170626
46813CB00006B/2594